The Wedding

Imraan Coovadia

Picador USA
New York

www.picadorusa.com

Picador® is a U.S. registered trademark and is used by St. Martin's Press under license from Pan Books Limited.

For information on Picador USA Reading Group Guides, as well as ordering, please contact the Trade Marketing department at St. Martin's Press.
Phone: 1-800-221-7945 extension 763
Fax: 212-677-7456
E-mail: trademarketing@stmartins.com

Library of Congress Cataloging-in-Publication Data

Coovadia, Imraan
    The wedding : a novel / Imraan Coovadia.
       p. cm.
    ISBN 0-312-27219-7 (hc)
    ISBN 0-312-30612-1 (pbk)
    1. East Indians—South Africa—Fiction.
2. Durban [South Africa]—Fiction. 3. Bombay [India]—Fiction. 4. South Africa—Fiction. 5. Weddings—Fiction.
I. Title.

PR9369.3.C65 W4 2001
823'.92—dc21   2001031947

First Picador USA Paperback Edition: December 2002

10 9 8 7 6 5 4 3 2 1

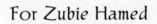
For Zubie Hamed

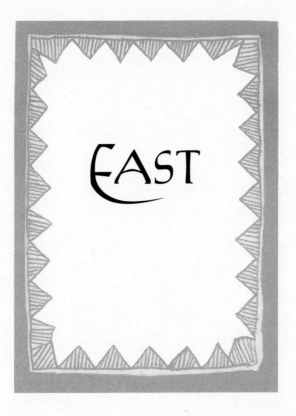

EAST

Chapter One

Four score and seven years ago my grandfather looked out of the window of his train and saw the most beautiful woman in the world. Unaware of the looming cataclysm he'd been buttoning and unbuttoning his waistcoat, yawning in the heat that came in from outside, stretching his legs into the aisle, picking his nose—and looking suspiciously at the family of Sikhs sharing his compartment.

A slovenly, turbaned race, he thought to himself, glancing across the bridge of his nose at the father, on whose lap two children were bunched up with ribbons in their hair. Then there were three children sprawled over their mother on the next bench. How these people bred!

Imagining, he saw before him a vast human pyramid—young, old, wiry Sikhs; clawing, drooling, spitting Sikhs—clumped up together, waving and jumping, chewing one-way. The horror!

Ismet Nassin was a businessman at heart, an enthusiast of the economist Ricardo. Asked what he believed in, he'd draw in his breath a little, hold up his right hand, and proceed along through his thin fingers with their thick white fingernails, flaking, pink-rimmed:

"Temperance"—he'd crook a finger—"Moderation," crook a finger, "Balance," "Restraint," "Thriftiness." If he was encouraged he'd go on through the other hand, "Continence," "Frugality," "Sobriety," "Discipline," and "Reflection."

Then he'd frown, "These are things, you see, our modern Indians do not understand. Too many babies, and because why? Because why? Ignorance, that is the reason, and that is the real enemy. On top of it, it is not good for business. We are not like the English. They understand"—brightening—"they know about this modern world. Ricardo and Malthus, ha! They knew a few things about what is what!"

Ismet was quite fond of these English and their elastic bands and their cricket balls and brussels sprouts. Each day he read the London *Times* front to back, though it arrived a fortnight late, tied into a tube with a piece of string and tossed on the straw mat by his front door. He respected the English character, their serenity, their sense of what was most judicious. Yes, the Englishman was a creature after his own heart. From a professional point of view—from what nation stemmed the accounting handbook, the blue-stained slide rule, the soft-lead pencil on which he depended?

Now Americans—new-smelling, milk-fed, moon-faced, raised on beef—were a whole different story. Wild, savage beings with mercury in the blood.

But these speculations (he told himself while unfastening the blind on his window), they weren't worth a pinch of salt without particulars and specifics, concrete examples, hierarchies. What if he himself, without anybody's two cents, had to hire an employee—say the choice was between an American and a Sikh?

(He saw no reason not to be prepared for eventualities. It could only help, that was for sure. Eventually he'd come up with enough preemptive wisdom so he'd never need to recalculate. To be immediate, decisive, efficient, that was really his dream. The Ismet-Nassin-Universal-Calculating-Machine.)

Well, these Sikhs were a little on the cheeky side. A soulful, dolorous, gap-toothed, tight-lipped bunch. And there was no ignoring a certain hostility that he'd experienced, quite uncalled for (he could see the station coasting toward the train from the window, nothing more than a shack really).

But whatever the obvious drawbacks, there was this advantage: They were a known quantity. They could be factored into the equation, no matter their funny underpants and concealed daggers. Was he prejudiced to hold customs and traditions in contempt—no question of that! He had met these Sikhs, exchanged views, done business.

Whereas it was only in the newspapers that he'd read about Americans. Print was his only real contact except when he'd caught a glimpse of one in a horse-cab one time on the Malabar Hill, wearing a brown serge suit and a panama hat with a white brim. That was not enough, as plain and simple as the hands right in front of his face. The dangers, those appearing in his head, those unknowable in advance, the possible perils of these beast-men, these Americans—to take a shot in the dark!

Yes, he'd hire the Sikh, he concluded with a sigh of relief. Of course.

He looked over at the man on the other side of the railway carriage as if to offer him a job.

The Sikh stared back.

Ismet felt uncomfortable. He flinched and turned to the window. He reached inside his nose. He sank back against the faded red linen on his seat.

And that's when it happened. That's when he saw Khateja Haveri. Khateja Haveri: the most beautiful lady in the world.

He knew that even before he got the chance to see her up close. What he glimpsed was a nose, a chin, a head around which was knotted a white cotton scarf. A pair of strong village legs. (Two big skittles virtually.)

A few seconds earlier and he'd never have got that.

Khateja might have been standing in the same exact spot, her eyes glued to the place—eight feet above the ground, thirty yards east from the ticket office—where his window finally materialized.

Standing there with her bucket and her white cotton scarf: wistful, downcast, expectant by turns, tapping her feet impatiently against the siding because it was hot and the cylinder of smoke was still a ways off in the foothills, full of white flares and blue diamonds, and she was thirsty. Her rabbit heart pounding in cadences.

She could have been shouting out his name into the white teeth of the tempest.

Waving a banner trimmed out in gilt and fine red cloth, "Mr. Ismet Nassin, here I am, Khateja Haveri! The Most Beautiful Lady In The Whole World."

But if the train had dallied, say, gorging on coal, or if it'd been helped by a favorable lime-smelling southwesterly from the Balaghat hills, then Ismet would've rumbled by unawares, unable to hear Khateja above the clamor, the clinking of track and wheel and iron-blackened cog.

Khateja would have been zip, zero, scratch, nada, nothing at all to him.

Actually Khateja, for her part, hadn't the faintest notion of Ismet's existence, let alone of how he'd descend upon her that particular morning in such a singular way.

"Ha!" she told him on their wedding night, going to sit at the farthest end of the bench so everyone could see in case he tried any funny stunts, "Ha! It is the illest fortune that you have come along from out of the blue. Chance in a million. Ha! I just do not believe my bad luck. Really, I just cannot comprehend. No definitely, there must be a purpose behind this suffering. I must be paying for the sins of the whole world."

But as the fields rattling past slowed, settled into the green-brown earth with its stone-tiled irrigation furrows and enclosure fences, why was Ismet not alerted to the significance of the train of events he was setting in motion?

Did a chill run down his spine when he turned toward the window and through it spied Khateja Haveri standing there with her bucket and white cotton scarf and the sandals she'd borrowed from her auntie Rabiya (who was so switched off she would never notice they were gone, not one time in a million years)?

Alas! There are moments when the lightest touch or a kind word can bind up a chain of consequences. I can't say that I have any real belief in history's curative powers, but at least it

reminds us when everything went irretrievably wrong. That
long-ago morning will reverberate through each subsequent
morning to infinity, because there's no such thing as an individual human life.

For who can tell where the past ends and the self begins?
Something quite as ordinary as holding out a hand at the end
of a sentence, for example, or a way of telling a joke, could have
been transmitted within a family for a thousand years. Well,
there's every reason to suppose that one's romantic constitution
has also been handed down, and that the ever-spinning movements of the heart have followed an identical pattern from the
very first parents to the latest offspring (although strictly speaking, some characteristics, like wickedness and charm, come
down in the family but skip every other generation). It is purely
on the basis of my own experience, in fact, that I suggest that
feelings are the most conservative human institutions: we love,
irrevocably, with our grandparents' hearts. So this is a letter of
explanation—accounting for and confessing to a bad history—
but it is also a love letter. A love letter, to an unknown ad-
dressee . . .

All this wicked history to which I refer hung by a thread
when an angel was sent down to strike Ismet Nassin on his
crown: a warning, divine intercession! The angel arrived in the
compartment. Ismet heard a ringing in his ears. He imagined
that bells were clapping against the side of his head.

The angel settled itself down very carefully on the other
side of the Sikh woman. It leaned across the compartment
without touching her and it blew, gently but very distinctly,
into my grandfather's left ear. Ismet felt giddy. Spots twirled

before his eyes—triangles shuffled—there were dark spots in his vision.

He fell back from the window and put one hand to his ear, which itched inside.

"Allah!"

He pulled a handkerchief from his jacket pocket and mopped his forehead, thinking he should have stayed home in the first place since he hadn't been feeling exactly up to scratch. (In the future he would have to pay more attention to his own needs, otherwise these little upsets were the price he would have to pay.)

"My God, my God," he went on, a little inconsistently, when the itching in his ear wouldn't go away.

The angel stood up smartly and knocked thrice on his head. Bam! Bam! Bam!

Feeling it had done all that could be expected under the circumstances, the angel squeezed its way through the half-open window. Anyhow, it had never been fond of earthly business.

But disgracefully, farcically, it had hit my grandfather too hard—and it sent him spinning. Ismet spilled off his seat, cartwheeled across the floor, and cannonballed into the Sikh. His left hand, trailing behind him, clobbered one of the children on the woman's lap. The child exploded into tears.

Huffily, its mother gathered her sari about her and glared at Ismet.

"Don't worry, *bachoo*," she comforted her baby. "This man is just Clumsy Two-Fists you know. He is not sure where he is going to on earth. Better we go sit somewhere else with your father when the train stops, then we will hope we have eventually come to a few minutes of safety and sanctuary without this sort of criminal behavior."

She kissed her child on the forehead and held its nose between two fingers. She spread her hands protectively around its middle.

The perpetrator stood up speedily and smiled apologetically, as if that would put a better look on things. He reached out his hand to tap the child on the back as a gesture of reconciliation, but it recoiled as if from a firebrand, the whites of its eyes showing from pure terror.

"Sir, I am most apologetic," he explained. "You see, it felt like someone was knock-knocking at my head. Hit me once-twice-three times, just like that."

"Then in that case you must best go see a doctor about it, *ne*? About the knock-knocking on the head. One-time two-time one-time-two-time-three-times, ay? To my head it sounds as if it is a medical matter then. Clearly," noted the Sikh, frostily. "Oh ho! You cannot just go about tearing at an innocent man's child with your hands. This is not the done thing in our part of the world, I must warn you before you have gone any further."

"Ayah!"—the wife interjected—"And then to go blaming someone else for what you have achieved. Then to turn around to say it is because someone has given you a few slaps on the head, no, it is much too much. You are convinced that my baby reached over like this invisibly and pushed you? Or was it I?"

A hysterical note crept into her voice. She shooed the children from her lap and drew herself up to her full four feet eleven inches. She opened out her hands before her.

"Look, sir, we are not that sort of person. We cannot be treated like dirt. We cannot just be accused."

"Or assaulted," her husband reminded her.

"Yes, yes, we cannot be assaulted and accused like this."

"Really, it is completely out of the question," the man said very firmly, as if to put a stop to that possibility.

The injured child started howling.

The other four children followed suit, rubbing their eyes with their tiny hands, tugging unhappily at the ribbons in their hair, sliding behind their parents for protection.

The woman retreated to the seat and set to quieting them.

"See what you have done to my family. Only see! What it is you have done to us who never laid a finger upon you!"

"I am extremely sorry."

"Sorry, ha! Sorry, ha!" said the man. "What does sorry do for us, eh? Sorry-sorry will pay the money to the bank, that is your feeling? Here you have come and made injuries to our person. And we have not yet laid a finger upon you. Even though you have been staring suspiciously. You hoped we would not notice this? You think we are stupid?" The man touched his forehead lightly with his open hand. "So because we are stupids, then it is all right from your point of view, you can go ahead to assault and accuse us?"

"Now look—"

"Of course if you would look, then likely you would not do these terrible things. That is the hope. But here it is you explaining to us that we must look! Us!"

"The cheek of it!" exclaimed his wife from behind Ismet.

"Assault and accuse, and then you can tell us to look! We are blind now?"

"Is there anything I can do?"

"What can you do?" the man inquired hopelessly, putting his outspread hands behind him for his children to hold. "What can you do? Just to leave us alone. What we have asked is to be left alone. That's all we have asked out of anyone."

"Well, I'll go then."

"Yes, just go then," his interlocutors chorused. "Better that way."

"Well, sorry anyway."

Ismet retrieved his briefcase from under the seat, snapped it open, folded his newspaper into it, and cracked it shut. Fez in hand, making perfectly sure he didn't trip over the children, he stumbled into the corridor of the train, not even noticing that the train had stopped and there were whistles and shouts outside where a group of men from the village were unloading a crate of crockery and curtains and an open box filled with tins of waterproof shoe polish for the village store.

Leaning against the side of the train, Ismet took a welcome breath. What could it mean? He'd caught sight of the woman through the window when he was swept from his seat and hurled across the width of the carriage by an invisible hand. Then there was that mysterious draught and the way the window had opened all by itself, the handle on the side rattling away as it did so. Was it providence, the hand of providence? Magnetic emanations? Perhaps radiation?

Nothing of this sort had ever happened to him. He was a moderate man, and he prided himself on that quality. It meant that he was unsuited for violent eruptions. To say the least his nerves were not up to it. No, such an affair could not be accidental (he saw that with great clarity). There must be a meaning. Under what conditions would He (whom Ismet affectionately regarded as a sort of very high-ranking clerk), under what circumstances would He meddle in this fashion?

What if—God forbid—he'd brushed up against the woman's breast, say, while tumbling accidentally across the compartment, and thus given the wrong impression?

A sign had been offered to him. A sign had manifested itself directly. Otherwise, it was too horrible to contemplate. (Angels that must punch him in the eye for no reason whatsoever—that was totally out of the question!)

Manifestations were not unfamiliar. If that was what was going on here, there was no cause for anxiety. Though he personally hadn't been manifested to, his mother was constantly receiving dreams, messages, even short nursery rhymes from above.

"My son," his mother Rashida announced from time to time, "I do not think you should be chit-chatting it up with these people, my child," referring to one or another of his card-playing, whiskey-drinking companions. "I have been led to believe it is inappropriate."

"Ma?"

"Yes. I have been informed. It is extremely dangerous for you now to do this and carry on irresponsibly. Otherwise why would He waste His time warning me, your mother," she'd conclude with impeccable logic. "He has better things to do, you don't think?"

Ismet invariably fell into line with such a diktat. He broke off his ties with the parties concerned. He left their invitations unglimpsed in their envelopes. If it came down to it, he'd cut them in the street, if that was what it came down to.

Of course he was a grown-up man and Rashida—but that was missing the point. To put it that way was to miss the point totally and utterly. Such phenomena cried out for attention. Otherwise upon what did one confer significance? What bedrock?

Somehow though, all along he'd thought of these communications that encroached upon his mother's sleeping hours as electromagnetic signals. He regarded his mother as a sort of Marconi telegraph, beating quickly somewhere inside to the tune of invisible waves, her leathery heart moving in her breast like an egg timer, her scarf trussed around her head so she wouldn't be woken up by any old noise because she was a light sleeper.

("Such funny ideas you are having about women," Khateja would scold him. "It must be the fault of this Rashida. Oh yes, it is she who is responsible for such hatred of women in this world, although I am sad to be the one to say it.")

But the facts were crystal clear: These signs were not an intangible disturbance in ether. They were physical signs, brutal—to the extent they'd cast him across a railway carriage and bruised his two elbows to boot. One never knew! No wonder his mother had been so certain of the advice she passed on.

Presumably, he reflected (leaning against the side of the train), this was what had happened: He'd been singled out for some grand communication. Something big. And it must have to do with the woman through the window, since he'd seen her at the exact same instant (the same exact instant!) that he'd the distinct feeling of breath blown upon his ear, as if through a six-*rupee* ear trumpet. The two things must be connected. One extraordinary thing, then the next following right on its heels. There was a clear relationship here which would be obvious to the greatest fool in the world. Could it have been a warning, an omen, a signal that danger lurked?

Certainly not (he decided, putting his briefcase on the floor because it was hurting his arm now). Why omens? Omens now? Omens when he had other problems on his plate? Why, he was in need of a wife. He'd been searching for a wife for two months counting from next week, since he'd risen to a senior position. That was the preeminent question in his life. No, there was no justification for omens.

But that was it! His future wife had been pointed out to him. Framed in the fleeting window by a symphony of head taps, there was no other explanation. And what incredible cost, what expense to bring him together with her out of the whole of India! Now to squander the chance when opportunity came virtually . . .

"You cannot only be standing here in the middle of the corridor, blocking things up," warned the conductor, who'd sauntered up without his noticing. "Where is it you are sitting?"

"I must be getting off here. That is how it has turned out. When again does the train stop over here?"

"Next week."

"Next week." Ismet sighed. Nothing for it. He must make a move against the quotidian. Put aside particular things. Grasping his briefcase tightly, he circled the conductor and tripped speedily down the steps onto the platform. Not three seconds later the train shivered, shuddered, shook, bellowed, blew out a cloud of smoke, whistled, and rolled away to Bombay.

He looked up at it anxiously, catching a glimpse of the Sikh family glaring at him through the very window from which he'd caught his very first sight of Khateja Haveri. Glaring with their knuckles on the green iron beam that divided the top section from the bottom that opened, stacked on top of each other like acrobats, steaming up the glass.

"A tide in the affairs of men," he repeated to himself anxiously. Then he strode out of the station and into the village to find Khateja Haveri, the most beautiful woman in the world.

Chapter Two

smet pulled a handkerchief from the pocket of his jacket
and mopped his forehead. Whew! The sun was right overhead, the width of an orange, simmering angrily, light in the
sleeves of cloud among the hills.

The plain was cut up by stone walls and fence posts into
bright green squares, here and there a desultory cow, a stone
well, a telegraph pole. Lit up in places by running water, the
plain rose up in the distance to blue hills right near the top of
which he could see the tree line and, on the tallest of them, the
snowcap, slate-colored, sparkling.

The station consisted of a wooden platform and an open-
face shack with plywood benches arranged in a semicircle inside
it, a green table on which sat a partition that served as the ticket
booth, two large umbrella-shaped trees in front, by the side of
the track. Beyond was the village: thirty or so shacks with
lengths of plain cream cloth in their entrances, made out of
banded wood for the most part, though a few had corrugated
iron roofs. They were set in lines progressively further from the
station, toward the grazing land and the fields.

About fifty yards away Ismet made out a clearing in which

women were standing, buckets in hand. Apart from these women, no one was to be seen. Presumably they'd fled from the heat, preferring to sweat under cover, drink water, chew *paan*, spit on the ground, as was the custom.

He noticed the train disappearing with unsuspected speed into the hills on the far side of the plain, a black-blue smoke column shining like a mirror in places, trailing into white and blue doughnuts, which he could see because, like steam, they altered the quality of light.

He did up the buttons on his waistcoat to the top, smoothed out his shirt by tugging on the sleeves, tipped his fez smartly on his brow, and set off for the clearing with his briefcase under his right arm, the newspaper carefully folded inside it so the print wouldn't rub off on all his files.

Unlike the cultivated land he'd seen from the train, which had been carpet green, the ground here was red and sandy, strewn with pebbles and twigs. There were goats, mangy sedated creatures that untucked their heads, looked him up and down with their rusted eyes. Then they yawned and curled up again.

Standing around a water pump set smack in the middle of the open ground were the village women. They too glanced at him with busy eyes and went back to leaning against walls, swinging buckets and talking amongst themselves, carrying to and fro chickens piled up in wicker baskets, squatting on the ground with wide-open knees, wrapping individual eggs in tissue in sleeves, sorting through wallets of chickpeas and heads of garlic. (Making it quite clear that if he wanted something in whatever connection, then he must jolly well be the one to open up channels.)

Holding up his spread-out hand to keep out the sun—there she was, the woman with the slender shoulder, the lyrical ankles, the one spotted from the window. Miracle of miracles!

He hurried up to her.

She paid no attention.

What now? He was meant just to come out with the whole thing? He harrumphed—he cleared his throat—he sucked in his breath—he guffawed and gallumphed—he scratched his head—he stuck his hands in his pockets.

By now all the women had abandoned what they were doing and were staring at him—all of them, that is, except the very one before him.

Indeed, Khateja deliberately turned around when she noticed him hovering about with his fluttering hands and expensive briefcase.

Feeling, why must she be bothered and hassled by these big-shot train travelers who must just arrive off the train for everyone to start with the bowing and scraping?

The bowing and the nonstop scraping and the wide-eyed fawning on every last word with the tongues hanging out on the ground to collect the dust and the black dirt—as if they were backwater savages or what!

Really it was too sickening. She was going to play no part. She was just going to stand there and not do anything.

Hopefully he would get one eyeful of her back and that would be that.

One big eyeful, she for one didn't have time to waste around

for a casual chat.

She went on picking at her fingernails which had ribbons of green from picking in the field morning time, waiting for the chance to fill her bucket at the pump.

"Er," said Ismet.

She whipped around very quickly.

"What er? Ay? What er?"

She'd calculated perfectly. She'd surprised him totally and utterly with an unexpected bolt out of the blue.

(Actually, it had to do with razor-sharp wits and exact timing, it was not too difficult a thing to achieve.)

"Er . . . Ur, um."

"Er, er, ur. What?" she said, snarkily.

The other women chortled, spreading their haunches, sitting down on upturned crates, offering heavy-lidded looks to one another.

These were the peaceful village ways his mother ruminated about from time to time during *ramzaan,* or on *bakri eid,* grumbling against unfeeling cold-fish Bombay? It was unthinkable. Must be some sort of ambush. Because why must he be treated with baseless hostility?

"What is it that you desire, Mr. ur-ur Man?" Khateja asked again. "You want to stand here making ur-ur sounds at me all day? Like one fat creature to make sounds and whatever in my ears so it is impossible for me to hear what is going on in the world? You think because we are village persons we have plenty time to be burning up for your personal benefit?"

"No . . . ur, not at all," said Ismet, sensing that events had taken a horrible turn sometime back, that he was losing his foothold in the normal world, the world of blue-lined ledgers and desks and glass bottles of ink.

(Because she was busy praising to high heaven his newfound itinerant lifestyle at company cost, had he not one week previously warned Jairam Reddy's wife, Roshni, "But Roshni, you must not think it is a matter of fun and games only, because there is an opportunity to do a certain amount of traveling on the firm's behalf. Fun and games, oh ho, that is not the case, ask Jairam, he is an educated man, he will say for you what are the true facts. The truth is, such a responsibility is frequently exhausting. Furthermore, there are dangers which cannot be anticipated because it is impossible to be acquainted with the customs and traditions of every region. As a matter of fact, that was a difficulty with my own father, I can give you that information." Had he not said those very words to Roshni, and, look, he was already possibly over his head in some sort of hot water!)

Khateja went on, "Because if it is that you want, to chit and to chat and to be busy with the futile conversations only, then maybe it is better you go talk to our Ahmedu Akhbar. That is my recommendation. Just go talk, waste no further time. If you give to him a few pence, just one-two cents in the pocket from you to him, then there is no doubt in my mind that he will be only too glad to be listening to your oohs and ummings and *urr*ings all day. Maybe weeks, who knows?"

At this the women broke into a gale of chuckles, exposing orange, gappy teeth stained by *paan*-chewing, chipped by buckets and stones, glinting in gold threads. Ahmedu Ashook, known as Akhbar in reference to his religious delusions, was the local idiot. He spent his days wresting bones from dogs, staring at a copy of the Koran he couldn't read, ambushing carts, listing under shrubs, snarling at insects, tolerated only by virtue of his family, one of the best to be found anywhere within a hundred miles, wealthy folk.

(Khateja: 30.

Ismet: Love.)

Despite the humiliation—the cabbage-ladies grinning and cavorting and squeezing one another's hands, taking out snuff from rectangular metal tins with mirror-lids to further pump up their pleasure at his discomfort—turning figuratively from these distractions, Ismet held his head high, straight as they'd forced the pupils to stand by the blackboard in school, on pain of being rapped on the knuckles with a ruler.

"I just want to know, all I want to know is your name," he inquired with great dignity.

"Oh look," yelled one of the women in the front. "He is blushing, man!"

"He is, it is a true fact, only look, ha! ha!" shrieked another of the sirens. "Ha!"

"Like one big beetroot, so red," Khateja remarked, smiling, girlish, with very great charm.

This was followed by a crescendo of open mouths revealing sinister cavities, by wave upon wave of merriment. One woman drew a leg up underneath her, pointed it at Ismet, balanced it toe-wise on the ground, and danced a quick jig, circling about it. At the end she sank to her feet, threw her head in the air, and yelled, "Mr. Blushing *ur-ur* Man, Who Wanted to Know the Name of Madam Khateja."

Actually Khateja, recovering from a fit of chortling and giggling, was more ticked-off by the inclination to turn everything into an opportunity for dancing and fussing (that was definitely some sort of collective deficiency in the culture), almost more teed-off by that than by this nosey parker from the train who had one great red circle on each individual cheek, his hands folded nervously in front of him, clown-like. What harm could be in him?

"My name is Khateja."

(Anyway, that cat was out of the bag.)

"I am Ismet Nassin," he said, stretching out a hand which she ignored, so he quickly retracted it. He continued (in for a penny!), "And your family?"

"Now that is none of your business, Mr. ur-ur Man."

Then she picked up her bucket, hoisted it over her shoulder, and marched out of the clearing, announcing as she did so, "At this point really I am quite fed up of this ur-ur person's interrogation tactics."

She was immediately lost to view behind a hut.

Ismet wrung his arms—he beat upon his breast—he pulled the hair out from his chest, draped himself in sackcloth and ash—he weeped and he wailed—he sank down into the earth! He disappeared forever, neither to be seen by human eye nor heard by human ear nor touched by human hand ever again!

Actually, these things ran through his mind. He considered them very seriously, he weighed pros and cons and folded up his fingers till the knuckles were gleaming white—saw on balance this was no time to lose his head in grief and needless abasements.

Hadn't he been specially blessed, specially gifted, and helped out by angels?

But what rose without thorns, eh, what silver lining without cloud, what spineless porcupine? Indeed, what spineless pineapple!

No such thing. Things have their price, the market and all that. Think fast, squander no time!

"Tell me what family Khateja is from?" he asked firmly, looking hopefully to the throng.

A kindly grandmother stepped forward. She was wrapped about in a red and green sari, bespectacled, rolls of fat around her torso, thin streaky hair pinned up in a bun, thick feet in open leather sandals.

"She is Khateja Haveri, the daughter of Mr. Yusuf Haveri who is a member of our village over here, one of our cleverest men."

"Thank you, madam."

The madam touched him softly with her hand.

"But my son, Khateja is not for you."

"No?"

"Indeed she is not for any man in this world. She is strong, head-stubborn, most obstinate. When her heels are dug in she will defy everybody there is, the *imam*, next-town *moulana*, her own family all including. She is like a mule you know. Oh, she has gone against everybody and everyone in existence. She thinks she is being the most beautiful lady there is in the world, for one thing."

"The most beautiful lady in the world . . ." he repeated, perfectly entranced.

"Well, that is certainly what she is thinking. Just two years ago she drove a man to leave the village behind. It has gone that far, in fact."

"She did?" said Ismet, not really paying attention. He had actually found out her name. And she was single on top of it all. Now what were the odds?

Seeing the lady through the window, unnamed, unforeseen, the unnatural unearthly trumpet blowing and beating away in his right ear, the unglimpsed hand jabbing at his organism—and then to hurry from his compartment and speak with her against all odds and discover her name?

Despite these uncertain beginnings, wasn't it possible matters were proceeding according to plan? How much else might not have gone wrong, that was the real issue.

"Oh yes. He was being wildly in love with her, a simple man. Simple man, ayah!" exclaimed the granny, drawing her hands in fists through the air, getting a little lost in the sheer horror of her story.

("No definitely, he was not a complicated fellow," someone observed from the back of the crowd.)

"Poor Sataar"—the old woman dragged out the *a*'s, sucking in her cheeks a little—"and when she found out that he was what-what besotted, then when she had received that information then she must start to tease him. Must start. Must proceed in that particular direction. Even though we all went and pleaded with her. 'Dear Khateja,' we said for her, 'Do not go on with Sataar like this, always tease-teasing him about his ears, his feet, all the time pointing out some of his shortcomings and deficiencies which is the same for every human being on this earth. You know he is still shy with you. You know he is a sensitive type. You know in his heart he has a certain amount of admiration for you. You are aware of all these facts of the situation. Now you must be finished with the mockery and the ridiculing, please. We are requesting this from our side.' But would she put an end?"

"Well . . ."

"Would she?"

"Really, I am not in a position to know," he admitted.

"Of course not! Of course not! Oh ho, she just went about it even more worse. Criticizing-criticizing, you would not believe! 'Hey funny face! Is that an extra toe I see, or is it in fact your leg? Does your nose really look like that all the time, or is it a thing you wear on top of it specially when you get out of the bed morningtime? There is so much knobble in your knees, Sataar,' she must say to him, 'You must give someone else some knobble. You must offer. You must donate. What is the reason for selfishness and keeping only to yourself? There's knobble in sufficient quantity for much of our Bombay, *ne*?' "

"Not really," said Ismet, not particularly listening.

"Yes really, ended up Sataar must go away to Delhi to escape the pain and the mental torments. Ended up with tuberculosis and driving a rickshaw, and him with his poor knees and all. Must be terrible suffering, never could walk straight in the first place. We have not even seen him one time since he has left from us. Just a letter every so often. 'And give my love to Khateja Haveri, I am often having her in my thoughts.' How is his poor family feeling now, eh?"

"That is a terrible thing to happen to anyone, most unfortunate," said Ismet. "But tell me, where is it that I can find the father, Mr. Haveri?"

The old woman's face dropped. Now Mr. Nassin must learn by himself. Better this way probably—Khateja would not be causing innocent men blushes and tears and two burning cheeks around this village for a while. Anyway, the effort of telling her story had tired her out. She could do no more.

"They are living"—she pointed—"in the hut behind the one behind this. Mr. Yusuf Haveri."

"And is there somewhere I could be staying in the nighttime, until the train has arrived again?"

"You can be staying with us," said a young woman who had stepped forward next to the old woman. She shook his hand. "Ayesha Moderi. We have a bed in the hut, now my husband is gone to Bombay because his father is dead two weeks past. Only little money."

She directed him to her hut.

"Well thanks, I will be seeing you soon, hopefully," he accepted, thereby disappointing the other women who had been preparing to offer their accommodation for hardly a charge at all. Just a few pence could always come in handy, who knew.

Ismet made off in the direction of the Haveri hut, expecting the women to stay in the clearing. Instead, they followed him at a distance, all in a pack, not saying anything. He passed a goat, a shrub, a rake stuck in the ground at an angle, a rusty wheel, an old railway timetable scattering in the breeze, and found himself in front of the designated hut.

There was a slatted door, whitewashed, acid-smelling. There was a postbox too, nothing more than a old tin with a hole cut in the top really, standing out in front with HAVERI painted on the side in shaky white letters, a damp round straw mat to wipe one's feet. He could see a dim interior, shadowy human shapes, the illumination of a lamp turned down low, chinks between the planks that stood against the walls, water stains close to the ground.

A chicken pressed against the slatting from inside and turned its bright, glaring eye upon him. It squawked, raised its dead wings, and half-fluttered, half-shuffled further inside. Clearly, it was shaken.

My grandfather knocked resolutely on the door.

"Yas!" came an aggrieved man's voice from inside. "Watch your pounding! You want to bring the door down upon us? Allah!"

The offended door opened mysteriously and Ismet plunged into the gloomy cavity, holding on the edge of the frame for balance.

"Oh, it's Mr. Blushing-blushing ur-ur Man," said Khateja.

She had been sitting cross-legged in one corner, plucking long beans from their cool green shells, laying the shells on the ground by her, the pale white beans in a metal bowl in front. Now she laid the unshelled beans on a piece of newspaper on the ground, uncrossed her legs, collected her bucket, and strode smartly over the chicken and past the intruder, exiting the hut through the door that he was still holding open, like a rubber band.

Despite his joy at receiving divine sanction (what a rare and precious item, eh, in this contingent world over here?), including his encounter with the most beautiful lady, Ismet was a little shaken. Things seemed to have lost their concrete edges, their definitions. In this new climate would a *bharfee* be a *bharfee*, a three-cornered *samoosa* a three-cornered *samoosa*?

Compared to what he'd imagined, immersed in his parochial, urban, clerical ways—he'd taken it for granted that village life was slow, steady, chained to the rhythms of season and field; maintaining that these people were, like grain, without guile, slow-moving, plain-speaking, and forthright—how little he'd known!

A man of middle age, clad in a *kurta*, barefoot, emerged from behind the door.

"So you are Mr. Blushing ur-ur Man."

"Well," Ismet said modestly.

"So Mr. Blushing Man is also Mr. Pound-his-Fists, Bring-down-the-Hut-of-People-He-Has-Never-Met-Man, eh?"

But it was accompanied by a kindly expression, sweetened by a smile.

"I didn't . . ."

"Oh," the other waved. "Do not be anxious about it, it is not a serious concern. But really, what is your name now?"

"Ismet. Mr. Ismet Nassin. Bombay Registered Clerk."

"I am Yusuf Haveri yes." The two men shook hands. "Tea?"

Ismet declined.

"*Lassi* maybe, a cup of *lassi*," Yusuf offered, displaying no particular enthusiasm.

"No thanks. I am fine. The train, I ate you know," said my grandfather, though he was parched and famished in fact.

But business came in first place. There was such a thing as priorities. That was the great lesson in life.

"Well, that is all right then. That is perfectly fine by us. We do not want to force things down your throat. Sit down now," Yusuf said slowly.

They sat down together on a bamboo mat. The chicken laid a tentative foot on the mat, but Yusuf shooed it away. It scurried into the deep shade in the corner of the hut, red and brown in its wings.

"I have come about your daughter."

"Ah, Khateja."

"The thing is . . ."

"Ah, the thing. The thing."

Haveri extracted a wrapped-up *paan* leaf from a wallet lying next to him. Ismet accepted when it was waved at him like a flag virtually (feeling that he must make an effort to acclimatize with the customs and traditions).

Yusuf tore off a large piece and stuffed it straight in his mouth. He gave the rest to Ismet, who put it in his mouth and gagged.

"*Chevra* maybe," Haveri suggested, registering his discomfort and revealing a small glass bottle in his right hand, filled with nuts and dried rice, a piece of green ribbon tied around the brim.

Ismet declined.

"You are a man with strong tastes, Mr. Ismet Nassin. Strong tastes. It is true I have only made your acquaintance very recently, but it is clear to me already, I must say."

"I want to marry Khateja, Mr. Haveri."

"Please, Yusuf, we are friends," responded Yusuf agreeably.

"Yusuf."

"Even Yusie if it would be making you more comfortable. For your information, that is what my old, passed-on father was always calling me with. 'Yusie, do this, do that,' he'd say," Haveri explained, sighing at the memory. He took his feet in his hands. "Who's your father again?"

"The late Ebrahim Sikander Nassin who was a tax inspector from Kathiawad in Surashtra, although he worked for a certain time in Bombay. But about Khateja?"

"Khateja." Yusuf ruminated, rocking slowly back and forth. "She is a difficult girl, you know. Difficult. Very difficult. Can't marry her off, royal terror. Royal terror. Mother's blood in her."

Ismet did a quick calculation: savings, inheritance, what he might borrow from the All-India Savings & Commercial, future earnings (taking into account he'd risen three notches already).

"I can give two hundred, maybe two hundred and twenty *rupees*."

Despite his deference to the wishes of Those Above, Ismet winced inside at the magnitude of the sums involved. Maybe he'd been precipitate. There was such a thing as negotiations and give-and-take.

For such a sum he might purchase a personal rickshaw and driver, a dozen Afghan girl brides on the side! Spend his summers on the beach in Goa lifelong! Raise a mortgage on a house in a fashionable section of Bombay and have change jingling in his pocket!

But the best-laid plans—and anyway, flexibility was the thing!

"Two hundred and twenty"—Yusuf Haveri whistled—"Two hundred and twenty *rupees*. For that I could get one personal rickshaw in Bombay. Driver too, man!"

Ismet flinched, this time visibly.

"I suppose so," he granted, "if you are careful with the money."

"And a good wife furthermore for my son, Ahmed," Yusuf observed, pointing to a angular, stumpy, grimy-visaged boy fiddling with his toenails in a corner of the hut.

My grandfather hadn't noticed him.

"Maybe and perhaps, I cannot say for sure. Anything is possible on this earth."

"Mr. Nassin"—florid Haveri grasped his hand and got to his feet, bringing Ismet up along with him—"this is really great news. Really great news, it has made my morning! Fixed up." He drew my grandfather toward him, hugged him, kissed him on the forehead, and pumped his hand up and down. "Fixed up! We are to be in-laws, then. We are to be in-laws. Excellent! Excellent news! Most extraordinary development! Be here first thing tomorrow morning. We will talk further then, set things up, rolling ball. Only thing, we must have references you know. We must be certain that Khateja is going to a good family. Not that we have any doubts, it is not a question of doubts and distrust from this position. Just to be little-little more certain, *ne*? That is how I look at it. After all, a daughter's life is precious to her old father." He thumped his hand against his belly. "Her old father, ha!"

"I can provide names, no problem."

"Names! Names! What is the need for names? We will wire

now-now to Bombay. My brother has a little business to do there this week. He will check up and he will see what there is to be seen and we will know this evening return, *insha'allah*."

"*Insh'allah*," Ismet echoed, caught up in the swing of things.

"Just an address then, if you please."

Yusuf Haveri bent down, rummaged about and produced a dirty scrap of paper and a pencil stub. Pressing on one hand Ismet wrote his address, where he lived with his mother, in block letters, underlining the street address twice.

"Someone will be at home, *ne*?"

"My mother," said Ismet, suddenly wondering if his dear mother wouldn't be unsettled by the wholesale investigation Haveri seemed to propose, "Rashida Nassin."

"Great! Fine, fine! Ha! Well," said Haveri, ushering Ismet out of the hut, "tomorrow morning then, eh? Excellent news."

Ismet found himself outside. The door shut hastily in his face. The women had disappeared. Wind blowing across the plain, clouds blowing along.

He stood there for a moment. His first moment alone since first stepping off the train, disgusted by the behavior, the hypersensitive jabs and gibes of his compartment mates—half the reason he'd felt unable to continue on that particular vehicle of discord.

His shoes were covered with dust. He stamped to shake them clean, then took out his crumpled handkerchief and cleaned his hands.

Inside the hut could he? Well, he thought he heard Haveri saying to his son, "Ahmed, Ahmed the son of my loins, we have found a madman to marry your crazy sister. What good deeds have we done to deserve this madman, that is the question. This is the greatest gift. Ah, they'll be a good match, the madman and the crazy Khateja! And we must order a rickshaw, maybe an Afghan for you so you also benefit from this stroke of good fortune."

But he couldn't be sure—the voice was indistinct and he suspected by now he might be feverish. Was he hearing Haveri slapping his hands together?

Was that Haveri saying, "But we must not be counting these chickens first!"?

Owing to how the human mind worked, the village heat induced suspiciousness. So Rashida had informed him. That was the explanation. My friend, trust a little!

He set off for the hut where he'd been offered a bed. Some water, a curry, maybe a *roti* or two, a nice cup of tea and he'd be restored, no doubt. He would gain perspective from a good meal and a few minutes to just think with his hands on his head. Glancing back, he saw the chicken was staring doubtfully at him, yellow eyes glued to the slatting.

Second thought: "If you are going to be hanging around in these villages, just in case you end up in one of our Indian villages, then it is absolutely crucial that you mustn't be drinking the water, you understand," Rashida had told him years before, putting him down in a chair and putting on the kettle to fix him a cup of tea before work. "Otherwise it will be on my head when my son is dying away in the countryside. Dying away in the countryside and I will have all the trouble on my hands. Well, I am not interested in dead sons, Ismet, I am telling you. I do not have the time. So, no water. No water whatsoever. Do not drink it no matter what the circumstances. Also, avoid the meals if it is possible. Eat chocolates, eat a packet of biscuits, eat on the train when there is an opportunity, but do not sit down and tuck in the moment any Jagjit-from-the-farm invites. I have told you this now, I have said what it is my duty to say."

Mindful of this warning—which came back to him now clearly in the same ominous tone in which it had been delivered, arms akimbo—Ismet realized he might have to go hungry for a period.

"I can make you a nice mutton curry," Ayesha Moderi offered, showing him the mattress in the corner of her hut vacated by her husband, "You sit here and put up your feet, you must be tired, shame, and I will just put one nice little dish on the fire." He declined with a hand.

"Not to worry, not to worry, it is no Big *Tamasha*, I am quite accustomed. Believe me. It is no trouble at all. Actually I will be absolutely delighted to show a bit of hospitality, since you are interested in our Khateja and all."

"So kind of you, but it is not necessary. Since I have eaten on the train. I am quite full, but it is too sweet of you to suggest, I appreciate that fact. But I will just lie here and have a little rest. A few minutes of resting, that is my number one priority."

He sank onto the mattress.

"You mustn't be embarrassed now, it will be my pleasure, I have said," Ayesha pointed out.

"No really," Ismet said firmly, "I am only tired."

("Do not sit down and tuck in with any Jagjit!")

"If you are sure . . ."

"I am sure."

("I am not interested in dead sons, I am not having the slightest interest!")

"I am quite sure."

("Dying away in the countryside and what it will mean is that there are more commotions and agitations on top of my head. You just take some elementary precautions from the outset. That is the ideal situation here.")

He put his feet up on the mattress beside him.

Ayesha conceded good-naturedly, went off to fetch him a cushion to put behind his head, saying very brightly, "Well then, allow me to get you a nice cool drink of water."

At 4:37 that afternoon a message sparked across the telegraph wire that linked the area to the Bombay region.

> To Mr. Yusuf Haveri. House is well situated. The mother is a bit of a witch, but that is to be expected from a certain section of our Bombay Indians, as you are well aware, dear Yusuf. Considerable assets on hand. I offer many thanks that our High Hopes and Expectations in our Khateja have been fulfilled in this wonderful and unexpected manner. Please to convey my regrets owing to the unfortunate circumstances of my absence. And to you Many Congratulations on this Happy Occasion.
>
> Faithfully,
> Your brother, Yacoob Haveri.

It stuttered reluctantly onto a piece of paper in the Reuter's Telegraph Office in the next village, situated in the part of the land to the north where the green land looked white to the eye because of the wind, and where there was a dam under construction on whose wall the paraffin lamps burned all day long in blue canvas tents. The message was torn off by the local operator, a Calcutta-educated man who wore green-shaded sunglasses and smoked a pipe out of boredom. He gave the paper to his runner to deliver.

The boy, who'd been flying a kite made with string and two sheets of brown paper, reluctantly wiped the snot from his nose, hauled in his kite by winding in the cord on his wrist, and set off on his long thin feet to the Haveri hut, four miles distant. When Yusuf opened the envelope very quickly, making very sure not to tear it in the middle, a smile curled across his face.

"Go, Ahmed"—he nudged his son—"tell that damned sister of yours to come here. No," he corrected himself, "first tell her mother I am wanting her on some urgent business." He smiled. "It's looking like we might get rid of her. Well and truly rid of her. Must be our prayers had an accumulating effect after all these years."

He popped a triangle of *paan* into his mouth and leaned philosophically against the corner of the hut.

When that evening Khateja, whistling, swinging the half full bucket around her wrist, picking her way past the chicken, at peace with herself and with the world—when she pushed open the door of the hut, she discovered the Haveri family squeezed inside.

They were all there, sitting pretty, talking in low voices.

Ahmed had been sent to fetch stools, cushions, two scratchy wooden chairs from the neighbors, a bench on loan from the station. On them were assembled the greater Haveris: septuagenarian Chotty, Omar, Mamood, and Amina-ma in the front ranks; Salim the butcher, Salima, Fatima, Fazel-*bhai*, Ayesha-*bibi* who had brought with a bowl of dahl specially, and Firoza reclined behind the venerables; her mother, Shireen, stood behind them, holding Ahmed's hand stiffly.

The two mattresses had been folded carefully and stacked behind the door, a cloth spread over them. Everyone was drinking tea. There was a festive mood.

The Most Aged, Most Durable Rabiya, Yusuf's great-aunt, was seated by herself on a chair next to the bench, worrying away at a string of orange prayer beads, gurgling unobtrusively into her cup, rubbing the rim against her gums, the black and brown dots on her neck showing when she lifted her head, silk scarf down over her eyebrows.

She hadn't said much in a decade, however, ever since her husband, Rishaad, lost his life to the smallpox, after which she'd suffered a severe stroke. A practical assessment relegated her to the corner, where Khateja could hardly see her at all, though the lamp was turned up.

Standing behind the lamp, Ahmed was bored, his free hand straying to scratch his thighs, fumble behind his ears, hitch his trousers up.

Shireen scolded him, "Ahmed, keep still! Keep still, you mustn't always be fidget-fidgeting. People will think you are abnormal!"

She squeezed his hand tightly, hoping to hurt him. When

she saw that her daughter had come in, however, she pinched him hard once-twice and fell silent.

In fact, everyone in the hut fell silent. In keeping with the dignity of the situation, the chicken had been expelled and was rootling around on the outside, pecking at the weeds, strutting, showing off with the other chickens, occasionally poking against the door to follow the proceedings.

In a way, the chicken represented Yusuf Haveri's hopes. It stood in for his optimism. His lips smacked only imagining its fate . . .

"Just think," he'd told Shireen, "when that aunt of yours dies away and we can sell her rings off, then we can cut that chicken, serve chicken *biryani*, chicken cutlets, chicken curry, *masala* chicken what."

"Ha!" Shireen replied. "That chicken! That one useless skinny-skinny chicken. Not enough on it for one good breast."

"Ha!" she muttered to herself when he'd gone out, feeling quite hurt, "he mustn't come and count his chickens over here, personally I am not interested."

No stander on filial pieties, still she was annoyed by her husband's cavalier style of dispatching her aunt via the process of imagination. How could he think such thoughts in advance? Thinking ahead to the future, she would have none of it!

Nonetheless, she didn't interfere when Yusuf defended the chicken zealously against those who proposed its speedier destruction. Not for her to cut up her own husband's heart, feathers flying, in a metal bowl. In fact, she sympathized without saying as much.

Yusuf had been standing by himself next to the door, leaning against the mattresses, stepping on the cloth.

(Skulking behind doors gave one that small advantage, the first opportunity for the overall picture. What was the game of life if not a struggle to accumulate these small-small advantages that mounted up in the final end?)

Now he stepped forward and took Khateja in his arms.

"My daughter," he intoned, kissing her on the cheek, "my one daughter."

At this everyone else in the room with the exception of Ahmed murmured, "My daughter, my daughter."

"What is this?" demanded Khateja, freeing herself from her father's embrace and stepping back a little to appraise the position, dropping the bucket softly to the floor by her feet. Not that she was intimidated. "What is going on? What you are all doing sit-sitting over here, eh? What are you relaxing around with tea in your hands as if it is Sunday?"

Yusuf had expected nothing less of his daughter. He could have played the situation beforehand in his head as if he had a gramophone record. She wasn't going to take the sea change just sitting down on the floor. Of that he was well aware.

Sternly, "Khateja, my daughter, my own baby, my *kaleji*, we have found you a husband."

He wondered if he should allow maybe a single tear to slide down his cheeks. On balance, he decided, he'd better not: If this didn't work out he was going to need every last one of his tears. Every last tear.

His lachrymose glands would be working overtime—oh yes, missing that rickshaw, that slew of Afghan brides, those fine sweetmeats, those lamb curries, the scores of chicken cutlets he'd promised to himself in exaltation in secret moments. What would that mangy fowl outside (oh, he secretly recognized its manginess) be to him then? A tidbit, good perhaps for an afternoon tea sliced cold with crackers and butter. Served on two dozen white saucers . . .

If only he could keep his cool now, and push his damnfool daughter kicking-screaming blue-murdered into wedlock with the blushing ur-ur madman before the crazy lunatic changed his erratic little mind and disavowed what had been declared in the hot light of the day.

(That was the sad truth about human nature, no matter if one wished to look as much as possible on the bright side.)

If only . . .

"Khateja," he repeated very firmly, "you are twenty years old now, one unmarried *galoot* of a daughter, and we have asked around a little and we have chatted with a few people who know facts about these situations and we have found you a good husband, a man with a good family, a husband who is right for you and also compatible from the point of view of personal relations. That is how it stands, Khateja. Now we want to arrange things, get the matter straight, everything understood on your side, everything clear and fixed up, ball rolling."

"It's the ur-ur man isn't it?" Khateja said with perfect serenity.

Quickly she evaluated: was this the correct strategic instant to throw a tantrum? postpone for maximum effect? the relative advantage of an epileptic fit and an asthma attack, gasping, choking for breath, screaming out loud so the cups in the drawer rattled, over a mundane temper tantrum, say? a seizure? In desperate circumstances the effectiveness of a well-thought-out, clearly enunciated, curdled-blood suicide threat shouldn't be underestimated.

Khateja was completely familiar with this sort of campaigning, having been forced to resort to extreme measures in the past to put a wrench in her family's connubial ambitions. This wasn't the first time, don't be fooled. It was becoming a continuous thing, trying to get her shacked up with one charlatan with two pence rattling in his suit pocket, one after another.

A continuous thing virtually, it was almost getting so she could predict the next move from their side. She'd ward off their designs on her virtue. In the dark, blindfolded, with one hand tied behind her back. Which was just the measure of the sordid nature of the whole situation by this point. Frankly, she was thoroughly sick to her stomach.

Unfortunately for Khateja, this time the Haveris were set to go.

"Mr. Ismet Nassin, Bombay registered clerk, that is the name of the fellow we have picked out with your interests in mind," Yusuf said patiently. But what was the point of triffling and trifling? "Yes, it is Mr. ur-ur Man. Mr. Blushing Man. Mr. Pound-His-Fists-on-the-Door Man, what you will, the name is unimportant, my dear."

Yusuf sighed. This wasn't going to be easy any way you looked at it.

"Well," said Khateja, "that is simple then."

"It is?"

"Yes. An easy thing."

"An easy thing?"

Yusuf allowed himself to relax a bit.

"Easy. I won't do it. I won't be married to that man. I will not be sold away as if I am a box of the vegetables for you to give to any passing stranger who is on the street. No matter how much money he is offering to you for the pleasure."

Khateja, in turn, allowed herself to relax a bit. Why, this hadn't been difficult in the least. What a pack of clods her family was! Really a pack of clods!

They really thought she'd give up? Logically, how many times would she have to rub their collective noses in the facts?

Maybe they were all retarded, she the only one blessed with an Okay brain? Her personal opinion, it was something in the blood, some retarding agent passed on from the older generation she'd luckily evaded. Had her mother Shireen been dilly-dallying with another man when she, Khateja, was conceived? Such was her suspicion.

Otherwise, honestly, could one explain how she, a free, quick-thinking intelligent individual, had landed up in the world with these ninnies and blockheads to call her family, to pinch her cheeks with their bony white-stretched manipulative fingers, rotten to the very core?

"Khateja, that is not good enough, that is just not good enough. This is an issue on which we have all decided. Your mother and"—he pointed generally toward the collected Haveris—"your aunties and your uncles, Rabiya, your grandfather, your brother Ahmed, your grandfather. We have all chatted about this. We have decided."

The indicated relatives assented with great vigor, "Yes, we have decided."

Khateja peered into the depths of the hut. Was it eye trickery, or was her brother, Ahmed—unlaughing-glumming Ahmed—smiling broadly, ghoulishly, monsterlike in his wretched corner? That . . . that worm! That donkey! That snake!

But it was a time for steely nerves. Self-control. Clearly these were serious Haveris before her.

Serious Haveris, you could see from their expressions. What were they thinking? Card-sleevery afoot?

"Your mother, your aunties, your uncles, your own grandfather and grandmother," Yusuf reiterated, "they have said what a great"—he paused— "what an excellent thing this proposal is."

"But my grandmother," Khateja pointed out, "is quite dead. In fact"—honing in—"both of them are dead. Both of my grandmothers are dead. They are dead-dead, the two of them. Completely. Totally. And Utterly Dead . . ."

The hut cringed visibly. There were oohs and there were aahs, there were tiny shrieks, expressions of pain, hissings and suckings-in of breath, muted murmurings and murmured mutterings.

Yusuf could feel the disarray spreading. A miscalculation that?

He racked his brains. He folded his hands almost shyly.

He looked extremely upset.

"Khateja, how could you be saying this in front of ev-eryone?

"Khateja, how could you do this?" he put it to her, raising his eyebrows a little to indicate he was waiting for an answer from her.

"Well, it is true, isn't it? They are both dead, two grand-mothers both, admit now, it is useless to practice this sort of a deception. How could my grandmother have agreed? This cannot be, oh absolutely not, it is an impossible thing. An impossible impossibility! What do you think I am? One big fat stupid?"—move to the offensive—"Shame! Shame on you who are in cahoots to use the name of my grandmother, such disrespect for those departed who really deserve our respect!"

"Rabiya!"—the solution came to Yusuf—"Your grand-mother appeared to Rabiya in a dream and was all the time saying what an excellent match indeed, what great luck Ismet was for her beloved Khateja. Great stroke of good fortune, that is what he represents for her. Certainly that was her feeling."

Yusuf turned to the audience who hummed their assent.

At the sound of her name, Rabiya rustled uneasily. She didn't say anything though, just fingered her way through an-other circuit of prayer beads. Shireen reached over and put her hands on Rabiya's shoulders for reassurance, pushing Ah-med behind her back so he wouldn't derail the whole process with funny stunts that Khateja could pick on to deflect atten-tion from the central issues (which was just like Khateja to do, that was the regrettable reality).

Yusuf pressed on, "Yes, yes. Your grandmother was in Rabiya's dream."

"Both of them I suppose."

"Well," he admitted, "I am not sure if it was both of the grandmothers, but it was definitely the one. My dear mother conveyed this information. But who knows, maybe it was Shireen's mother too, behind it from the beginning, that is a possibility. On this earth who will say they can set limits to what is possible?"

He looked thoughtful. He raised his eyebrows a little and looked upward for just a second (even though ideally he should keep his eyes on the target, he knew perfectly).

"I don't believe it for one second."

"But didn't Rabiya just tell us this? Did Rabiya not stand and say clearly what was on her mind, due to how she was concerned that we must be conscious of the situation's full implications? One minute ago did she not stand here to participate with the family on this decision?"

From the back Shireen, "Yes, Khateja, you must be listening. These are precisely the words Rabiya used a minute before you so delightfully put in an appearance."

"Ha! Rabiya hasn't been saying anything all these years, and suddenly this? Suddenly she comes out with this? I am not a believer. No chance! Why she doesn't say it for herself, eh? Why she doesn't say it with her own mouth? Here I am and here is Rabiya under the same roof. Rabiya, say it now!"

"Don't be like this now, Khateja," pleaded Yusuf.

"Ha!"

A tantrum was overdue (Khateja decided), a good cat-

erwauling crashing thudding banging throbbing thrupping
tantrum!

(Probably in this regressive society that was what it took
for a woman to prove she was no one's puppet.)

But something, a glint in her father's eyes, held her back
for an instant. What else was up?

"Khateja, you know it simply does not matter what you
are believing or thinking or deciding. Not one bit. We are
decided on this, firm-firm. There is no place here for 'yes-buts'
and 'buttings,' I am telling you. Or else. . . ."

"Or else what? What?"

The bagged cat, the dropped boot, the gauntlet cast: "You
will be married to Ahmedu tomorrow!"

Ahmedu the idiot, Ahmedu raven-chaser, Ahmedu swal-
lower-of-sparrows, Ahmedu the brainless, Ahmedu the drib-
bling! Oh Ahmedu, Ahmedu!

(Game, set, match: to Mr Yusuf Haveri.

Best supporting cast: the Haveris. Special mention to the
grande dames.)

"What!!!"

"Yes"—try not to gloat, she is your daughter, after all—"we
have fixed it up."

"You can't do that. I'll refuse. There, I just did. I have
refused to marry that moron."

"Refuse—fiddlesticks!" Yusuf shot straight back. "Refuse—
fiddlesticks! We have it straight with the magistrate, who is
being Ahmedu's uncle. Tomorrow"—tapping his foot sharply
on the floor—"we will do it if you do not step into line. Tomorrow. Early morning, we will send a message with Reuter's.

And then his family will come take you away to their house.
They have already chosen a room that will be for you and
him, they are looking around for furniture at this very moment, I can tell you that much."

(What need to raise one's voice when the loopholes had
been closed up? Relax. Enjoy the pleasures of a deed well
done.)

"You wouldn't do that. To me?"

"Yes, we would," chimed the family, Ahmed's voice distinct among them. "If it is necessary."

"If that is what must be done. If that is what it comes down
to. If there is no option for us. Yes we would," Yusuf inter-
preted patiently for his daughter's benefit, in case she hadn't
got the point through her brain.

"No?"

"Yes yes."

"You want monster babies, eh? Little Ahmedus? Ahme-
dudus? Cripples, vegetable heads, *aloo* brains, hoof-clovens?"

Yusuf sighed, the brutality of the world weighing heavy on
his heart. "If that is the price, my daughter."

"I am just not believing it. The cheek! Ma, are you agreeing
with this mad dad?"

Shireen nodded her head, feeling miserable. Conflict
wasn't her forte.

"Papa, grandfather you too? Chotty? Mamood? Amina-ma?"
They nodded their heads.

Yusuf felt uneasy at this brazen appeal to his base of support. Phase three.

"And Khateja . . ."

"What?!"

"If there is any tantrums, any epileptics from your side after we have had this discussion, then what we must say is that maybe Ahmedu is for the best. You will be suited together, *ne*? Crazy both."

"You, you, you snakes," Khateja shrieked, unable to inject the venom she was feeling into the words. "You are all . . . I hate you all . . . You're all . . . all worms! Worms! Worms, hear, worms worms worms!!! Except you, Ahmed, you're worse." She shook her fists at her brother. "Worms!"

Alternating between "Worms!," "Snakes!," "Dogs!," "Pigs!" and "Rats!" she hurled herself out of the door and careened away from the hut, speeding past the chicken and almost slamming right into a half-buried rake. The village women, who had been clustered outside the hut gleaning what they could of the proceedings, watched her go in amazement. Such things!

Buzzing like an angry hornet around the village, kicking at dogs, hissing at chickens, possessed by images of rutting Ahmedu, thighs lusty like a goat, so furious her head was swimming with black dots, her eyes filled with red fluid, Khateja ran into the two people who didn't know well enough to stay out of her way and hadn't been warned to do so by the wisdom of the village communicated in significant glances.

The first: Ahmedu Akhbar.

Ahmedu was looking through a telescope his father had bought for him for his twenty-first birthday from a Portuguese shop in Panjim, where import-export business had taken him

the previous year—a factory-reject shipment of Manchester
cloth.

Ahmedu had just finished rubbing the whole thing—wood, lens, metal screws, all—with spit, bringing the instrument to a slightly moist varnish. Spinning the front bit back and forth, he watched it sink into the back bit and then emerge when he reversed the process. He put it to his right eye, knocking himself in the head.

Switching hands, he placed it gingerly against the other eye and squinted through it. He could see the moon, large, dry, yellow-floating, cratered and cracked.

A hand grabbed the far end of the telescope and forced it down.

The red eye of Khateja appeared in the place of the moon, shining wrath down the cylinder, vast in its turbulence.

Then she let go.

The telescope went flying.

"Aaargh!" she screamed at Ahmedu, who recoiled, forgetting his new toy. "Aaargh, you worm, you hoof-cloven, you knobble-knee, you ham tongue, you bastard monster bastard, you helped them plan this, admit it. Choke, you worm, choke, choke. Die, bastard, die!"

Then her rage swept her away. It was impossible to scream as loud as she felt inside. Her throat felt like sandpaper inside and anyhow being at a standstill with this moron vegetable was the last thing. She pelted off in the direction of the railway platform, where the day's arrival was smoking a cigarette, elated at his good fortune. Ismet had spent a quiet day in the village. After Ayesha Moderi brought him a jug of water over his protests and set it down beside him meaningfully without a word (was village hospitality not good enough for this Bombay Ismet?), he decided to take a walk, see a bit of the country. Who knew when he'd get the chance again?

He drifted about the vegetable patch at the back of the village, where the women were digging up potatoes and onions, packing them up in wicker baskets, squatting down on their hard knees, bundling up their saris above the elbow. Later, he went and stood by the station where for three rupees, the ticket seller sold him two Cadbury's chocolate bars wrapped up in silver paper and a bottle of lemonade.

By now his anxiety dissipated. What spineless pineapple indeed, but how sweet and golden the fruit when the bark is offed, how soft the flesh!

Yes, he could see now, a lovelier and truer and more complete life was at hand. Need be he'd surmount greater obstacles, jump a million and one hoops, if such was the expressed desire of angels. He'd fly through fire. He'd whistle and keep both hands in his pockets while passing through the circle of the flame. No problem.

He lit a cigarette and looked up. There were clear, sharp sparkles, rough cloud banks, the firmament hill chipped at the horizon. The train tracks led elliptically away in both directions. He imagined staying on the train forever, briefcase lodged on the overhead racks, business abandoned, appointments missed, traveling along in circles that wound round and round the planet but never came back to the same place.

"Aargh!" Khateja screamed for the second time, seeing him standing there with his cigarette in one hand.

"Aargh!" Ismet responded, jolted.

His future bride was bearing down on him, red-faced, hands in fists and suspended above her body like hammers.

For a moment Khateja feared she'd burst with rage. Explode! There was a heavy, heavy pounding in the vessels in her head. Her lungs contracted; her heart galloped within her chest.

Had she punched Ismet at that exact moment, he would have been smashed into the ground like a drill bit. Not even his head would have remained above it.

("Remember that handsome Bombay Ismet, eh," they'd have told Khateja when she was fifty plus, "that Mr. Bombay Ismet. How he was going to marry you and all with his big promises, then he disappeared just like that. Whoosh! Zip! No trace, gone from the earth. Gone away from the earth with his big promises. Always thought he was a shifty sort, personally. Wily customer. Even in the beginning, couldn't bring myself to trust this *Memon* chap with his big-big talk, I remember clearly.")

(That would have been better.)

But Khateja didn't strike him. Because the universe cooled in an instant. Everything became perfectly clear and transparent.

Holding up her hands flatly before her to forestall a response from his side, she said, very slowly, "If you make me marry you, I swear I will make your life one long misery. You will know nothing but sorrow. All you will experience is pain, suffering, and traumas like you have caused to me on this day. Pains and traumas, I will never forget. No, I will not put it

behind me. You will wish how you had never been born, that
is my promise to you."

"You don't understand," he explained, "it was an angel. . . ."

"Then I will make the angel too regret the fact that it has
been born," she countered, curiously satisfied.

"You and the angel will go and cry together," she forecast.

"The two of you both," she reconfirmed, "you will go
and cry."

Then she turned around and walked home in no hurry.
Savoring each pace.

As for Ismet: Well, what silver lining without cloud? Now
destiny must take its course. The way things worked out was
always so unexpected.

Surely his new wife must learn to love. When all was said
and done, that was His wish.

Chapter Three

"Mr. Blushing ur-ur Man is still here?" Khateja inquired pleasantly the following morning when she came in from an early stroll by the field where the cow was sleeping, wet and shining amid the plants.

"Yes. He is still here in this place. There has been no change in the situation."

Yusuf fully expected a second uprising.

But he steeled himself; the apparition of a rickshaw revolved in his mind, to say nothing of some peace and quiet once he'd ejected this daughter.

"And he is still wishing to marry me? That is his desire?"

"And why not? Are you not my daughter, the child of Yusuf Haveri, fine stock?"

"Of course, papa. Of course. Well, fine."

"Fine?"

"I will marry him."

Yusuf said, "My own darling!"

He said, "My chicken!"

He was overwhelmed by a tide of affection. He flung his

arms about her and spoke down to her gorgeous crown, enchantingly parted right along the middle.

"I knew you would see what is sensible for you after all these years. Only last night I was telling your mother how I suspected you would come morningtime not downcast and sulking and pulled up at all, but in fact you would be happy at how you could be married up to a good man. 'In fact she will be looking forward, she will have a certain amount of anticipation inside of her heart,' these were my exact words. Ask, ask if you don't believe."

"Yes, papa." Khateja freed herself from Yusuf's effusive arms. "You were perfectly correct. From the very beginning I should have listened to your opinion, that was my big mistake. Now it is clear in my head."

Within a month (she calculated) she'd be returned directly back to her village, he'd actually offer his whole money supply only to get her off his bleeding hands—there'd be ample, oh, oversufficient time to settle accounts.

Then they'd all see, yes, the little joy in their lives would disappear under her exceedingly careful ministrations, how they'd suffer, the worms! She'd half a mind to learn some magic on the side: not soul-damning stuff, just hemorrhoids at a distance, diarrhea, ingrown toenails, malignant breasts, warts, that type of thing. This whole one village would rue their treachery, yet they'd never be able to pin their miseries on her. Their miseries and laughable village tragedies that would haunt their whole lives.

And the lives of their village-children's village-children.

("Leave me alone," she'd say. "I am just a poor sad woman

abandoned by her husband. And I must be accused like this. I
must be made into the scapegoat for what you have brought on
your own heads. Shame! It is a little too much now.")

"I will marry Mr. Nassin," she repeated dutifully.

"You must be getting married very quickly now, Mr. Nassin.
Who knows but she might well change her mind if there is a
big delay. I know my daughter. Unfortunately she is what-what
fickleness itself, that is her only real fault. But nobody on this
earth is perfect, that is the sad truth. The important point is
that we can't be too careful."

"Yes, yes."

"Under the circumstances. So we have arranged for the
nika'a tonight. Ahmed has gone to fetch plates from the next
town. Shireen is cooking, samoosas, biryani, everything fixed
up"—why not justifiable exaggeration?—"Khateja too is helping, getting the tables straight and all, going for the knives and
forks and whatnot so there is a weight off our backs as far as
the preparations are concerned. A weight off our backs. She is
happy about this now, sure to be a good wife, mother's blood
in her. Very good girl actually. Twenty fine years. Ha, I could
even sign a guarantee, in a manner of speaking, of course!"

This very day, Ismet reflected, he would be shacked up with
Khateja. That was how things had turned out—and why not?
Tonight was as fine as any other night.

How would he explain to Rashida how he'd gone in the
morning and returned three days later with a wife at his side
and a couple village in-laws on the side? Maybe her feathers
would be a little ruffled, since she was always one who wanted

to be consulted on important decisions. But surely he'd receive the same help from above that had already smoothed his way so miraculously, was that asking too much?

Certainly not. He anticipated no insurmountables. Maybe strained introductions and then settle in to domestic bliss. His mother was no monster that she would block up her ears to what he would tell her of these remarkable events. She knew some things about these signs and messages. She would sympathize and take Khateja into her heart straight, that was his prediction.

"No need, it is fine," he agreed. "Tonight. Only thing . . ."

"Anything," Yusuf vowed precipitately.

"I need clothing, jacket, trousers."

"No, no, you are fine as it is, perfectly all right."

"At least a clean shirt."

"No," Yusuf countered. Where on earth would he find a correct-fitting shirt for this fruitcake? "Absolutely not. On no account. I do not even want to hear of this again. Why, you are looking so handsome I hear the girls next door whisp-whispering, 'But we are truly jealous. If only this Mr. Nassin were not marrying Khateja we would take an interest ourselves. And what nice clothing, what a good shirt, what good trousers, you must just take one look, really make the man in this case.' Yes, that's what they are saying. Mustn't be embarrassed now, fine young fellow you are. No need for a new shirt. No need whatsoever. In fact, I want them to say, 'Look at this Mr. Ismet Nassin. Doesn't even change his shirt and still he's the most handsome, best-dressed man we have ever encountered. How fortunate is our Khateja, and even more her old father, this chap Yusuf Haveri over here, to have this well-dressed son.' That's what I want them to be saying. Make me proud of my new son. What a man indeed!" He reached forward and pinched Ismet's cheek firmly. "Ha!"

"Well, if you're sure."

He was blushing again. No one, not even his own mother, had thought him so comely, and here was a sizable village lining up to marry him on the strength of his looks virtually. It went to show: India was a big place, and it was never possible to say with certainty what was sitting up just around the next corner.

In Bombay many women wouldn't give him time of day. And he'd just about had enough of that sort of behavior. Sick to his stomach of the Bombay situation, the Bombay maidens and their airs and put-ons.

Here was a besotted village, charmed by his every mannerism. Every little thing he did! Well, he wasn't going to let it go to his head. Though he must admit that being smacked across the cheeks by an angel, being found so attractive in the village from the advent, it made reflection necessary. Thought about his place in the greater scheme of the world. It raised the question of destiny.

(And when there was sufficient justification, it was equally foolish not to consider destiny, ne, as it was worthless in the opposite situation to speculate foolishly without two real hopes.)

"And, er, son, there is the matter of the money."

"What about it?"

"We will be needing some to pay for the ceremony today. Also to give to relatives, friends who come and all. For good luck in the future."

In for a penny.

"Well," Ismet said doubtfully, "I can wire Bombay Savings if it is an urgent necessity."

"It is an urgency, my son, you know, cash on hand and all that. A hundred and ninety-five now. Two hundred. The rest can follow later if it is necessary, week, two weeks not a problem. After all"—Yusuf leaned forward and stared deeply into Ismet's eyes and took his hands firmly in his own—"we are family now, *ne?* What is a week when we are together for all life?"

As it happened, my grandfather did find a clean suit. The local merchant, a short, heavy man with sad, heavy eyes and heavy feet, offered to lend him a suit at a nominal charge.

"Hardly a pittance," he said expansively, "hardly a pittance. Just to keep the books straight, you know."

He took the opportunity to place before the groom an array of goods and services—boot blacking, shirt pressing, general and luxury laundering, best-quality shoelaces, top-class wristwatches, patent umbrellas—which, even if they weren't of immediate use to Ismet right-straightaway-on-the-spot, would come in handy at that unexpected moment, unquestionably. That was the meaning of the word "caveat," *ne?*

And where would such bargains, such reasonableness, be found a second time? Certainly not in Bombay, home of sharks and wheeler-dealers, crooks, thieves, bloodsuckers, fiscal leechers. But why was he explaining this when no doubt Mr. Nassin was more familiar with such people's shenanigans than he?

Also, didn't Mr. Nassin, village darling that he was (one must admit directly to his face), didn't he think it appropriate to purchase a few choice items to distribute to his new relatives and well-wishers at the ceremony, which he himself was planning to close his shop specially in order to go to?

How about saying good-bye for the moment to a few special ones? A few choice articles, a few select ways to say a special "thank you" in a most unusual fashion?

"Actually," Ismet said anxiously, "I do not have too much money at the moment. Just the suit really, that is what I will take."

But he was cajoled into taking with him a bag of confections for the children, a set of framed portraits of Queen Victoria for Yusuf and Shireen done in permanent ink, a bicycling guide to the Lake District, a dog-eared copy of *Moby-Dick* for the sophisticated, educated types.

The suit itself was an inch or so short, and his ankles flashed out shyly from the trousers when he walked.

But that, the merchant rushed to assure him, was the current vogue in trousers among the younger generation in the village.

The village was abuzz. Yusuf had squandered fourteen *rupees* on milk, a block of sugar, paper cups and spoons, and was seated under an umbrella at a table by the water pump pouring out glass after glass of *lassi* for the thirsty, who were enjoying his largesse immensely.

(And for himself? It was a perfect occasion to liquidate his holdings, everything saved up over the years for a celebration. "Better be kissing that chicken good-bye," he'd told Ahmed. "This time tomorrow it is going to be in a *biryani*, oh yes. How I am looking forward to meeting it on my plate!")

By the time the next-town *imam* arrived, summoned in the greatest haste to perform the *nika'a*, everyone was involved in one way or another in the wedding. Khateja had consented to wear her mother's prettiest sari and the two gold bangles Shireen received from her own mother on the day of her marriage to Yusuf—on the understanding (Yusuf made clear) that she'd return them chop-chop that evening.

"But today, my dearest daughter, we are wanting you to look your best."

Nothing must go astray.

Still, if anything did, if Mr. Blushing ur-ur Man developed the cold feet that any minimally sane person would, Yusuf would be 170 *rupees* in pocket, deducting the cost of the *lassi* and the *imam*'s fee. No chance of a refund on that money since he'd already handed it over to the safety deposit at the station, from whence it would fly within the hour to Yacoob for safe-keeping. Best, though, he scoop the rest and dispose of the vex-atious Khateja.

Khateja did look good. Shireen, who honestly believed this match was in her child's best interests, spent half an hour cir-cling her, tucking away folds of fabric and pinning up bits until the bride of the afternoon felt dizzy just watching her mother go round and round about her like a solicitous pendulum, springing around on her knees, watching like a hawk for any imperfection.

"There," Shireen crooned, "my daughter, my child," and kissed Khateja once on each cheek.

Khateja glowed. She twinkled. The dimples in her cheeks swirled about. What with the laughter lines in her cheeks, the charming set of her shoulders and her exquisite eyebrows she was a very pretty young woman. Looked at the right way, she had the luxurious mood of a panther about her. She seemed to bound over the earth. Her nose was short and sharp, flared at the nostril. Her eyes and thick hair were a lovely brown. Her skin was a trifle darker than she herself would have picked out but otherwise entirely satisfactory. Her chin was quick and elegant. Her breasts . . .

But put her breasts to one side for the moment, please. She was a very pretty young woman: fine figure, fine face.

The sari Shireen lent her, hardly worn at all, was made from fabric bright bright green, mixed in with silver threads and copper stars that glowed and twinkled too. Her hair, normally bunned up behind her head, floated loosely through the air. Shireen had drawn around her eyes with a piece of kohl. Her eyelids were smudged with green, her eyelashes wept with black, and copper circles swung from the lobes of her ears.

She was sent on a walkabout first, from the hut to the railway station, thence to the store, thence through the clearing east, west, north, from which ten southerly paces led her, on Shireen's arm, back into the hut to sit on the matching pitchpine chair next to her fiancé, where she would finally have the chance for a little rest and a cup of tea and a saucer of sweet-meats sliced into thumb-size rectangles. The village assembled to salute. It whistled and clucked and threw little bits of things into the air.

"I am absolutely delighted to introduce my son-in-law, Mr. Ismet Nassin. For the information of the public, he is a registered accountant and a senior chap in this here Bombay. But as we have all seen over the past few days, he is not one with a big-city attitude, oh no. With him there is no question of adopting a highfalutin tone only because we are village people with Simplicity in our hearts. Truly, this is a man of the people before us who my little Khateja is marrying with." The father of the bride announced all this with a bullhorn he'd dug up somewhere, since this soft-spoken Ismet (why must he blow his own trumpet?) politely declined the chance to say a few words himself. Yusuf continued, "A man of the people and a chap who understands what is the meaning of the word 'modern romance.' Like my lovely only daughter, Khateja, who we will miss so much, who will hopefully be back soon for a visit with us to tell what she learned in the world that is outside, the world that has many great dangers but in addition many greater opportunities for advancement and future happiness."

There was a rousing cheer.

Maybe this marriage thing was Okay, Khateja caught herself thinking.

Right there and then she scolded herself: Don't be fooled, deceived, don't be led astray, my Khateja! This man is a worm. They are all worms. And they are going to pay.

Immediately after the marriage ceremony Yusuf gripped Ismet by the arm and led him off for a word.

"Here my son, my present to you on this happy day."

Proudly he handed over two train tickets, wrapped up in a brown paper envelope with the relevant information penciled on the front in big block letters.

"Tickets," he explained, "for the train tonight. Seven-thirty." He glanced at his new Waltham wristwatch and added informatively, "Twenty minutes. Not much time, necessary to hurry, can't be squandering the minutes, we do not have all the time in the world. These are the unfortunate facts, what can we do?"

"Twenty minutes!"

Ismet had loosened up, gotten into the swing of things, smiled and yelled and thrown things back at the crowd, pressed a hundred sweaty hands and accepted embraces. His arms had been squeezed up to a froth, his legs clutched by children.

The truth was, he was enjoying this. In fact, he'd be on top of the world virtually if only Khateja could bring herself to say one single word to him at this early stage of the game.

But even taking her intransigence into account, the experience was most pleasant. Here he'd stumbled on a place where he was loved, yes, loved: the word was not too strong! Why leave so soon?

"So soon?"

"Yes. It is important. Keep from hitches, you know, unexpected changes. And you have our address, yes? Can always write a note if something crops up, keep in touch. Most fond regards but there is no such thing as a good thing which will last forever, my dear Ismet, my son. You will find that out for yourself one day, I am afraid."

"But . . ."

"No." Yusuf was adamant. "Certainly not. Shireen and I have talked about this and we have come to a decision. It is important for you and Khateja to get away from things, obligations, you know, responsibilities, commitments, so you are able to take some time for yourselves. You must spend time just the two of you, that is our feeling." He smiled. "Honeymoon a little."

Honeymoon a little . . .

"But the train to Bombay doesn't go tonight. I have made some inquiries, you see. It is only coming following week."

"Exactly," said unblinking Yusuf, "and this way you will both have a holiday." He stretched out his arms. "See something of the country. Beautiful places, historical places"—might as well be honest—"Hyderabad."

"Hyderabad! But that is located in the opposite direction!"

"Oh," Yusuf said smoothly, "but that is precisely the point. Leisure time. When you get to Hyderabad all you must do is buy a ticket and lo! you will arrive in Bombay quick-snaps. You will say, 'My good father Yusuf, he was absolutely correct. In fact, my holiday was too-too short. A fleeting thing. Pity we didn't get a chance to see more of Hyderabad, it is one of our oldest and most interesting Indian cities.' I give you my personal guarantee."

Then he quieted his voice and said confidentially, "Besides, it is Khateja who is wanting this thing, you see. Always wanted to see Hyderabad even as a small kitten. 'Daddy take me to Hyderabad, Daddy take me to Hyderabad. Daddy can we pay a visit to this Hyderabad for a few days tourism?' Don't know why exactly, just always had a thing about it."

"Hyderabad?"

Ismet grimaced. He thought of it as a grimy, enfeebled, hill-set city, sun-cudgeled, raisin-peopled, camel-walked, rain-drained.

"Oh, oh, wonderful city, wonderful city. Never been there myself but heard only the best about it. Best reports. Brother Yacoob, your uncle Yacoob, saw it on one occasion many years back. Never got over it. Never got over it, it is the most amazing thing. Still to this day he is always talking about it, always has a good word for it, Hyderabad has this, Hyderabad has that, in Hyderabad they know what is two and two, and so on. He'll be too happy when he hears you've gone. Always been crazy about Hyderabad. Where Khateja got the idea, I suppose." He handed Ismet a chipped blue luggage bag. "Here, these are Khateja's things, packed them myself with my own two hands. Keep safe, please, she is your wife now. And the suit too you can keep. I have arranged with the store. Think of it as the little present I can give you out of my own pocket, only sorry it is not more."

The village accompanied them to the platform, Khateja still not saying anything to her new husband, looking down at her feet as if in deference, smiling shyly at her childhood friends, tapping children's necks. Everyone plunked themselves down on the raised portion, their feet swinging over the edge by the track.

They crowded around Ismet for another round of handshakes, the women insisting on kissing their beloved Khateja for the nth time.

Only Ahmedu wasn't present, excluded at the bride's insistence.

"I am not having him there," she'd said that morning in an isolated moment of bad temper. "We must provide bones for him to gnaw, the worm?"

She'd been 100 percent compliant on every other issue and hadn't even grumbled much about her brother's attendance in a brand new *kurta* with cream-colored silk stripes. Surely there was some such thing as nuptial privilege, such was the general opinion.

Ahmedu was duly banished and spent the day by the river trying to glue together the glass shards of his telescope with a tube of adhesive paste and a tin box filled with yellow rubber bands.

Presently the train ghosted into view and chooked to a stop right beside the newlyweds.

"Go now, go," said Yusuf, hustling them into a second-class compartment, "your life lies ahead of you. Do not be forgetting us, eh?"

The train shook, the village roared, Khateja groaned, and the two of them found themselves alone underneath a roof for the very first time.

Two whistles, a cloud of gray smoke and they were off!

Chapter Four

yderabad? That dump? Hyderabad, that is our destination? What is this? What sort of husband is this?"

"But your own father said that was where you were always wanting to go. Plain as daylight he told to me, 'I am sending you to Hyderabad. Khateja was always dreaming, talk-talking about it. Great city, great city.' "

"My father, fiddlesticks!" fumed Khateja. "I suppose he told you how to be going about getting a baby too, I suppose. Hyderabad!"

She was most annoyed. If this thimble-wit was going to pretend to marry her, then the least she could get out of it was a trip to Bombay, souvenirs perhaps, a glimpse and glance of the big city, the English fellows, and their ridiculous red-cloth empire.

Experience, tourism, contact with different perspectives. At a minimum she'd want to take in a couple monuments. But here she was sent to Hyderabad, and for what?

She pushed herself further back on the bench and stared out the window, watching the brown earth and trees and telegraph poles slide by. She glared at him.

"I suppose you think now I am at your mercy, you can do what you want with me, that I am an innocent girl who it is possible to abuse, so you can go ahead to perpetrate some things because I am a lady from the rural areas. You think now you can have your fun, eh?"

"No, no." He was grieved at being misunderstood. "I would never do such a thing to hurt you. It is out of the question. As a matter of fact, I am respectful to women, that is how I have been raised up since I was a little child. It is part of our culture virtually."

Thank heavens she hadn't misjudged this madman: timid as two lambs. Two shaking lambs. She'd be able to protect herself against him quite nicely, that was her feeling.

"Well, not a finger," she warned, "not a finger," and waved one at him. "Just one and I will scream. I won't stop. No sir, I will be screaming from now to Bombay and when the polices come I will tell them about the finger. I will explain the whole situation. 'I was alone,' I will say, 'and this man comes in and lays a finger on me. Two-three fingers!' And then they will take you away to the prison and there will be no escape for you."

"I would not do it anyway, do not trouble yourself."

"I will be watching. Don't think I am stupid at all."

Ismet decided that nothing would be served by his insisting on his good intentions. And he was exhausted. It had really taken everything out of him. He took off his jacket, folded it up, and laid it on top of his briefcase. To this pile he added his waistcoat, pocketwatch, wallet, his increasingly crumpled fez. Then he untied his shoes, heaved them off, stripped off his socks, rolled them into a ball, and stuffed them into his shoes.

"Well," he announced, "I for one am going to sleep so I can be refreshed for Hyderabad."

"Ha!"

Khateja folded her arms.

For eleven days they traveled in a mighty loop 450 miles in diameter, through Jaina, Parbhani, Nanded, Nizamabad, Secunderabad, Gulbarga, Solapur, Karmala, Sihngarh, Mulshi, Roha, Alibag, Khopal, and Karjat.

First there were the high passes through the Balaghat mountains, which they reached on the first afternoon: rock, frost, high overhead white slides of ice and iron-stained vertical stone faces, crowns of rock, great vaults of air below and above, the visible blue of sky appearing at a great distance before them and off to the sides.

The track sidled along the vertices where cliff and base met at wide angles, which formed by means of shadow and reflection blue volumes that straddled the range and stood out in their eyes.

In among the low-lying brush of trees below the railway, which showed now and again striking, pure moments of black wood and filtered emerald light on the ground, there were timber huts, their walls long, wide, green-speckled trunks. Smoke lines rose up from them in ellipsis, rising islands in cold space and miles of air and the lost weight of cloud.

At the occasional platform, little more than a cleared, fenced-off space by the track, the people who boarded wore canvas shoes and flap hats and carried sacks full of vegetables and didn't speak much; thin, quiet folk, content to rest with their legs apart and watch the great gutted land go by in its blue-black variation.

When these travelers turned to one another to communicate some observation rapidly, they did so with obvious reluctance. Then they turned back to their solitude, stretched their legs across the floor, wiped the glass by them clean using spit and fingers.

Khateja followed suit but her fingers got chilled almost immediately. Because clearly her body was not adapted to the cold chills in this environment. She listed unhappily beneath the blanket the conductor had offered her, seeing she was without. Later he came in with a pillow, which he gave her also, and a bedsheet for Ismet, who tucked it around his shoulders and under his lap. He was wearing a cotton vest under his shirt and two pairs of socks, one inside the other. There was a draft from the opposite side of the carriage that was gradually refrigerating his neck.

The mountains gave way to open, water-racked plains, folding away from the railway tracks like a spread of palms, a giant's invitation, a green and white *salaam*. There were beached cattle, legs folded up underneath them, their large bodies seemingly set in the earth for all time. A pith moon glimmered during the day, shone down at night in its pitted majesty, skipping on the temperate circle of air that replaced the mountain current.

The people who got onto the train were plumper, better fed, glad-chinned, merry-voiced. They brought with them jute sacks filled to bursting with nuts, desiccated sugarcane, jute, bales of silk tied up with string and held safely on their laps. Satisfied, they tapped on the seats, they whistled once the train was moving, they joked with one another. One time a *carrom* board was produced and set up on the floor by two children.

Khateja decided to try her luck. She turned to the old man sitting next to her. His clothes were old but a clean white.

"This man"—she pointed across the compartment at Ismet—"he has been bothering me. Molesting. Won't give me peace, that is the real root of the problem over here," she surmised.

Ismet cringed. The old man nodded and smiled agreeably at every word, revealing sharp, stained teeth, thin gums white in places, silver fillings.

"Yes, yes," he said fondly, and patted her three times softly on the head.

But either he hadn't understood a thing she was saying or he was indulging her, since he didn't feel moved to do anything further. An hour later, when he rose to his feet to get off, he went up to Ismet and patted him, too.

Then he shambled off, taking a box of old sandals along with him.

"Khateja. This is not nice, what you are doing. Imagine! I could be ruined."

"Ha! And your opinion is it is nice to drag off a girl you don't even know from her home so you both can chase the wild geese over to Hyderabad? That is nice?"

Looking forward to a brighter day than this one, she added, "Best you are ruined. Teach you a lesson, you kidnapper. Kidnapper! Take him away"—she addressed an invisible policeman—"he is Mr. Blushing ur-ur Man, dastardly criminal. Nothing but a worm really, no loss to society."

Nevertheless, she didn't get around to denouncing him again.

Partly she was dispirited by the old man's reaction; partly she was too tired to wage an effective campaign (the only one worth the while waging) and she needed to replenish her energies for the titanic struggles that lay ahead; partly she was suddenly frightened at how this idiot Ismet might react.

Sure he was quiet, unassuming, docile, ill-built, unshapely, ill-starred, that was taken for granted. But the truth was, one could never tell with these types. Still waters, etc.

She'd been thrust upon her wits in these chancy circumstances; they told her in no uncertain terms to wield a prudent foot, she must turn on the discreet ankle.

Oh, she would never abandon her freedom struggle! This Mr. Nassin could hardly hold on to her for a month without acknowledging the futility of it all. It was totally and utterly useless for him. For of course she would never submit.

From her perspective, the only real danger was that this man might lose his sense, beat her to a pulp, injure her, seize her, tear her hair, throw her against walls. Who knew?

At times it had even been a close-run thing with her own father (her own father!), what with his black tempers and his grudges and his propensity for aggressive, preemptive actions that made violence, physical violence, a black-breathing possibility in the corner of her mind (oh, she had been well aware though she had tried not to make any inflammatory comments).

If things were steered away from violence, eruptions, and such, then her victory was certain. Only the timing and the circumstances of triumph remained to be decided. These were the certainties, she told herself, that would sustain her spirits in what could not but be a trying time.

So, in stalemate, Ismet and Khateja Nassin rolled across India. They plunged down old hills, rocketed up the silver sides of mountains, sped under a bled sky past millet. There were baobab trees, old brown veritable-forest trees, brambling across acres, canopies touched by leaf and light and bird. The sun baked train and earth, plummeted away at dusk. The light flooding into their compartment was metal-stained, blue-fringed like an outspread fan. In the nighttime the air was still cold. It flowed down their throats like water, made heavy by the day's heat.

After each stop the conductor passed through. After the first day though, he didn't bother to pause in their compartment, which mostly they had to themselves. He hurried through smoothing his hair, absorbed in his feet. Sometimes he offered them tea from the urn in the corridor, which they drank in small brown rim-chipped cups held in both hands, the upturned cones of vapor steaming up the window above where they were sitting.

The few people who came in were for the most part Muslims, the women veiled, the men stern-countenanced, the children flinty. Neither Ismet nor Khateja felt moved to strike up a conversation with these others. Sometimes they would talk a little with each other, about the wind, the temperature. It wasn't friendly exactly, but it was a distraction. After a few days the conductor loaned them his miniature backgammon set so they sat by each other and played with the board sitting between them on Khateja's bag.

They came to a great river, in the middle of which tiny green islands were scattered. Visible just underneath the water were mud bars made gray in places by mineral salt. The sand along the banks was as white as bone, and there were pebbles as big as pigeons' eggs by the waterline. There were boulders as big as houses.

The railway bridge was strung by wire three-hundred-odd yards above the water. The train lunged over the crest of a valley and the river appeared whole underneath them, shining out far in the west as a lit filament in the earth. It was impossible to ignore the whining of the galvanized pins.

Khateja was worried: Was the carriage swaying from side to side? For the first time the great momentum that had carried them hence was made into a danger. If the track gave beneath them there would be no grip worth clinging to. Nothing could possibly hold up against the locomotive's mass.

They'd soar upward for an instant, pitch infinitely deep in the water in steel diameters. She'd never much trusted machines so she kept a close watch as they crept across the bridge. She quailed inside at every oscillation. There were white marks on her palm where her nails were, so she tried not to look after a while.

But they reached the other bank safely and pushed on toward the great crowded plains, citified, bricked in, laden with temple and mosque and a thousand thousand feet, bifurcated by a green river that fed the oceans with ash and bodies and branches.

It seemed to Ismet as they lurched forward that the land they were traveling through had been racked by age. The land was old, broken, worried apart at the seams, overrun by long-worn races, cut up by rain and rock. History itself, ten-twenty thousand years' worth, brick and pottery handicraft everywhere and everywhere pressed into the ground, pushed under by those teeming feet.

Like Russian dolls, each hoary old India was squatting right on top of another India squatting right on top of the one preceding, a thousand forgotten kingdoms, untold ranks of the soul. Where was the possibility for individual advancement?

When they stopped at a large town and it was still light, both of them got off, taking all the little luggage they had with them on the off chance. This happened a few times a day, and it was welcome respite. The hallucinatory spell of travel was broken.

Absent the clanging of the wheel on the track, and the labor of the bronchial engine, it was as if their powers of hearing were reborn: the quietness around a footfall, the rain landing on absorbent earth, the squealing of a cart wheel on a pebble path.

First things first: Khateja found the waiting room, which was usually on the first floor, sat outside on a bench and waited for a cubicle if she had to, undressed, cupped water from the tap in her hands and rubbed it over herself, under her arms and between her legs and through her hair.

She'd brought with her a piece of white soap wrapped in a cloth, stamped in the middle with an impress of a crown, which the storekeeper gave her free as a wedding gift, "so you will keep us in mind for all the time you will use it, my dearest Khateja."

She rubbed it against herself, and then rinsed off again. Then she washed the clothes she'd been wearing, squeezed them out in the sink, put on something clean from her suitcase, and combed out her hair in front of the mirror.

Meanwhile, Ismet had also changed. He'd be sitting on a green railway bench where she'd left him, smoking, his briefcase tight on his lap, pushing his hair back from his forehead.

"Maybe a bite?" he'd ask Khateja when she appeared, spotless with damp hair on her shoulders and water on her neck.

They'd go and find something in the few minutes left before the train departed.

The first time they stopped, all that was to be found was a man selling bread, tea cakes, chocolate bars, a single packet of water biscuits, a few bottles of ginger ale, his wares set out lovingly on a table lined with wax paper that he'd set up on the steps that led down from the station.

"What are you in the mood for, Khateja?"

"Everything."

"Everything?"

"Yes, everything, Mr. Tight Two-Fists. A bit of everything, that is my desire. You not wanting to spend money on your new wife, is that the case here? Not a day gone and already I must be deprived. Ho, you will not get away with that."

So Ismet bought a *nan*, an *aloo paratha*, a *methi roti*, a tea cake with pink frosting, the packet of water biscuits, the chocolate, two bottles of ginger ale. They took them back to the platform and sat inside the waiting room. Khateja swung her legs impatiently and looked at the dirty white walls. She took one bite out of each thing and then left it. Lying there. Just lying there.

It almost broke poor Ismet's heart in two, the waste of it, but he said nothing deliberately.

And lo! his young bride seemed almost happy when they got

back on. She whistled; she plaited her hair, drawing it between forefinger and thumb, weaving it quickly into a single rope with spidery fingers.

Then she left her hair and said, "I hope you are not thinking to mitigate me."

"What?"

He'd been watching her knead her hair, perfectly enchanted.

"I am just telling you now, so you won't be going around objecting later. I am not going to be mitigated. No matter what. You should just know that. No mitigating me."

"Mollifying?"

"Or mollifying neither. No, no, there will not be any mitigating or mollifying me, that is a sure fact."

"Did I contradict?" he asked, suddenly irritated.

"I just want to be sure, you know. So you can't be saying you were not warned."

When they reached Hyderabad, the farthest point of their journey, Ismet realized with shock that it was already Friday afternoon. Already time was flying by. He donned his toppie and announced that he was going to mosque. The train wasn't scheduled to leave until evening, so he had the time.

"And what am I supposed to do?" demanded Khateja.

"I don't know, I don't know. See a few things. I will be back right soon. I have not missed attending mosque in fifteen years. Wait here. It is one of those things."

"You, you are one of those things, that is how it looks from where I am standing," she countered but, busy unpacking his rug from his bag, he paid no attention.

So Khateja sulked in the waiting room and Ismet, on the stationmaster's recommendation, found a short white mosque not half a mile away. He was very late and barely had time to doff his shoes, squeeze his way in, and say his *namaaz*. Afterward he turned down the offers of *paan* and cigarettes and water from the locals, who were happy to chat, and hurried back to the station along the unbridled bullock-ridden streets on whose corners men sold coconuts from wicker baskets and sweetmeats on paper squares.

He could have sworn that his wife was happy to see him return, though he had long since resigned himself to her inscrutability as far as he was concerned.

In fact, Khateja had been thoroughly bored, with only the clock set high on the wall for entertainment. Perpetually on the verge of breakdown, the minute hand quivered painfully each time before moving on. A beetle trapped inside the glass was constantly being caught unawares and shoved gently but firmly across the yellow clockface. Stupid, stupid creature!

"Tick-tock tick-tock." She was half hypnotized when Ismet rolled in at long last. "You can't be abandoning me like this in the future. It is not right, what you have gone and done. Hours tick-tock-tock."

"Not hours."

"What does that matter, seemed like hours. What is important is in here, *ne?*" She tapped her head. "Not out there. Lasted hours in here. Relative duration."

"Well anyway, I thought we might be going to the castle."

"The castle?"

She had never seen such a thing. Exactly what she'd hoped

for: travel-adventure, new sights, experience, something to take
back with her.

"Old castle. It is maybe a thousand years. Maharaja's Castle.
I believe it is the property of the *nizam* who is over here, but
he has opened it to the general public."

"Where?"

"Oh, not far, ten-fifteen minutes' walk, right around the corner virtually you could say. I have made inquiries at the mosque.
It is very beautiful, as they were explaining"—he smiled extremely graciously—"but, eh, so many minutes' walk for me
could be a year for you. Can't know what counts inside your
head, that is what I have realized. I wouldn't want you to be
walking for a year just for a castle." He touched her lightly, ten-
derly on the arm, just to see her reaction. "A year, even in your
brain it must be quite tiring. Must be. Really, it is too much to ask
at this early stage. Please to forget I had mentioned it."

"No, no," she said firmly. She made a face to protest his
literal-mindedness. "I want to go and see this castle. Let's go
right now. Really, it is a thousand years old?"

"At least. Here before the English."

"So old!"

She whistled.

The castle was indeed ancient. Only some of the rooms had
been opened to the public by the maharaja, who was off hunting tigers. They paid the thirty *paisa* entry fee and climbed all
about it, peered though the carved wooden windows, tripped
down narrow staircases, up battlements and towers, around the
edges of unused halls, along the stone balconies.

The rocks were chipped white and gray, worn smooth like

teeth. Water trickled down here and there, soaking through green fungus. Khateja put a finger into the stream and tasted it. It was sweet and cold and evaporated on the tongue, leaving an iron taste.

"People were living here?"

"Well, I am not sure. Must be, else why would they have gone about building it?"

"No reason, I suppose."

The journey back to Bombay was uneventful: yellow fields, blue-green marshes, more mountains, a wide plateau on one side of which they could see the beige outskirts of the Satmala hills near Aurangabad.

Khateja was quite confident, quietly confident: It couldn't be long now before this dolt gave up and returned her to her village. He'd got not one bit of encouragement out of her, that was for sure. She'd been recalcitrant, defiant, niggling, naggling. She would swear that already this Ismet was looking at the rest of his life as a long gigantic horror.

No, this insect didn't have the strength to hold her. He'd burnt his fingers; he'd parted with a sum of money; been wild-goosed halfway across India on the soonest train; gulled, tormented, put down in public view, rebuked with vitriol (oh, she had no illusions about her talents in this regard).

No doubt he was quaking like jelly inside, just waiting for a face-saving moment to dissolve this nightmare. Why, he'd already snapped at her four times in as many days. Mr. Nassin was losing his grip.

Soon, very soon, he'd see through these religious experiences. The awful truth would rise up before him: He'd made a big, big-time mistake. He'd fallen into sweet temptation and come up with only the thorns in his fingers. It would be time to cut his losses. That was how his brain worked, she would swear.

But he'd fallen in love, madly in love.

Was it her feet, dusted with talcum powder, sliding like a teardrop, had they sidled into his eye, which was connected by rods to his heart? Her shoulders like butterfly wings, on which she rubbed Superior Skin Cream from a round tin? Her way of folding a nose between thumb and pinkie, edging toward the end of the bench? Her cheeks, apple-bright, dimpled, drenched in rosewater? The hair lustrous from a piece of white soap and a shilling's worth of egg shampoo?

Even her surliness, in fact, her brow-clenched moodiness, her barbed sallies, her general cussedness found a place in his affections. She couldn't put an unwitting foot wrong, oh no. Everything she did was just perfect and exactly right.

The game was up for the old Ismet Nassin, Bombay registered clerk, bachelor.

Webbed and spidered.

The end of the road.

Hadn't Yusuf Haveri warned him? "We are family now, *ne?* What's a week when we are together for all life?"

Chapter five

How did they end up in South Africa?

Of all places.

Why scatter a packet of mothballs among one's clothes, close up the account with Bombay Savings & Commercial, send exploratory telegrams to the proper authorities, quit a good job, arrange for correspondence? Why pack everything into two iron trunks, one of which had a big red dent in the top, scuffed all around and kept together with arm-thick envelope-bands? Why peck a mother on the cheek—and set sharp sail? Why this migration thing?

Three reasons.

One. Khateja and her new mother-in-law, Rashida—Rashida, in her own right a lady of great expressive powers and capacities, given to complex gestures of disavowal and speculation and exaggeration, a repertoire handed down and refined to sinuous, violinlike perfection—they didn't exactly get along like a house on fire. (In fact, Khateja nearly burned the house down.)

Not entirely recovered from the first shocks and defeats of the past weeks, the new arrival mooned about the place. In the room at the top of the stairs, which Ismet cleared out first-thing for her, Khateja moved the dressing table and the chair around, trying to decide how she liked them the best, keeping everyone awake with the sound. The thuds rocketed through the wafer-thin ceilings and the papered wooden wall. Above the sink even the twice-divided kitchen window rattled, it was that bad.

Khateja lounged about in bed and drew her curtains so the light wouldn't rouse her, clapping a pillow on each side of her head if she was wakened too early, to muffle the daytime clamor. She wandered in the streets and took a day trip to the Malabar Hill. She left peach pips lying right there on the lounge table with its neat lace tablecloth and brown ceramic vase standing with reeds, the Peach Pips of Shame.

She didn't even bother to make conversation! "Morning," that was all she'd say—"Morning" or "Afternoon Already" or "Is there Maybe an Orange Left-Over for Me from Night-Before? I am Having a Little Craving for One Little Small Orange, you see"—oh ho, Rashida reflected angrily, it just wouldn't do! It was quite so clear, perfectly transparent that this moody, quick-fingered village belle with her desires and her whimsies and her restlessness wasn't interested in chitchatting with her new mother in particular, yes Rashida was no fool she couldn't see!

Now every single bone in Rashida's body resented this blood-sucking, leechlike manner of behavior which was very revealing of a whole attitude (a whole attitude!).

Every single last bone.

She was being trampled on, that was what was happening

over here in front of her own two eyes! There were ways of behavior, *ne*, there were ways to show respect and considera- tion, was that asking for so much (she would like to know)? There were unwritten codes, customs.

But instead she must be cheeked like this in her own house (under her own roof!) by this quick-stepping maiden who wouldn't even think to offer a hand, though she must see with her own two eyes how she, Rashida, was slaving away to keep everything in its place and shipshape.

And when there was more work in the house than ever before, with one more mouth to feed, one more additional basket of washing to hang on the line, one more person's mess to tidy up—now was when she needed the assistance more than ever. Otherwise, she must just spend her whole life cleaning after this village Khateja who was happy to spend her life making dirty constantly, that was her lot in this world?

Oh, Rashida burned inside. In the afternoons, returning from the market with big brown-paper bags of vegetables in every hand to collapse in the armchair by the front door for a few minutes, then every footfall of Khateja's resounded in her head.

Each time this upstart country wife laid down a damned toe upon the linoleum it was the same as fastening an electrode to the brain of Rashida. She was wakened from her sleep when Khateja went to the bathroom at the oddest hours and opened the tap full and turned the lamp in the passage up high so the light flooded underneath her door. When in extremity she roused herself and went and stood by her door and glared up the corridor as if hoping the diabolical eye-force would shut off the lamp, then Khateja would appear after forever and pretend not even to notice her there, leave the burning lamp, and stamp off to her room, with not so much as a by-your-leave.

In the mornings Rashida (by this point she couldn't help herself) sat there by the sink and tapped her fingers against the table and couldn't get on with her life and counted the hours of luxury before the bride roused herself and combed out her dilatory hair before the glass in the hallway while she watched through the open kitchen door.

"What is this woman you have brought into our home, eh, Ismet, my own son? I am asking you a question. Do you have the slightest idea in your head what you have done? How is it possible you have gone and sneaked out and married without even asking what are my opinions so you can take into account? But from your side, you don't send one telegram, apparently that is too much to ask after my sore bones. I am worried so I am virtually sick on the floor, and then you are back with a wife and a little-little tiny smile in the middle of your face as if nothing has happened! Little-little tiny smile. Is this a nice thing, let me know your opinion?"

"Ma, I know it is a difficult thing to comprehend and it has caused you a certain amount of heartache. I am extremely sorry. From the very beginning I have been struggling to come only with apologies and explanations. But it is very hard to explain to you in a few words the exact circumstances of what has taken place. Maybe there is an angel. . . . All I am asking is not for you to agree with me about this straight off the bat, but just that you are patient and show decency to her. I am quite confident that everything will turn out for the best. It is something in my bones."

But was Rashida quelled by her son's hinting at deeper, darker things? Was she chastened by his shame-faced, half-spoken allusion to an "angel of intervention"? In this area she had considerable experience.

"Oh my! An angel is involved, now this is news to me. Now an angel is responsible for the catastrophe that has come down upon this home. It is an angel that has been poking its fingers into my family affairs. Well, thank you for this information. Thank you, my son. Really, it comes as a relief. Show me this particular angel if it can be arranged, but otherwise you must please not go around telling these stories to people or they will be taking you away. They will lock you up in chains and put you in the dungeon and they will not be interested in the stories you come with. Oh ho! An angel, my foot, you cannot make me a fool, my little honey drop. A pretty face, that is what is responsible here, a pretty face and one nice sari and where is your brain! Where, I say, is your brain? On the spot it has ceased to function despite all the education in the world. Your father was just the same, just the same. One pretty-pretty sari and it is all over. Brain Shut Down. The real surprise is you think you can trick me so easily with this card-sleevery. That is the most interesting part of this whole situation. Revealing of a whole way of thinking in fact."

"I am not up to tricks, ma. I am just asking for a small amount of patience here. You behave properly with my wife Khateja, and it will be a big trouble taken off my heart. Please now."

"Please now yourself," Rashida snapped, but the tacit understanding was that she'd try, oh how she'd try, even though the trying might kill off her old heart.

Maybe (she granted) this funny-funny Khateja girl would get her act together. Hopefully she just needed a little time to get used to the big city, the nature of the household, what was expected of her by her new family in the way of duties. Soon probably Khateja would start lending a helping hand around the place, join in to participate, wield for the general benefit a spoon. Anything was possible.

But late one afternoon—a fortnight after Ismet had arrived on the doorstep with his briefcase and Khateja's luggage bag and Khateja herself (the "little-little smile" in the middle of his face more from embarrassment than what Rashida supposed), fourteen days from that moment that remade the order among men and things—his new wife curled up on a chair in the kitchen and picked at her toenails.

There was the smell of cooking, which Khateja had always been fond of. She was drawn straight downstairs like a calf on a string to a bowl of warm milk.

This Rashida had been laboring away since morning, and just relaxing there in the atmosphere—dimpled lids clattering, water bubbles chattering on the flame, a black triangle of cut-up fried onion waiting on a plate—it made Khateja feel, well, almost like home.

Anyway, it was too boiling outside to go wandering about in the streets or along the beach, as was her wont, buying a nice fresh mango or a few *samoosas* for a bite, escaping from this morose Ismet and his silly mother, Rashida, who was all sulks and funny, abusive glances.

But if she was going to be staying indoors and not doing any trips and sight-seeing and accumulating experiences for mulling and general intellectual benefit down the road, then it was definitely a consolation to smell some good cooking, she must admit. It was an excellent sensation at the very top of the nostrils. Without actually looking over in that direction, she kept an eye on Rashida, who was wearing an apron over her sari.

The older woman had been busy like a bee the whole morning from the time Khateja seated herself there. Without a break shelling recalcitrant beans, burning one finger on the stove, slicing open another one with a knife while peeling potatoes in the sink, why her right hand was virtually hobbled.

Must be virtually hobbled, Khateja thought—not unsympathetically, for basically the thing was she couldn't bring herself to hold the old woman responsible when it was her wretched son's fault that such a dreadful standoff had resulted.

Then Rashida tasted a spoon to check for salt and the water scalded her tongue and she spilled all over the floor. She groaned in total mental agony. She said something indistinct about help and sticking plasters in the upstairs cupboard.

Khateja looked up at her for an instant, back to her toenails.

That was it!

"What kind of a woman is it who won't help her mother, eh, her old mother? Look, I am an old woman and I am scorched up to the bone virtually and there you are just sitting on the chair, so strong and healthy, only fidgeting. Won't lift a finger. I am wrong sorry, only lift a finger to twiddle with a few toes. Lazy bone. Lazy, lazy bone. Can't believe Ismet married you. He was always such a fine boy, very popular with the girls, he may not have made you aware. Now look what he has landed up with. Just cannot see what qualities he has seen in you because they are quite invisible as far as I can tell. Maybe it is I who am blinded."

"Maybe," Khateja agreed thoughtfully, putting her feet back down on the floor and spreading out her toes experimentally.

"The cheek, always talking back."

"Look," said Khateja, "I agree with you completely regarding this issue. You are correct here. Completely, no doubt about it."

"Eh?"

Rashida had been prepared for anything but this.

"Oh, you are completely in the right. I also have difficulty believing your Ismet son has gone and married me. The worm! Paid my father good money, when he knows he will not ever lay a finger upon me. Useless investment, worthless investment, time- and money-wise both, totally and utterly. And he is supposed to be a businessman-capitalist."

"Worm? How you can call my own son a worm when it is him feeding you up with his own two hands. Virtually. Feeding you up all the time. All the time, does not even stop to take one breath for his own health. He is always thinking about what your feelings will be. In the morning when you are busy sleeping still, then he will come and tell me to make sure you can get whatever you want and need, I must keep my eye out because it will make him that much happier when he is at work. In the evening time he will wait until he is sure you are properly satisfied before he can take a second helping, he will watch closely with his eyes to make sure you are happy and content before he can take a moment's peace. But then you are here under his roof busy making a commotion and running him down! You think this is your grandfather's house?" Rashida inquired, shaking her burned finger vigorously and biting on her tongue to stop the pain. "You aren't a big queen person, you know."

"And you," Khateja parried, "you aren't my mother. You are just not my mother, it is not even a question of possibilities here. How you can be talking like this to your own son's wife? So old, so old, and no dignity. All pickled up. Sour as a mango. But don't worry. Personally, I do not want to be around here for long. Only thing, I am a prisoner. Tell your son to let me go and I will go. I will go directly. I will pack my bags in two seconds. Gladly, too too gladly. Two chops! You will never be seeing a second glimpse of Khateja. Such stingy people, the pair of you. Wouldn't want to see you again. Know which side my pat of butter stands upon," she remarked, feeling increasingly bitter, feeling like all her compromises, her bitten-back, choked-off, unconfrontational attitude these past days was getting short shrift because the personal cost to her of such restraint was totally unappreciated by these people. "Not like your worm son Issie Issie Mitty Mitty. Mr. Mitty Mitty. Ha!"

"Ha HA!" was all Rashida could come up with, taking her cue from this refractory bride.

Rashida was getting along, year-wise, and wasn't as quick as before. (That was it, that was half the problem to start with. Oh, those were the days, wasn't a woman in Bombay could fence with her and escape without being well and truly bested.

The *Memon* menace. Yes, she'd been a veritable Rashida-the-tongue, her tongue a lioness among tongues. And now with the inevitable depredations it had evaporated so completely she was grasping at straws in the face of some village lass with a front-tooth gap, though she'd planned for so long, so many years to be a mother-in-law and had hoped she'd stocked up a few reliable strategies over time. Well, it wasn't the case sadly.)

Ismet pushed the door open just in time to save his mother being caught flat-footed, Khateja having joyously deduced her upper hand from Rashida's minute of silence. A day poring over ledgers, blanking ink, and blotting papers with the sleeves of his shirt rolled up to the elbow meant he was totally unprepared.

It was the kind of thing one must work on every hour of every day at the very least, no use just arriving with a half-numb brain in the thick of it. No use because it was all in the training and upkeep, because one wasn't equipped at birth with this. The constancy, reasonableness, and patience of numbers was no sort of groundwork for the utter slipperiness, the logical leaps, the ferocious speed of women's intellect.

"Good evening," he sighed, having gained an inkling of what was in store from the clamorous voices he could hear almost all the way up from the street corner where he was dropped. But he could hardly turn tail and head off, that would be sheer cowardice even if he was totally drained.

"Good evening, what good evening, eh? Here is your wife cheeking me in my own house. Cheeking and swearing and sulking as if it is a full-time vocation. Fulminating, you know. I think it is time you are telling this woman up to shape a bit, Ismet."

"Ha!" Khateja swept into the fray. "What species of man are

you, can't protect a wife from your mother-witch." Finding herself incapable of expressing the depth of her feelings, she picked
up the lamp and shook it at him, then at Rashida. "Why must
I go through this? Why is it necessary for me to undergo this
suffering and anxiety? Better you divorce me now."

Crooking a red-boiled ginger fan-hand more weakly than
she'd have hoped ideally, Rashida concurred, "Yes, yes, divorce
her. Send her back. Dispatch this woman back to the fires from
where she has come from in the first place. She also will be
happier in the natural environment. Do not even worry about
the money, it is gone and it will not come for a return visit.
This way we will be happier in the end. We will be the ones to
come out smiling ultimately, I am convinced. What is money to
have this in one's own house? Just look how she is playing with
our lamp as if it does not cost money. It is irresponsibility, that
is what is at stake here. Her peoples should have been the ones
to pay thousand, ten thousand *rupees* to find a house for this
crazy-in-the-head Khateja where she can play with the lamps
and all. I am acquainted with a very rich man, Mr. Ashook Hassan. Recently he gave his whole fortune, *lakhs* of *rupees*, to
marry his daughter off. Take this shrew Away from me, and I
will be Happy no matter, he told right to his face. Even though
he must live in poverty, virtually starving, he says for me every
day when I walk past in the street, Rashida, Rashida, I have
never been happier. If I had one hundred times more, then I
would have given it to get rid of this daughter. . . . Yes, Ismet,
send her away. We must act firmly. From the start I knew it
would come to this, after I was not even invited to the wedding.
That for me was very revealing of the whole mentality."

"For once this mother of yours is telling a true thing, first time so far that I have heard." Khateja quivered, as a result of the self-restraint needed for passing up the opportunity to retaliate against Rashida in order to strike at Ismet—

"Let me go!" demanded Khateja, waving the lamp furiously this way and that—"My freedom! Now!"

And then a crash, a bang, a *whoom!*

The lamp flew out of her hands and smashed against the wall. The room was plunged into a patchwork darkness: by the passage door a cool blue daylit rectangle from the outside window over the street door, by the kitchen sink a white illuminated cross from the candlelit tea-shop across from them.

The flames exploded in every direction. They licked across the floor, engulfed one of Rashida's carpet slippers and roared, flew upward with dizzying velocity, and wolfed at the ceiling. There were blue-white hearts, red arrow-tongues, vapors that burst into ankle-high stars. Everywhere there were battalions of orange-helmeted sparks.

Appalled, Ismet threw his jacket over the lamp. He ran outside and fetched an iron basin, filled it with water from the tap, rushed inside and threw it over the jacket, the incinerated slipper, on the table, up at the wall with a heave. The fire sighed sadly and poked a vaporous finger up through the jacket.

He went and filled the bucket again and poured water more carefully around the room. The fire gasped, smoking carbon that caught in one's throat. It collapsed into flowers of wet smoke that rolled along the walls. Scattered about on the floor were chips of glass from the broken lamp.

Everyone was quiet for a moment. Silence . . .

Then:

"I knew it!" Rashida announced triumphantly. "I had a dream about this. To Perdition, that is the final destination where she is taking us. An arsonist, a firesetter you have brought to our very home. A wild woman." She went on, more supportively, "Now *bachoo*, is the time to be a man. It is His wish she must go, so you must make her go. The Wild Lady must take off from here, end of story. This Madness has cost my slippers already, what next, who can know? This ordeal must come to an end now. Now this minute."

Ismet was unconvinced.

"Ma, I simply do not agree with you that for Khateja to go is the wish of any god. In that case where is the possibility for free choices, eh? No, no, in this you are quite mistaken, I am afraid. Also, we have plenty lamps, that is my feeling. We can afford it."

"Ha!" shot Khateja, scowling at Rashida. "Plenty lamps!"

Khateja looked down meaningfully at the floor where there was glass everywhere, and Not Very Many Lamps.

Rashida wanted to take the big spoon from the sink and hit her with it.

Khateja turned back to her husband who was standing with his hands clasped together in front of him: "But what nonsense-business is this now, really, Ismet? Excuse me, but your own mother informs you about this wish from her dreams that a divorce has become necessary—and you say she is a liar! That is what you say to her face! No respect for women. Oh, I knew from the start. Not for your wife, that was always clear, but here it is your mother who has taken the trouble to make you aware of facts and information. But no, Mr. Ismet won't be listening even to his own mother, the one who bore him inside. All that trouble you went to"—she turned to Rashida—"all these years and what has been the end result?" She shook her head. "No, Ismet, my friend. This time you must listen."

Brave Ismet! "No. I do not agree. It is not true. You both are twisting things, that is my feeling. The two of you both are making it impossible to see what is correct in this situation. Making it impossible, which is a real pity."

Rashida wasn't sure whether she was more incensed by this Khateja's disrespect for property and propriety, whether that was the greatest thing getting under her skin here, or whether it was her son's rank insubordination.

Taking the long-run perspective (increasingly a concern for her as she got older) Ismet's filial intransigence was more pressing. This young customer was getting totally out of hand, heavens!

"*Ayah, ayah*! Ismet, my own one son! How can you say to me I am a liar in front of this woman who calls you worm? Now it has gone beyond the worst tragedy. Well, this is giving me pains in my head, all this argue-arguing. Sharp, shooting pains. I am going to my room. I mean, this is what extravagance! You want to be throwing lamps away, you and your wife you want to destroy lamps, then you must just find your own supper. It is as simple as that. Who knows, maybe Madam Arsonist will be fixing a few snacks?"

A bitter laugh and Rashida retreated upstairs, taking the steps two at a time.

"Well," Khateja said very quickly, "don't look at me like this.

I am certainly not going to be running around slaving in the kitchen. Oh no. Do not expect and then you will not be disappointed in the end, that is a good lesson for you. Now you can go tell your witch mother sorry, go running under her sari like one baby. Probably she will just use her spells, clap-clap. Go now and she will read some spells for your benefit. Please, it is for your own good. Go. Just don't be looking at me, that is all I ask."

He struck back with, "Actually I wasn't looking at you like anything," but his wife had already disappeared into her room and slammed the door behind.

The next day Khateja confronted him in the morning and demanded five *rupees*.

"Your mother certainly won't be giving me anything."

"What is it for?"

"How can you be asking me, your own wife, to account for each and every cent. It is a true instance of stinginess. Time and again you display the worst features of our Indian character, I am telling you. Well, don't I need money to live? You would rather have it that I am starving away to death, ragged clothes, no shoes, eh? You want to be killing women?"

"That is a crime in many countries," she added when she thought he was hesitating but in fact he was wondering where he'd kept his wallet.

He handed over the notes—ten altogether, including a five-*rupee* conscience-salve—and slumped off to his office.

Outside, Bombay was a furnace: knives of light, hot ground, the air a bludgeon. On the corner a man on a footstool was peddling coconuts for fifteen *paisa*, opening them up with a knife, fresh fruit in a cardboard box by his feet, milky empty shells piled up behind him. Khateja walked past the tearoom with its blackboard chalked up with prices, past a man squatting by a pile of newspapers weighted down with a stone, past the boarded-up shack where the young Ismet once bought frosted cakes wrapped in paper and tubes of gelatin sweets, past the bus stand, home of a vast intemperate Tamil clan where a young woman in a yellow sari was sitting on the front veranda and peeling potatoes into a bowl of water.

When she got to the post office, she informed the clerk, "I want to send a telegram. I will be waiting right over here in this spot for the reply. It should occur chop-chop."

In large block letters she wrote, "To Shireen Haveri & Yusuf, Will be coming home very soon. Mr. ur-ur Man is one worm. One real worm. It has caused too many marriage difficulties. I could not have dreamed. Going to be divorced quick-snaps. Can't be helped. The man is a monster. Return post soonest. I will wait over here in this spot in post office so please to make a hurry."

On an afterthought she added, "Mother also a monster," and handed it over to the clerk.

She stood in the post office the whole morning and most of the afternoon as the men with lunch boxes stacked on bullock carts rattled through the streets on their deliveries. Two English soldiers, rifle-toting, red-cheeked, came in to collect a parcel that turned out to be a fruitcake, which they sliced up on the counter next to her with a pocketknife. A wide-chested merchant, his hair parted on the side and slicked back with oil,

arrived with a box full of pencils to send to Ahmadabad. Struggling to place it on the counter, he dropped it on the floor and
it spilled over and she helped him tie them up in bunches of
ten with rubber bands, and put them all back in again.

When in gratitude he offered her for her own self a free
pencil (yellow with a pink india-rubber top), she refused.

"Why must I take a pencil for my own self?" she declared.
"Am I one of these novelists that I must go around the place to
collect some pencils. That is definitely not the case. So, no pencils, it was my pleasure."

After he left she told the postal clerk where to find her when
the telegram came if he couldn't see her from where he was.
Then she went and squatted by the door on a stone block. Later
she bought a cup of tea from the vendor right under the poplar
tree who was selling to pedestrians and men from the shipping
offices and the rubber factory around the corner. Then, because
it was getting too hot for her and her sari was getting sweat-
damp and uncomfortable, she went back and waited on a bench
inside the post office.

Eventually the clerk called, "Telegram is here for Haveri, K."
She went up to the counter.

"Please, do you mind reading it to me."

Khateja knew the telegram would be in shorthand, which
she wasn't good at, although her literacy skills, overall, couldn't
be beaten.

The man smiled, "Not a bit, not a bit. It is saying, 'Excellent
news. Come home chop-chop very happy." He paused. " 'Marriage with Ahmedu fixed up soon as possible tomorrow if can
take soonest train. Best Regards. Yusuf Haveri.' "

His smile broadened.

"It is time for congratulations, eh? Good news, eh? Best telegram all day, all week, in fact. Makes me happy just reading it. Look, I am one smile!"

"Good news, good news, my foot, those worms!" Khateja screamed. "They are grass snakes. And what is love today? What are parents' feelings today to commit this crime against their own children?"

She stormed off without taking the telegram.

"This calamity is your fault," she assailed Rashida on reaching the house.

"What have I done, eh? I am quiet for my son's sake, not saying anything, bone-working my fingers and here you walk in and just accuse, just like that! What is it my fault? Tell me. Now I am actually curious."

"Parents today, they are not aware how to behave with their own children. No love left. I am afraid there is no respect anymore for anyone. At this point I am starting to lose faith with the whole of humanity. People are just cruel like that, don't care a bit."

"Well, that is true. It used to be different."

"Ha! What you know, what you know? You cannot know what it is these people have done to me. You can't be knowing how cruel these monsters can be," and then Khateja found herself on the hot, bitter brink of tears.

She remembered the clerk's "Look, I am one smile" and felt a hot flush, from what she wasn't sure.

She turned away and went into her room, closed the door carefully, crawled under the sheet and cried and cried and cried

until her eyes were red and sore and her hair was thick with
salt and washed in tears.

Ismet also was troubled. But see, he'd never been a happy
man. Oh no, he for one had never been a joyful jovial go-lucky,
never a lark in the winds, never a honeybee in nectar. Oh he'd
play cards once now and then. He drank *lassi* with sugar and
ice in summer. He read the newspaper in the mornings with a
cup of tea by his elbow, although of course that was in the past
now. During the monsoon it was his wont to lie in bed on the
weekends and watch through the open windows the rain and
the clean gray light that followed. In contemplation the wet-
flurried wind and white water gutters on the street side afforded
him silent thrills.

When offered a square of *bharfee* or a *laddoo*, for instance,
his whole face would light up! He'd smile a little smile, frown,
hold up the sweetmeat to himself in his large hand, smile again,
break off a small piece with thumb and forefinger—and then,
for all the world like a trained seal, toss it from above onto his
tongue, chop-licking.

Then he'd grin out broadly, tap his fingers against his trom-
bone arm, snap them one-two-three times very quickly, and
wink larcenously at anyone who was looking. Now and then—
returning late from playing cards with tonic-sweetened companions in upper-floor club rooms—he'd defuse his mother's ire
by raising his eyebrows and pinching her cheeks (fast-fast so she
couldn't duck).

But one wouldn't expect to catch him dancing alone in his
room with the door closed and the gramophone turned up high,
that was for sure. In fact one wouldn't think of him dancing at

all. If he were to be found at a wedding in the first place, then it would be on the sidelines, relaxing in a chair by the lobby where the little children played and the old men smoked, his feet spread out wide, chatting about tariffs or adding machines with cup and saucer balanced on his knee, carefully with two hands so it wouldn't fall and break.

And if from time to time he did look up wistfully at the dancers in the center of the hall, with their jewelry and fancy suits and whatnots, done up to the nines, all smiles and weaving about, he wouldn't make so much as a move in that direction. If he were asked to do a jig he'd say no. Nicely but firmly.

"No," he'd say, "Really not. Feet falling off and all that, you understand. But enjoy for yourself, enjoy for yourself. Life is too short."

But that period of his life was over and done with: the half defiance, the self-understanding worked through to acceptability in his own head, where it really counted, the only place really. Now he was in the dumps. Noticing a palm-sized smear on the page, he found a large tear had trickled onto his blotter, without his even realizing. Ismet put his hands up around his ears and squeezed his head between them, and questioned himself.

In a way it wasn't even an unusual thing, that was the real tragedy. The real tragedy. Say he forgot himself for an instant— out these tears gushed: pear-shaped what with their sagging watery middles, sliding down his face in salt trails.

Whether he was sitting by his desk, walking home the long way down Marine Drive, playing draughts with Khateja, lying

on his bed in the middle of the night with the windows open
and the hallway lamp nudging the door and his eyes listing into
his cheeks, at any moment he was liable to burst into tears. He
was actually afraid to look anyone directly in the eyes lest they
see his face was moist because he'd run out of tissues to stanch
the flow.

What was getting him down? Not just the domestic warfare
to which he came home after work, the histrionic belly-
clutching behavior, the intemperate red-cheeked rhetoric delivered with pots and pans brandished from the safety of the
staircase. Really, his mother's bickering he could handle.

So what could it be?

After his own fashion he'd been content before. But even if it
hadn't been obvious immediately, from the moment Khateja
had appeared in his window standing with her bucket of water
with her scarf half in her mouth, from then he wanted more.
With Khateja by his side, he saw himself forging a commercial
empire, founding a dynasty, patronizing culture. A sea change.
Riches, dragons, treasure barrels, roaring crowds, strange terri-
tory, trading delegations. Nothing less for the husband of the
most beautiful lady. And this was the second reason, above and
beyond the drastic situation at home, that drove my grandfather
across the great pea-green ocean.

Hope and Love, love and hope: a bastard couplet.

Struggling with his emotional condition, Ismet also had to
reckon with a wife around whom he couldn't raise a finger, and

a mother enflamed, prowling about in her printed apron with nary a word. The deciding factor was that he had to face up to all of this on an empty stomach. A culinary showdown.

The morning following the innocent lamp's demolition, Ismet's mother, hanging up her apron behind the kitchen door as he left late for work without even the chance for a breakfast roll, made it quite clear: "I will not pick up a spoon first. No, not so much as a spoon. If she is going to be staying here she can make supper once. She will organize and get the vegetables and the meat from the shop and then clean the dishes afterwards. That is all I am asking. And then I will be happily cooking. But she must first do this once. Tell me if I am being unreasonable? Just tell me?"

"Ma, but—"

"But I am not interested in Buts, Ismet. She must cook just once, or you must send her home. Or we will all just be starving straight to the death, *ne?*"

Rashida smiled. She crooked her arms at her side, just daring him to try wheedle a meal from her.

An alarming image occurred to Ismet: the three of them continuing to waste away like this. Inside a week they'd be bare skin and bones. Skin & bones without a handful's worth of flesh on the midriff. Eventually they'd be too weak to stand. They'd lie on the kitchen floor, squabbling when they found the energy. There'd be grumbling stomachs, blinding moments of red weakness, spitting out nothing.

No one would visit and they'd be marooned together right in the middle of the floor, too weak even to move the forbidden finger. There'd be maybe one chicken leg on the counter: oh, hardly a feast but there'd be flesh on it, enough to save them, rough yellow meat. Their eyes would be glued on it. They could almost taste . . .

But Khateja—lying closest to it, the only one able to reach it—would refuse to get it.

"Tell your witch-mother to fly there on her broomstick," she'd say, refusing to address Rashida directly. "That is what she must do."

Anyway, Rashida would absolutely forbid Khateja to take it. Nothing doing.

"It is my leg," she'd say, "maybe we are not royal queens or anything. Maybe we are worms, but that over there is my leg of chicken and you cannot go around the place stealing it," and her body would throb with rage at the thought.

She'd say, "It is all I have now on this forsaken earth now the two of you have broken up my lamp."

And both of them would refuse to let Ismet have it.

"No," they'd say, "you for one are certainly not having it. Look at the misery you have caused to us. Look at this devastation you have triggered single-handedly. Why must you benefit now by consuming that leg?"

He would plead, "But if both you won't have it, and I cannot have it, then we are all going to starve to death, right here in the middle of the kitchen. We are all going to be dead, no doubt about it. Dead. Dead. Dead."

They wouldn't budge.

Sticking to their guns, "Put us out of the suffering you have just gone and put us into. Much better to be dead than to go through another week of this. To say nothing of a fortnight or a year. So: just leave that chicken bone alone! And don't think we won't see if you've taken a bite in the middle of the night, quick snack or something. Oh, then you'll be really sorry. Then you'll see. Then you will know all about what is two and two. So just leave it and let us starve."

And they'd all three of them be found months later, dried up, shriveled, husked, black on the floor, charred by hunger, brimming with green spite. . . .

Ismet shivered involuntarily at the thought. Ugh!

"What is this, eh?" Rashida demanded, "you are a performance dancer now to be shaking and shooking like this? Rolling about like a madman with wild and crazy eyes? Maybe you have caught the rabies. You'll be foaming at the mouth in no time, who knows. Better go see the doctor."

Considering this—her son foaming and choking and bubbling from the rabies, raving and twisting in his sheets— kindness returned to Rashida. By no means was she temperamentally cruel.

"Oh Ismet, my Ismet, you were always a good boy, such a gentle one. Big fat baby. Not smiling much, but not crying either. I was so proud, talk-talking with everyone about Ismet. And you should have seen your father. Beaming, it is a definite fact! And now look what has gone and happened. Ah! Maybe you will come right in the end. A mother can only hope, a mother's heart cannot all the time be breaking like what you have done to me. Ah."

Rashida sighed and retired to her room, where she'd stored a *roti* and a jar of jam in her cupboard. She was feeling peckish. Not being able to eat in front of her son and his slovenly wife was taking a toll on her. A *roti* was just what she needed, dipped bit by bit into orange marmalade, maybe some *achaar*.

It was also what Ismet needed. His stomach had actually gone numb from deprivation, and it hung in the middle of him like a giant iron ball. Why, all he'd had today was a vegetable *samoosa* from the shop near the office, yellow-crusted, warm, filled to bursting with peas and pasty potato and slices of wet orange carrot.

And then the man at the next desk, smiling hungrily, chop-licking, had unwrapped a *poori* the size of a newspaper, stuffed with slices of mutton and spread inside with mustard and bits of green and red mango pickle.

Oh, how he'd wanted some, just a bite, maybe a little-little more. He'd just worked up the courage to ask for some when this man, noticing his devouring glances, actually offered.

"Would you like?" he asked pleasantly, pointing at his *poori*.

Ismet hesitated, oh, fatal instant, oh, inexpungeable delay.

"Really," the other man insisted, "I have too much as it is." He rubbed his tummy. "Getting round like a big ball now. It is the wife, you know, she won't stop feeding me. Must have more food, she says, no good to be hungry like a wolf—dishes it out like nobody's business."

But what would be thought if he seized the opportunity? That he was the sort who'd think nothing of making two funny-funny eyes at another man's *poori*? Two funny-funny eyes in his desperation? That, wretched man that he was, he would not spend a *paisa* out of his own pocket on his own upkeep? Would not his accepting the man's offer and scoffing up his *poori* right there be the most obvious thinkable sign of his predicament (he fretted) since what decent, self-respecting individual would come ravenous to work, bone-chewing, taking in his desperation to lascivious glancing?

"No really. I am trying to cut down also, you know, because of health worries."

"Oh," said the man and laughed out loud, "and there was I thinking you were hungry, all morning I was saying to myself, Ismet, he is looking starved, very thin, last few days. Sunken in, hollow eyes, the works. I was just now reminding myself I must make sure you are doing all right. And here you are just taking care of your health, keeping fit. Losing a little weight. I am so stupid, what a stupid I am being."

"No," Ismet said quickly, "don't think that."

"Ah no, I am used to it by now. Never was a bright star in school. Doesn't worry me. Always making mistakes. But this is a relief springing off my mind—in fact, you are dieting when all the time my imagination . . . But this has really come as a big relief. Well, I am sorry to interrupt."

"Not at all," Ismet replied, feeling guilty.

He wasn't going to make the same mistake twice. If his mother was going to deny him food, if his wife wasn't about to drop everything and conjure up a meal, then he'd turn else-where. Explore other avenues, follow up leads, go to a restaurant maybe, or drop in for a visit, enjoy a *biryani* or some chops, a lamb curry hopefully, a couple cutlets. No telling. Might lift his spirits. Only, where to go?

Money was tight, so a nice seaside restaurant and a plate of garlic prawns was out of the question. As for his friends . . . Well, he'd been avoiding his friends ever since his marriage. He hadn't even looked one of them up for a tea and a *samoosa*. It was not because he was embarrassed about his new bride, quite the contrary in fact, but really he couldn't see his way clear to explain the circumstances under which he tied the knot.

The facts, plain and simple as they'd look to anyone, were that he'd gone stark raving mad. Such wild, intemperate, ill-considered, downright maverick action! Why harbor illusion, it did look bad, this business of arriving from nowhere with a mercurial village-girl without so much as a warning telegram. And then to chitchat about miracles and throw angels into the conversation quite casually as if it was no big deal—it was asking too much, however generous his judges.

Anyhow, the whole thing was useless because he wasn't up to explaining himself on an empty stomach. And it seemed like he'd done enough defending himself for the time being.

Which left Jayraj, Jayraj Reddy, Reddy extraordinaire. Something of a madcap, not given to long, drawn-out explanations and sagas, Jayraj would understand. He wouldn't force him to talk. He would respect his friend's reticence.

Jayraj—Jayraj's wife, Roshni, rather—would spread a repast before his very eyes, surround him with sweet tea and chitchatter, grand plans, hopes, stories, distractions. Such entertainment was just what he needed. And if Jayraj Reddy was just that sort of gin-sipping, poker-playing Indian against whom his mother had enjoined him, then so what—ay, it was so much the sweeter!

Sure enough, after catching a rickshaw that carried him away from the water-stained seaside Bandra Flats along Marine Drive, past the lines of cypress and poplar, the wide avenues with their balconies and tea tables, the big-blocked offices with their shining glass and stairway vistas, he found festivities were in progress at the Reddy residence on Silver Oak Lane.

There was a garland over the door, lit incense sticks in brass vases by the matte rubber doormat. There were children whooping and hooping in the street outside, playing with a ball, throwing paper darts, flipping bottle tops along the pavement. Several grandmothers had been moved onto the front veranda, where they were swinging gently on the bench, chewing *paan*, smiling, wrinkling, eating off banana leaves with their fingers.

"Jayraj is here, yes?" Ismet asked them, trotting up the steps.

Impatiently, one said, "Go in, go on," dismissing him with a wave of her hand, returning directly to the point she was trying to get across.

So Ismet passed through the open door, green, paint-flecked, and down the carpeted passage into the lounge where there were easy chairs, a grandfather clock, a knee-high table for plates and trays and glasses. There were people of all sizes and shapes in the surrounding rooms, firecrackers in dozen-boxes, orange-juice jugs, ribbons and all. Ismet had seen nothing like it since Jayraj had tried to raise enough money to buy and operate a passenger ship.

"Just think," he'd told Ismet at that time, eyes gleaming, hardly able to stand still such was his state of enthrallment, "India's first Commercial Luxury Liner, first-first in the world, Symbol of National Pride and all that, bound to be a big hit, pots of money. Plenty opportunities for investments. Superb returns from a relatively small initial sum. Consider."

Ismet thought and thought and was doubtful. Still, he'd

ended up investing a reluctant forty *rupees*, more for his friend's sake and to show he wasn't afraid of risks, without which there could never be payoffs.

In the end, even after the party, only 1,230 *rupees* were raised, divvied up as part-shares on the enterprise books, and Jayraj settled on a sailboat to take travelers up the river on the weekends when he was free and could take charge. He bought himself a yellow raincoat, a bow tie, two starched white shirts and, with Ismet's help, even prepared a speech to deliver to the rolled-up boatful, on matters of general and ethnographic note, which he learned by heart.

There were never as many holiday makers eager for a floating tour as he'd hoped, despite his having contacted the various steam navigation companies and having sent out flyers in the post. But fortunately the Royal Navy needed a spare boat for beetling up the coast and offered to buy it from Jayraj, and they'd got most of the money back in the end.

Jayraj had been unhappy for months. Quite depressed.

"You understand, Ismet, it is not myself I am being sad for, oh no. It is this country. It is India, hmph. It is just not being ready for a commercial luxury liner. It is just not in the position of having grown up. Hundred years behind, you must only see the ships the English have. Oh yes, it is this country I am sad for, that I cannot help it, push along a little. Otherwise when will be progress, that is the real question. Poor India. So backward with the leisure industry no—"

"Ismet!"

My grandfather jumped. But then, Jayraj was always managing to startle him with his expansive greetings, his general effusiveness. It gave them both a kick; their relationship was 100 percent symbiotic.

Jayraj had managed to sneak up behind Ismet. He shook him by the shoulder, he spun him about the hips, he plumped his hand, he kissed him on the cheek, he drew him to his chest, he pushed him away, drew him back, sighed deeply, pushed him away again, he punched him on the arm.

"Jayraj."

"Ismet-Ismet," said Jayraj, "what is this I am hearing everywhere, talk of the town, everyone chitchatting, gossiping, no one knowing anything firm—just speculations, you know. Maybe you have gone out and found yourself a wife. Found for yourself one pretty little thing who is looking especially good in a sari. Oh yes, that's what they are saying," he concluded joyfully, jovially, exhilarated. "Is it being true? Tell-tell, don't keep us waiting, we have been wanting to come by, see what's up and all that, but I said wait, wait, Ismet will be coming to see us in his own good time, didn't I, Roshni"—this shouted to his wife who wasn't visible—"oh yes I was telling Roshni yesterday. But don't delay. Enlighten us."

"Well yes, it is true. Some weeks ago, only got back recently or would have come to see you sooner, first minute to get away—you know how it is."

"Please no explaining, no gaping need for explanations in this house. You are here now and you are sitting down with us and we are happy, *ne*? And where"—he looked at Ismet, behind Ismet, around him, down the corridor—"where is this new wife? We are most eager to be making her acquaintance of course."

"Um, she is at home, headache, you know. She is a sensitive girl, not in the best of health. Khateja."

"Please, didn't I tell you already, no explanations. We are all understanding people here. What business is it of ours indeed! We are not devoured by curiosity."

He stepped back the better to regard his friend.

"So"—a smile blossomed like a tulip—"Khateja is giving you hells. Already, eh? You should really have asked me first, Ismet. Hints and tips. Women today can be very cheeky. Well, as long as she isn't a village girl or anything. Few simple tricks."

"I am sure it won't take long. I have already been learning so much. A second education virtually. What is up here?"

"You must bring her, who knows, maybe we can fix her up for you, tell her how lucky she is to have caught our Ismet's eye. Around here? My brother, Tejpal, has returned. This is the first occasion we've seen him in seven years as a matter of fact. Left when he was just a boy almost and now he's back and taller than me, can you believe? My only brother, very fond of him, always a bit of a joker. But you must meet him, see for yourself." He called down the hall. "Tejpal! Tejpal!"

A long thin man, shaped like a green bean, thin-cheeked and twisty-shouldered, emerged from the nearest room.

"Tejpal, you must meet my friend here Ismet Nassin, great fellow, great fellow. Classmates many years ago now in Bandra Grammar."

They greeted each other.

"But you two must be talking," said Jayraj, putting a hand on each of their backs, "lots to talk about, I'm sure. Back in a second."

With that Jayraj hurried off into the lounge, zoomed through a sliding door, and was lost to view.

Tejpal was wearing a white shirt open at the neck and maroon cotton trousers to which a pocket watch was attached by a silver chain.

Ismet wanted to know where the arrival was from.

"South Africa, you know. Durban. Was in London seven years ago but in South Africa since then."

"Where exactly is it?" asked Ismet, who'd never had much of a sense of the world.

"In Africa. Right at the bottom bit. In the south."

"Oh."

"Wonderful place," added Tejpal, who hadn't liked it a bit, too sun-drenched, too open, too hilly and beshrubbed, the people nefarious and looking out for their own interests only. But he'd always been a bit of a joker, always willing to play along, tell people what they wanted to hear, trot out a yarn. "It's absolutely wonderful. One hundred percent perfect and all right. Many good features."

"Really?"

"Oh yes, yes." Tejpal warmed to the theme. "Superb country, one of the very best. And money! It's everywhere, lying on the ground, just waiting for someone to pick it up virtually!"

"No?"

Ismet wasn't so easily beguiled.

"Yes, yes. Virtually, not really. But all it takes is to go there, set up a business, cash comes rushing in hand over heel. Very, very easy. The blacks there, *ne*? They'll buy almost anything,

almost anything. Beads, whiskey, matches, flints sell for very
good prices. Easy life."

"So why you came back then?"

"Came back?"

Tejpal looked puzzled.

"Yes, why did you come back to India? If you were so happy
and all that side?"

"Come back to India? Why come back? Why come back to
this India over here? That is your question, I see. No reason really.
I didn't want to come back, as a matter of fact. It was the wife,
only the wife, always talk-talking about home, her friends. It is
what her heart was set on. Consequently we returned."

"The whole time she was by you?"

"Yes. And she was so difficult in the beginning, always com-
plaining, didn't want to go. She has certain traits in her person-
ality, you know."

"I know how it can be. I have met too many of these difficult
women today. New generation, I suppose."

"Well," Tejpal announced triumphantly, "a few years in
South Africa put an end to that for her. You should see her now,
completely obedient, asking me every minute what I am wanting, what are my wishes, what she can do for me. Absolutely
in love. Just seven years and it has done miracles on her."

"What you are talking about miracles?"

Tejpal, who as a rule of thumb would rather leave a man
with a little hope than without, sensed the surge of interest.

"Certainly. You should have seen her before. Kicking, screaming, raising up a big fuss and commotion, oh ho! Wouldn't lift a

finger. Ask Jayraj. Now you should only see! Think they're brother and sister now, or what. South Africa has put her straight one way! Perhaps it is the climate or what, I am not a medical scientific doctor, so unfortunately I cannot say for sure. But see with your own eyes."

He called, "Yavini! Yavvy, come, come! Yavini!" but gave up quickly. "No doubt she is unusually busy. But if she was here you would see plain with your own two eyes. So helpful, considerate, caring. Great woman now, tremendous pleasure to be with."

"Pleasure to be with . . . absolutely in love . . . pleasure to be with," Ismet repeated, as if stunned by the sound of the words themselves, just as he still said, from time to time while falling to sleep with the sheets over his head, "the most beautiful lady in the world."

Finally, the most perverse of my grandfather's three oddball reasons to migrate: he dreamed of founding a . . . a . . . a what?

An empire?

Not really.

A dynasty then?

Not the right word exactly.

A reputation?

No.

A charitable institution?

Never crossed his mind.

How about a bank? Was he thinking of founding a bank in South Africa, along the lines of Bombay Savings & Commercial? Oh, he wouldn't have turned anything down. But these aren't the core of the thing, the flesh of the pineapple, the heart of the matter, the navel, oh no.

(Retrospectively, it makes one giddy, the sheer magnitude of his desires—and from a man who'd been so quietistic. But love turns the damned world on its bloody pivot. And even the meekest human breast contains an infinite egoism, undetectable by the savviest observer.)

Get this.

Ismet dreamed of founding a new race.

Oh yes, a new race, a new class of beings, new mud filled up with the breath of life, new forms.

They set sail for Africa, a clean table of a continent: its long plain wasn't cut up by stone walls, wasn't swarming with a dozen peoples, and wasn't ringing from end to end with this endless chatter. The plants firm and green and white veined. There were rivers with high banks and white water, mountains rising up through air, air that hadn't been breathed in and out over and a thousand times over again.

Yes, unlike India, Africa had been spared the nonstop penny-pinching of the spirit. No pots in the earth from a thousand years previously, boarded-up mosques you couldn't avoid, no maharaja's palace wherever one turned one's head. Whenever one climbed off at a railway platform in history-free Africa, one wouldn't expect to stumble immediately upon a village.

The important thing: that there be a final break with this conniving, rhetorical, feverish India, this India of gambit and deception, this India in which it was beyond the capacities of

any man to build up something new and strong, this tropical
India in which it had become impossible to love!

Khateja the ice queen would melt.

As the ship pressed close on the African coast she would
reach for his hand and squeeze it tightly.

"I am scared, Ismet," she would tell him, her pale green-
speckled eyes spreading wide across her face like the breast-
warmed eggs of a pigeon. Although she would want to look her
best of course, that morning she has neglected to wash her face,
brush back her hair, it has gone that far.

"Do not be worrying and eating yourself up, sunshine."

He would put his free arm around her shoulder and fiddle
with her ears and tap her on the side of the head.

That aboriginal forge Africa would throw them ever more
tightly into each another's arms. There would be an untamed
volcano, a chop-licking leopard circling around in the evening-
time, the poisoned darts of the bone-nosed natives whistling
through the air to make sure they would turn always to the
other for reassurance. Cooing and mooning, adoring inaugural
twosome.

From Khateja's womb would spill a legion of children, a hud-
dle of them, limbs freshly shaped, new hair plastered on their
scalps, new toes, new everything, what. A hundred, a thousand,
peopling the vast land, young giants with easy knees, striding
over the ground. Sweet milk would be their fare, churned up
in quantity by Khateja's so fertile breast. They would lounge on
Ismet's knee, tumble about on the ground, vault ten—sorry,
wrong—twenty feet in the air, raise cities up from tree and
stone, fashion minarets, eat beef in the red. . . .

Chapter Six

outh Africa, South Africa! What is this south South Africa? What are you thinking, where is your brain, man? What is this South Africa thing you've gone and got into it? Where is it being anyway, just out of interest?"

"Below the Sahara desert. You know."

Khateja shrieked, "I know, I know, ha! What facts is it I am supposed to know? You are the one having these wild ideas and then I must know. Oh hell, do not be bothering, what do I care. I know only one thing: other women have husbands who do not intend to rush off to Africa out of the blue! Hyderabad is not enough to swallow? What have I done so wrong on this earth that I must be rewarded like this? I must have the worst luck in the wide world, even including this South Africa place, that is my theory. Who knows, maybe this place does not even exist and it is a brain figment." On reflection, "Only it can't be a what figment of your brain since it is 100 percent, oh clear that your brain has gone off on holiday. Maybe that is where your brain is, why you want to be going there. Ha! Off to South Africa to Get Mr. Ismet's Lost Brain Back. Ha!"

"But, Khateja, you have not listened to a word I have said.

Maybe you should be going to have a talk with Mr. Reddy by
yourself. Why is it you are not willing to listen to this when it
is a chance of a lifetime?"

Khateja put her hands to the side of her head and fanned
them out, radar-like.

"Look, I may not be having ears as big as you, but I can still
hear. Do not say I have closed up my ears and am acting as if I
am deaf, because I am not, by no means. I am listening closely
and what I have heard is how you are mad, mad, gone mad. No
hope. Brain On Holiday. So do not go and say, 'My wife, she is
a deaf thing.' I won't have it, these lies and distortions. Lies and
distortions and half-truths, this is more of the same from you.
At least I am getting accustomed," she pointed out on a more
cheerful note. "And also I don't care a bit what Mr. Tejpal has
to say. No doubt he is crazy and up to tricks as well."

He was getting desperate. Talking to his wife or mother felt
to him like he was trying to scale a wall crowned with thorns
and broken bottle tops. He could jump up and down and
shout—that was one strategy—he could negotiate carefully,
dealing with one obstacle, one objection at a time, but two more
sprang up in its place.

He hadn't scored one single point in a month of marriage.
And if one's word was not allowed to stand, then what?

But that was the wrong way to look at it: Just look now, he
was even thinking like them. He was growing accustomed to
the hostilities, as he'd grown accustomed to starvation.

Even if he made casual chitchat about the weather he'd be
sure to be opposed from the very outset no matter the levity
he tried to bring to the issue: e.g., "Don't people need rain,

decent people, but it is not as if you are interested in the welfare of agriculture for the majority of the people who are living or- dinary lives in the village."

Still, he was a fair man. There remained his customary virtue, which was half of the reason he could keep his self-respect even when he knew he wasn't the most exciting fellow. It was true that from one point of view he'd purchased this woman. But hadn't she agreed at the time? Indeed, Yusuf had positively pressed his daughter upon him, and had he forced her to do one single thing? He'd been completely fair and aboveboard. He'd fed and protected and housed her. He'd asked not a bone in return.

And he was not about to become a tyrant just because his heart throbbed with the desire for her to come with him and make a new world. No, a new republic was built upon consent, its walls sunk deep in agreement. If their paths must fork, then so be it. Need be, he'd live with a cracked heart.

"Look, Khateja, I am firm about this. I have decided to do. I am going to South Africa soonest. Maybe two, three, four years and then I will most probably be coming back with business capital to invest. If it is not your desire to come along with me, then that is fine. Oh, it will not make me happy, quite the opposite. But it is fine, I suppose. I will do what you have been hungering for."

"Yes?"

"Yes. I will divorce you since this is what you want. And you can go back to your family. I will buy for you the ticket, give you what money it is I have left over, and then you can go back where you feel you rightfully belong."

"Go back? Go back? What are you, a monster, a devil man? Forcing me back just like that! I am a married woman. What will people be saying? How I will be suffering agonies! Old witch they will constantly insinuate, and now her husband has sent her back. Oh, Ismet, what is this you are doing to me with your own two hands? How is this cruelty possible in one single individual who, after all, is only two arms and two legs and a head?"

"Wait. Let me understand now. You don't want to be sent away?"

"Well . . . no."

"But just the other day here you were standing, stamping your feet, right before me, saying, 'My freedom. Set me free. Right now.' Or was I imagining? Isn't that true?"

"I suppose so, if you're going to put it that way," she grumbled.

"So now, out of the blue, you want to stay by me? Now you want to be a wife? Now?"

The retreat was threatening to turn into a rout. From a strategic perspective, there were two ways she could go, Khateja realized with frightening clarity: She could be forced back grudgingly, pushing back with her weight at every blow . . . or she could swallow the hog whole and throw herself on the enemy's mercy, armed only with apologies, tender solicitudes, submissions, the tear-stained eye, and the sorrowful cheek, in itself a reproach.

"Look, Ismet, I will be honest and straight with you, that is just how I am. If I go back, they are going to force me to marry Ahmedu. It is a terrible thing and I have tried to keep it from

you since why must you also suffer from the realization that
there is so much wickedness from the people who are close to
our hearts. It is a painful thing only to be aware that such mal-
feasance is still in existence today in the universe, but I must
tell you now. They will make me marry That Idiot."

"Marry Ahmedu, eh?" He was starting to enjoy this. "Ahmedudu? Ahmedu the idiot?" Now it hit him. "They're going
to make you marry him? Ha ha ha. Ha ha ha."

And then he chortled. He chuckled. He sniggered and
snickered.

He laughed out loud. He giggled right in front of her.

He bent over double and roared!

The tears brimming up were transformed into tears of
delight that rolled majestically down his face. His cheeks
swelled up, red-dotted. In the general merriment his nose
started running, expelling in two moist lines the snot of triumph, the snot of delightfulness, the snot of just rejoicing!

"Look, my dear, there is no need to make such a commotion
of this," Khateja said, patiently.

"You are going to be married to the *aloo*-brain, the cloven-
hoof, the vegetable head? Ahmedu who eats sparrows? At least
you won't be having to cook, eh, Khateja? 'Don't worry about
supper, Khateja, my honey, I will just pick up a bird on the way
home, it is no trouble. I will bring one for you also in addition
if you are having a taste.' That is what he will say, I can hear
already in my head. Then you will have found your happiness.
Then you will be over the moon. I do believe I will come specially to see how you are married for the second time. With
Ahmedu who has plenty fingers for three ordinary fellows!"

"I don't think these are nice things you are saying, Ismet. Very out of character."

"Khateja, it is not my problem your family is plotting and planning to do this?"

"No, not really," she conceded.

"It is not my fault."

"No, it is not, all right."

"Well, what is it I am supposed to do? Here I am off to South Africa because there are some excellent opportunities opening up, and I cannot take my wife with, and I cannot send her back because basically I am a kind man here in my heart. Because I am One Big Softie. So now I am open to suggestions?"

"I don't know, I am not knowing at all. Why you asking me like this, interrogation tactics? It is not a nice thing the way you are acting. Unexpected. Frankly . . ."

"Look, Khateja, it is perfectly simple. I am going, so either you are coming with me or you are going back. There is no other choice, isn't it, so now you choose."

"How can you take such advantage of me when I am weak, Mr. Ismet Nassin, when all along you were bleating like a sheep, baah baah? I knew it, saw it in your eyes, hatred for women. But it is not decent before God, this blackmail, I am warning you for your own good. Judgment Day he will be telling you, 'Mr. Nassin, have you no shame, to do this to your wife, an innocent woman? The time is past when it was possible to overlook these kinds of offenses, I am very much afraid.' And there you'll be, blushing just like in front of the village but this time every angel, your father, your father's father will be there and so embarrassed they'll be! Oh yes, no doubt. I am Simply Amazed and taken aback by this arm-twisting card-sleevery."

"Khateja, it is your choice. I am not forcing you. I am not dragging you anywhere. The decision on this issue is entirely in your own hands, I am afraid."

"Ismet!" she shouted, "Ismet, just listen to yourself!"

"Oh no. I am losing patience. I am up to here with 'Ismet! Ismet!' Just choose, that's all. Otherwise I'll be sending a telegram to your father: Ms. Haveri Arriving Shortly. Spruce Up Ahmedu."

"I will not forgive this, I am warning you."

"Just decide."

"Fine! Fine! Fine!"

"Fine, what?"

"Fine, I'll come, three years tops, no more. Only thing?"

"What?"

He wasn't in a conciliatory mood. The frenzy of victory had left him with an appetite for blood. Under the right conditions, even the mildest person can become cannabilistic, by being raised in the right tribe, for instance.

"No fingers, okay? This is the least I can ask on my own behalf here. No finger raising?"

He could hardly do that without her consent. Anyway, surely she'd change her mind. Women needed things, needed children and . . . stuff. To have come so far, to have conquered so speedily—it would be a shame to move without generosity.

He agreed magnanimously and added, "But then it is reasonable for you to be cooking, *ne*? After all, you are my wife."

"Cook? But I do not know how to cook."

Khateja saw with a cold shock how people would take what they could from you. Cruelty was the way of the world. Here she was, back against the wall, strapped to the table, and her husband (of all people her own husband!) was rubbing salt into the stinging wound, grubbing after his own selfish interests, putting in the boot.

"You'll learn."

"Fine. Fine. Fine, I will cook also. But I am warning you I will not just be forgiving you for this cruelty and heartlessness. This is a pattern of mental abuse as a matter of fact. I will certainly keep it in mind for a future date. Now I am tired of hearing about this. Please to leave me alone, I am just exhausted of arguing and discussing. I am in need of a few hours to think and put my head straight after this shocking experience."

Holding her shoulders straight, her head high, Khateja walked with the greatest dignity to her room. She closed the door softly and sat down heavily on the bed and thought about revenge.

Three weeks later they found themselves on the steamer *Truro* bound for the port of Durban, in self-governing Natal. For propriety's sake more than affection (was she naive to just overlook the water under the bridge?), Khateja sent a final line to the village: "Departing South Africa. (Signed) Khateja Haveri."

For his part, Yusuf was getting annoyed at the need for these expensive communications. "Best of Luck. Regards from all here. Keep in touch, Haveri," he fired back, feeling completely frustrated at the image of shekels disappearing down the drain forever and all time, but he copied the address wrong when he gave it to the messenger boy. It never reached her.

So the two of them, beetle-backed migrants—bickering, feuding, mixing it up—disappeared from the face of India. They simply vanished. Somehow there's never enough ceremony at the migratory watershed.

Wasn't it the final end here of ten—sorry, wrong—twenty full centuries of rhetoric and maneuvering (twenty discordant centuries!)? Wasn't there ample cause for ceremony, a statue? There was cause for a really big palaver actually, but in the end they went, just like that.

Rashida burst into tears. She managed to hug and kiss and shed tears for Khateja also, "my daughter and I was hardly having any time with you at all, hardly even two minutes, it went too quickly," and she put her head on her daughter-in-law's shoulder and tearfully squeezed her chin.

And then the ship whistled and the gangplank went up and India floated away. A mist rose up around the shoreline, great white-smoking billows of cloud that steamed about the peeling buildings and the seafront hotels.

The ship had been bright red in the first place, but fused paint on the hull revealed stretches of gray metal sheets with great bolts spaced at arm's length for punctuation. Some feet above the water appeared the side of the orange triangle that would be entirely submerged under the maximum complement.

Khateja, leaning dangerously over the bow on the second deck that first afternoon with a level stomach, decided it all went rather well together. Ismet had been left behind in the cabin, green-cheeked, gargling sporadically with salt into an enamel cup, while she explored to her heart's content, reveling in health at every step.

There were three decks on the *Truro*, of which the topmost was for the exclusive use of the English crew and European passengers, who strolled about in white cotton slacks with atlases and spyglasses and chess sets that they put out on the square table to starboard, where there were deck chairs and bolted umbrellas. A smokestack loomed from the highest deck, once bright blue but now faded to the color of iron. The portholes in their five rows were accented by newly and neatly painted black circles.

The cabin, at the one end of a corridor of green metal doors, was smaller than she'd expected, thin metal walls, enamel basin in one corner, green tap bent over it, a square water jug with a square plug to keep it secure in turbulent seas. There were two bunk beds, clean white sheets with thin, rough blankets folded on top, which they spread out and tucked in, thin pillows, two per bed. Next to the basin was a cupboard into which the two trunks fit easily.

The first night she demanded that he turn around and close his eyes.

"How can I take off my clothes while you are look-looking with your big eyes all the time? It is not a nice thing. Turn to the door and just shut your eyes. Go on," she urged him. "Now put your hands on top of your eyes. Good."

"I am not going to be looking," Ismet protested.

"For what reason must I put my trust in you, eh? So far you have responded to my trust by ruthless betrayal, that has been my experience. You have not shown that you are worthy of my trust, which is a very delicate thing, you should be aware in future. So now you must just keep your hands up."

She unwound her sari, kicked her *chappals* onto the floor and, opening her nightgown above her head like an envelope, slid into it. The ship lurched. She felt ill. She scrambled onto the top bed, folded back the blanket neatly, and tucked herself in. Folding her arms behind her back, she peered across the cabin at his back. It was more comfortable than she'd expected, and she rather enjoyed having him in this position. Through the porthole she could see large silent waves, circles of darkness and light spreading out like ink.

"Can I turn around now?"

"Well, if you have to."

"Um."

"This umming again, Ismet? It is becoming familiar to me as a danger sign."

"Now you must close your eyes too, *ne*? That is fairness and justice."

"You are ridiculous. When will you grow up, that is my question."

"Look, this is just not fair, Khateja. Why shouldn't you also do this? When it was my turn."

"Fine, fine. I'll just lie here and shut my eyes. I won't be looking, oh no, nothing to see. Why must I be curious?"

So she closed her eyes tightly, demonstratively. Then (of course) she opened them a fraction.

He was standing mostly naked in the middle of the cabin, with only his underpants and his vest on. He was methodically buttoning up his shirt so he could fold it neatly and put it in his trunk so it wouldn't crease, as if it made any difference at this stage! But what an oddbod! His ears were jug-shaped, dried peaches. There was a large hair sticking out of one. It was the rest she was interested in (out of the intellectual curiosity that was her hallmark throughout).

His chest was thin, squeezed between his shoulders, the nipples separated by not a finger's length (and for a man who would be a father of giants—it was really too bizarre). There was a threatening bulge in his underpants.

Familiar as she was with the realities, nurtured in the earthy village without the baggage of indirection and the veiled quip, still Khateja had half expected not to see it there on him. Yet there it was.

She shuddered. Thank heavens he had vowed solemnly never to raise this finger upon her. For the life of her she couldn't prevent a snigger. Ismet whipped around so that his back faced her. Then he snuffed out the lamp's wick and felt safer.

"What is so funny over here in this place? You opened your eyes, didn't you? I knew even beforehand. I said to myself, this woman here is not a reliable lady."

"Oh, Ismet, I didn't know as how you were looking like a plant, just like a plant, spitting image. Otherwise I would have been watering you. I am so sorry, I have neglected my duties."

"Look, you are being stupid, Khateja. You are treading on dangerous waters because your imagination has run away with you. Metaphor, metaphor, it is not a healthy thing. In Africa it will be important to say what is a spade. You cannot only call a tiger or an elephant, for example, whatever name is coming into your head, it is very shortsighted," he observed, knowing full well he was grasping at straws. "It is possible they are sensitive about these sorts of things!"

She stood her ground even though she saw it was a losing metaphor:

"But it is a true fact. First is the legs. They are the roots, you understand. Then the chest, which is the stem. Finally the ears, which are the leaves, big to collect the sunlight. It is not necessary I must know all of biology."

He got into bed.

"Listen, Khateja, I have warned you what are the consequences of all these metaphors, but I am tired now."

But for a long time neither could sleep. They lay quietly in the gray light from the porthole, watching the water crack.

For three weeks there were winds with wet particles and damp handkerchief skies, squalls in morning and evening, rifts of cloud that brazened down upon them, a maritime sun far away in the corner of the sky. The ship smelled of spilled oil, fish, the sediments of grease that ran black on every available surface. The passengers around them hung uneasily on the railings and smoked or held their children up to look out over the smoking water or stayed sitting in their cabins with their legs folded up on their beds.

The sea divided into great watery slabs that crashed over one another, surged against the ship's plate, growled in the middle of the night. By early afternoon the horizon was nothing but a line of dark orange; light streamed out over the ocean, making angry bright smudges here and there on the infinite surface.

Right at the edge of the world was a single, clean white band, marking the point where the sky swept upward from the ocean. It seemed as if there were trenches cut into the sea, hard surfaces formed by shining water. Now and then lights showed through the gloom, but mostly the ship was alone, water-battered. In the night the wind beat on it, whistled across the decks, raised up the sea as Ismet and Khateja lay under the rough blue blankets that had the name of the British-India Steam Navigation Company printed in red block letters on both long sides.

Inside it was stuffy. The corridors were ill-lit and seemed crowded mostly because many of the doors were left open so conversations could be carried on from one room to the next. In the wider spaces on either side people squatted against the walls and played cards and *carrom* board. Faces marked by concentration, they flung card after card onto the floor or sidled up to the board on their knees, not bothering to look up when Khateja or Ismet stumbled past. All the while, somewhere below, wheels and cogs and levers ground away. Oil filtered out onto the walkways.

There were two solid days of rain and ragged, boiling ocean when the water sheets, bent out of shape by the wind, crashed down on the decks and washed into the hitherto dry corridors. A fire burst out in a starboard cabin. They woke to mornings filled with thunder and, in the far distance, lightning turrets that threw out white for an instant on the sides of the clouds and the waves. The biscuits sealed into drums with rubber and wax were the only dry food they could buy from the provision store, in paper wallets of five.

Just when Khateja thought she'd go mad in the gathered gloom, things cleared up. The clouds thinned and blew off to the horizon. The sky opened upward and folded open, and a bright white sun burst out. The sea remained choppy, heaving, but it was blue. There were splinters of light coming out from the whole of it, everywhere sparkling.

Best of all, there was the coast. The ship, renewed, steamed close on the shore. Birds swooped overhead, curious, hungry. The beaches were short and white. Vegetation pushed in hard against them, great walls of green fighting to reach the level of the water. Khateja could see huge trees with black roots and fronds dipped down, a blue-spreading marsh, a fold of yellow-brushed hills. She noticed the still watery sheets breaking inland, fingering into the land.

They glided past a mountain rising almost from the water itself. The side facing was ridged, with rocky outbursts spoiling the surface's smoothness. There were two split peaks, forked a thousand feet apart, iron-blocked teeth. There was inland forest, black-topped, rising here and there in slender pine trunks, gray and rutted. Some had forced their way onto the mountain slopes and grew straight out, almost parallel to the ground. Right up to the snow line were shrubs and bushes.

Still no shacks, no jerry-built harbors, no canoes, no people—just the clear light and the plants and the birds and the water and the land.

"It is making me uneasy," Khateja told him in a moment of mutual concern. They were standing on the bow. "Nobody is living here, not natural. Primitive, you know."

By now he was anxious. He remembered words of Jayraj

Reddy: "My only brother, fond of him, always a bit of a joker."

Oh, how they came back to him, positively haunted him. Was it possible? Had he been played for a sucker bet, his life, his hopes dashed at the whims of a Reddy? Would a man, would any living man have done such a thing to him, sent him off to green perdition? (Had his mother in fact not warned him, "The only place we all three are going together is to Perdition"?)

Were they going to be dumped on a wooden siding, not a city in sight, put upon by face-painted natives, disemboweled, left in scorn perchance to eke on cassava and dry roots in solitude? Was this the waterborne end of the Nassins, the African ellipsis, the trailing out of the dots in history's umbrage?

And what of his hopes, his dreams, yes, his illusions, his cherished damned illusions that had brought them across meridians to this infinitely strange land? What of wealth promised, hope held out, the migrant's beacon? What was to become of a great love, a new race, a new republic of man? What of the Nassins, what of Ismet Nassin, what of Khateja?

And then, in the blackest of it, Ismet rued. He turned upon himself—leaning on the bow, Africa spread out in front of him—and cut himself down. Yes, he poured scorn, he poured acid, he regarded himself in deepest spite, he spat on his ambitions, he cursed his immoderation, his vainglory, oh, his false heroism.

Stupid, footling clerk, stupid little man that he was, he half deserved it. But he'd had to drag a woman with him to the earth's ending, ruin her too, rope her to land's final instant before the world streamed into water and space and cockade iceberg. He'd had to abandon his mother, aged, claw-footed,

shrunk in her skin. Everything he had shirked—oh, how the
world is blasted neither by hero nor by villain but by the moderate men turned to immodesty and overweening ambitions—
instant profligates, half-baked prodigals, men with apricot ears
who rise up against their station, who charge from an unsched-
uled platform. . . .

"Are you all right?"

He'd turned pea green; he'd gone pale. He was shivering.
Should he explain himself to her, throw himself upon woman's
infinite mercy, lay his self-doubt on the table, furnish his hand
of wretchedness?

Second thought: Why bother, why spread the misery? It was
time to choke back the tears and the pity; finally it was just
about time to rise to his plight.

"No, no," he dismissed himself with a hand. "I am fine. Just
seasick."

Imagine, then, his relief two hours later when Durban un-
furls itself, emerges from beach and green hill, detaches itself
from white beach and tree, rises from the earth to embrace
them with harbor's arm, and lo! there are railways heavy with
locomotive and track, there are tall buildings, even a minaret,
clean plaster houses by the hundreds, sorry, thousands, there is
a city tabled out on the hills, oh shining city!

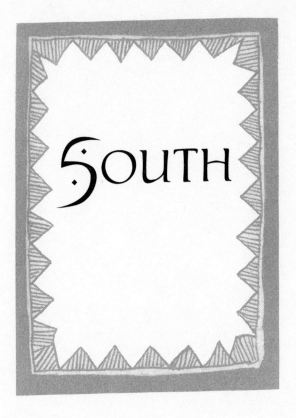

SOUTH

Chapter Seven

To recap: You may wonder why Khateja allowed herself to be whirled across the ocean because, dire as it was the force of circumstance doesn't altogether account for her persuadability. The truth is that Khateja long intended to widen her horizons. An appetite for travel—she was the first to admit to it. She had plans to see all the countries of the world, piazzas and pyramids and Aztec temples and the whaling towns of New England. Oh, it went all the way back to her least-remembered childhood thoughts.

As a little-little girl had she not asked her father—who was off to Bombay with his brother, Yacoob, to sell a roadside box of quality cotton shirts for a healthy cut—had she not asked, "Daddy-papa, if it is possible can I come sit by you and uncle Yacoob in the puff-puff train so it is possible for me to see for a few days our Indian city Bombay? Experience does not all come straight from a book, that is the lesson you have taught me yourself. It is also necessary to do a small amount of tourism, yes?"

Then, "Shireen!" he bellowed straight back, "Shireen, why are you teaching this daughter of yours all these expensive tastes, eh? When you are well aware we cannot afford! A small amount of tourism, oh ho! One day it is a puff-puff train and the next day we will make the discovery that we must fork out for the next item that has crossed from one side of Madam Khateja's brain to the other side. All this is leading to is bankruptcy, I can see clearly. So do not come with the Daddy-papa and the philosophy of education, you hear, Khateja! Only place you and me will go together is into Insolvency!"

Exasperated, feeling like his family was getting totally and utterly out of hand, Yusuf then went out and clipped the bankruptcy notices from the Bombay newspaper in the station office and brought them home and pinned them up over the dresser where everyone would have to notice them at some stage, with a packet of pink-headed pins he'd saved from somewhere.

As for Khateja—no sooner had she resigned herself to no tourism at all (oh, a next-town trip to swap Ahmed's shoes under the counter, an afternoon ride on the Ahmadabad-Srinagar train service, one time with her uncle Yacoob to help him carry tins of evaporated milk for the Hindu shepherds in the mountains—but that was by no means experience of a different culture), no sooner had she said to herself, most unsparingly, "Nothing doing, Khateja, it is most unlikely you will have the opportunities for travel"—then, in a few short weeks, she was whisked from one place to the next, as if she were a tennis ball.

So her husband brought her beyond her wildest dreams, to South Africa. To Durban on its northeastern coast, a beachy, subtropical, Commonwealth city one million strong: one-third black, one-third white, and one-third Indian. Since Durban housed the largest number of Indians in a single place outside India, it was, excluding the subcontinent, the most rhetorical city in the world. (And thanks to its piebald, multistriped composition, the municipality of Durban inculcated in the mind of the expatriate Mohandas Gandhi, who was currently residing there, the outrageous conviction that each disparate subcontinental belonged to the same nationality—and so, in a sense, Durban created the nation-state of India.)

Khateja looked with greedy, particular eyes as they came in from the harbor and the customs agent released them onto the land after stamping their passports in purple ink. Red stone smokestacks, a rubber factory, a street of warehouses, a cement mixer on the pavement. Beachfront hotels. Bottle palms in lines, black iron benches. Brown brick flats on the hill. A web of tramtracks. A Portuguese prawn restaurant. Clothing shops.

But to tell the truth, she was too finished to pay attention for a long period. Her eyes were shutting up in their lids, such had been the rigors of the journey. The whole time she kept very quiet, while her husband, sitting by her side, tapped her enthusiastically upon the arm, read out loud from his notebook, handed her Tejpal's pencil-sketch map to see. He had a thousand things to tell her about the city and its highlights, which he had memorized.

(Probably he would get it out of his system and then she would have some peace and quiet finally, that was her thinking.)

She only cautioned, "I am only a simple-simple village girl, Ismet. So remember, it will be on your head if I have contracted a debilitating illness from this constant motion, it is not out of the realm of possibilities."

Deliberately though, she mumbled (with the way he was looking, all smiles and jokes, actually one smile and one joke after another—really, she would have to be some kind of a monster to make undercutting remarks), so when he looked up she just shook her head slowly. They needed to find somewhere to live, that was the first thing. Even Shireen, her mother, had worried about them having a roof over their heads, to say nothing of a window to look out of!

The place they found was in a block of flats on Queen Street, not far from the central business district, the Grey Street mosque, the market. There was a ground-floor tearoom, the stairways were cement blocks painted red, flaking red halls with a knee-high gray band, washing line strung up on chicken wire, black-eyed children with spades and buckets and dripping noses, the smell of cooking vegetables and evaporated butter, dimpled copper pots left out to dry by the screen doors, large circular women with red dots on their forehead.

Supervisor and part-owner Vikram Naidoo was at home, rolling up to have a long talk with them outside. He wanted thirty-five pounds for the vacant top-floor flat. He showed them around happily, opening up the cupboard and the balcony door for their benefit, and then mentioned the figure very casually, putting his hands in his pockets. Clearly they had to negotiate.

Though she really had no clue about the value of money because of her semi-sheltered upbringing, Khateja said immediately, "Mr. Naidoo, indeed!" She told him, "We are not your wealthy-luxury Indians. This we cannot fork out."

Vikram looked hurt.

He turned to Ismet.

"Mr. Nassin, for this amount you will not find a place in the stable. But I am aware of what it is to face difficulties in the financial sphere so let us say twenty-seven pounds, rock bottom. Twenty-seven-pound bargain-basement. Let us agree, then we are finished."

He nodded and smiled trustingly.

They settled on twenty-two pounds, "please not to broadcast this information because it is one special favor due to how you two are a special case, but please do not broadcast it to the whole population, that is what I am asking from my side."

In addition then, pre-empting because he'd watched Khateja playing with the one window (playing: opening and closing and fiddle-fiddling with the screws which were a little loose anyway, owing to normal wear and tear), their new landlord offered to come the very same afternoon on a repair job "absolutely free of charge since we must be together as Indians. Must be."

Reviving, Vikram went with Ismet to collect the trunks and then invited them over to his place, "We must celebrate, this we must celebrate," and he set his soft brown hat decisively on his head. They went down the back stairway to a door behind the tearoom, "You mustn't be afraid only to knock if there are difficulties. We are right down the stairs, so you must not be afraid."

There was a comfortable lounge, sofa, matching chairs, a damask coffee table on which was a square glass ashtray, a wireless set draped with a cream cloth. Hailing Khateja and Ismet as "our new neighbors," Vikram insisted they make themselves at home. His wife, Pravina, would prepare all. Khateja took to this woman immediately. She needed allies.

Ah bright-cheeked, doe-eyed Pravina, sweet-lipped, all sorrys and pleases!

She offered trays immediately, brought sugar in a stainless-steel bowl, a pot of boiling water, tea leaves in a fragrant fist-sized wooden crate so they could take for themselves. Vikram went and fetched the windowsill flowerpot he'd made from an empty kidney-bean tin. He had manufactured it single-handedly the month before, piercing three holes in the bottom with a fork so the water could come out. As a matter of fact, he'd wanted an occasion to show it off to company.

They all sat next to one another on the sofa and accepted happily and poured warm milk in their cups and kept the saucers on their knees. One of the children, a girl with blunt features and paper bracelets on both wrists, came around with a very big pink plate. Around the edges there were biscuits in a neat arrangement. Khateja took one covered with coconut strips. It had a sweet, edible silver pellet baked on top and inside it tasted of butter. She had to keep one hand under it to prevent the biscuit flakes from falling into her lap.

Genial, middle-aged Vikram, easy-minded, unbuttoning the two bottom buttons of his short-sleeve blue shirt, told them about his stake in the building, the details of his arrangement with a G.P. doctor and his legal-eagle brother who'd put up the building capital to set them up. Oh, he talked and talked while they sat there, tired on their sea legs, a little disoriented from the change in time and light from the ocean.

Seeing how they both looked a little discouraged, with black crescents under their eyes, Vikram took another biscuit and drew an unexpected moral.

"Well, it only goes to show you, Ismet, Khateja, what has been my philosophy from day one. In the end, things must always turn out for the best, no matter how bad the thing looks."

It was with this happy maxim ringing in their tired heads that they spent the evening moving in properly, he sweeping out the built-in cupboard, she rubbing the sink and the tulip-neck tap with silver polish and a scrubbing rag that Pravina had provided. Then they could get around to unpacking, both of them trying to suppress the starts of homesickness that came up in their hearts.

From their trunks: four sets of light blue bedsheets, a pewter cutlery set in a heart-shaped box, five enamel cups packed in straw, a tablecloth, a backgammon set, white cotton curtains with lace trimmings.

It was Shireen herself who'd packed the curtains and the matching crockery in a cardboard box with a transparent window in the top and put that at the top of Khateja's luggage (so long ago!), adding newspaper to keep it from getting damaged, saying, "Take them, my girl, my baby-daughter, for your own happiness, what need do we have for curtains in this here place? No, no, take them with just in case. Hopefully they will come in handy at the correct moment. But just do not let your father see, that is all. Then he will insist to have them here for himself. He will say again how he is going to have a window in which to put these curtains at some point down the road. Someday he will have one window, oh ho! Better you go with them and leave him to his dreams about his window."

In much the same philosophical vein, in fact, Rashida had

laid out a dozen knives and forks neatly on the red-velvet inside surface of the box in which she had bought them in the first place, weeping out loud, polishing them individually by hand (why must they go and have to worry first-thing on the other end about making their belongings clean and tidy?).

Yes, India, multifold, many-fingered, articulated, cloth-covered India issued from their luggage: a Koran in a soft cream binding to put on the bookshelf that Pravina brought from down, a red-and-white-checked settee cover, the walking stick that once belonged to Ismet's father, Ebrahim; a collapsible umbrella stand given by the next-door neighbors on hearing of their travel plans; a lace mosquito net from Tejpal and Jairam and Yavini and Roshni, presented at the surprise party hosted in Andheri that Khateja actually knew about beforehand from Rashida, though she kept mum with Ismet not to ruin it for him.

According to her promise to help them in cleaning the flat, Pravina came with a mop and bucket. Later on Vikram showed up with a carpet brush from the basement, a length of industrial red soap, a bucket filled with polishing rags, a hammer, a holster of screwdrivers, a plate of vegetable *samoosas* from the downstairs tea room, which he set on the kitchen table for anyone to take.

Once things were a little clear Ismet took his *namaaz* mat from the bottom of his trunk and rolled it out proudly for them all to see. It was worn in places to a translucent dot. Now he could pray in a proper and respectful manner in this new land. He leaned it against the wall in the sitting room to let it breathe, until Khateja popped in and told him to take it to the room directly opposite, "sharp-sharp if you please," because that was where he was going to sleep.

Despite their speedy departure from India, it would be a mistake to think that my grandfather hadn't put some thought into the question of how the two of them were going to fit in, in South Africa. In point of fact, he was most concerned about it. Without some kind of adjustment on their part, progress was out of the question. They would be left behind in the mud and the murk. Onboard even, while lying in his bunk one evening, had he not—smiling broadly, making light and easy what was obviously an important concern because he'd learned full-well what it was to play the diplomat—had he not told his wife very quietly, "My dear Khateja, I am certain you are aware that in this country we are going to we cannot afford to cause some commotions. We will have to be careful to advance in this society and not to rock the boat immediately on impact. There is such a thing as customs and traditions, you see. That is my point," and then repeated, helplessly, "customs and traditions" because she was sitting on her bed winding up her hair in a ponytail, holding a piece of elastic open with her free hand and pretending not to hear.

From the outset, in fact, there'd been no need to remind him to watch his step. A proven track record: Gushing about Ismet's travel opportunities in front of a whole dinner party in Andheri, Jayraj's wife, Roshni, had been quickly rebuked by Ismet: "No, no, Roshni, in an ideal world what you have said would be true. But as it is, it is not simply fun and games to move around our India. Do not imagine that for one second!

Oh ho, there is a certain amount of danger associated with this
lifestyle, I am very much afraid. There is no getting around customs and traditions."

So he had readied himself for this new country even before
he stepped on the boat that brought him here. Nevertheless,
the mentality in this place unsettled my grandfather almost immediately. Probably there was no such thing as enough preven-
tative mental preparations. He hadn't realized how complicated
and messy the situation of South Africa was, and he derided
himself for it. It was the landlord in their building who tipped
him off to the realities:

Away from the ladies, Vikram (a devotee of Gandhi) first
took the bean tin with the flowers in back to the windowsill,
where it stayed to receive the light. Then he sat Ismet down in
a corner.

In great earnest Vikram explained, "So please Ismet, one
word of advice that I can give for you. In this country you must
not come with stories if you are this Bombay-Indian or that one
Tamil, one what-what Gujarati-Indian"—taking Ismet's hands in
his own—"No, my friend, what is essential is we must stand
together united as one, that is my point," while Ismet listened
without saying a word but fuming inside.

For him to be embroiled by this hand-grabbing, early-bird
Vikram, embroiled in funny stunts! As if he had any intention
anyway of "coming with stories"!

It came as something of a shock, then, his reception at the
Birmingham Van Fruit Company the following morning. Tejpal
had worked there when in Durban and had given Ismet an in-
troductory letter, which he presented to the manager, Roderick

Campbell, having made his way to the Birmingham Van's Pine Street warehouse. In Bombay Tejpal had reassured him that such a letter would do wonders for his prospects, so Ismet had treasured it, keeping it safe between two pieces of linen on the voyage over.

Campbell, the manager who happened to be in his office and who was an indulgent man, given to intuitive maneuvers, made Ismet sit down next to him and he read the letter carefully, confiding as he did, "I'll tell you, Nassin, I like Indians. As far as I'm concerned, they're the best damned people in this whole damned country. Honest, hard workers. We can't get blacks who work like that. And you speak the language."

My grandfather was taken aback at how quickly he'd been lumped directly into the Indian masses. How could this man throw these terms around? Even once had he counted himself among that point-scoring, black-eyed, fever-browed mob? Vikram, his friend, had warned him that this sort of thing was bound to happen with the whites. They had no conception of the subtleties in the world!

—But, "please my friend, you must not come with a Song and a Dance"—

He reminded himself of this maxim and pointed out, "Why I am very fond of fruit myself, sir. Very fond, that is why I have taken an interest in this opportunity."

Then, because he still liked to talk about her with others when the opportunity arose, he confided, "My wife also, always one for a peach or plum, you know. One thing she really appreciates."

Delighted also, Campbell showed his pride and joy, a tele-

gram from the queen. There and then he took it down from the
wall in its stainless-steel frame.

"And thanking you for the oranges," he read aloud, "Victoria," and handed it to Ismet to see for himself for a minute.

"No telling where this business will take a man, Nassin."

"Oh, it is most extraordinary, sir!"

Khateja also had kind words.

"Oh ho! An excellent opportunity! Great stuff, Ismet! First
class! Same time following year, who can say where you will be
if you are willing to put in the hours? Who can really say?"

"Certainly. Sky is the limit! Oh, Khateja, what a pity you
could not hear for your own self. Never mind, never mind, we
will visit by him one of these days. We will go and have some
chats, the three of us, and you shall see what I mean. Inspired."
He smiled and brandished two gently triumphant palms. "What
did I say for you, admit, big chances!"

"It is a definite fact. Great opportunities and chances, I was
quite wrong and incorrect. What has happened with my brain
not to understand this simple, obvious fact beforehand, that is
the real question," Khateja admitted most graciously.

Chastened, she pushed back the hair that was falling right
down now in her eyes so she couldn't see a thing. She opened
her eyes very wide and grinned.

Then she reached forward joyously (because by this stage
she was close to bursting) and pinched his two cheeks, "Indeed,
maybe short time down the road you will move up to vegetables, that is certainly my hope! Away from the fruit and into

the vegetable business! Just think of that possibility unfolding, my god!" In a moment of speculative optimism she tapped him on the head once-twice very speedily. (She almost believed herself, such is the effect of language upon the brain's functioning.) "My very own husband selling the cucumbers and the green beans and the *dhunia-jeera* for all and everyone, since who, after all, does not want a vegetable at the end of the day, after all? But what a wonder that will be! Forgive now and permit me to dream for one minute here, that is what it means to be a human being." Then Khateja remembered that this blockhead might miss her subtleties if she didn't underline them. " 'We took a risk,' that is what I will say. 'Right at the start we took a risk, that is true, but only see how it has paid off and we are busy reaping some rewards. If I want one pound lentils, a cabbage maybe, then all I must do is make a request with my Ismet, please to bring for me one pound lentils, one onion, what-what two onions! Two onions! If that is the desire in my heart, this dear husband will bring a nice pair of the onions, one-two just like that. Yes, it is a tremendous thing. You would not believe the comfort and luxuries it is for our lives on this earth. Who will cry out for money when there can be a tomato on the Tuesday, a few-few potatoes on the Wednesday, several carrots weekend-time. Several carrots, that is the case!' "

Then, "Well, this is the cross on top of my shoulders, *ne*?" Ismet burst out in a nasty tone, "This is my cross, you will never appreciate an achievement for what it is. Must be that is what is in your nature, must be also you do not even desire for me to progress because you do not want things to work out so you are wrong in the end because that is the worst-worst most terrible event to happen as far as you are concerned," he suggested, feeling exceedingly bitter.

Since she didn't reply (busy with her fingernails all of a sudden-sudden), "For your own good, Khateja, I will give some advice which is that in future you mustn't come with your opinions when it is a subject on which you are totally ignorant. Totally ignorant. It is quite obvious that you are unaware of the facts of the business situation. For instance, Mr. Campbell, I did not want to mention, he is one close personal friend of this queen there."

"Oh ho! My! This is a fact?" she wanted to know, glancing up from her fingertips.

This wretched man, he must only go on and on, must make some more discussions, must carry on to provoke one big argument. Since the time they arrived on the shore actually he was busy with the nonstop lecturing to her, chatting-chatting merrily so she couldn't get in an edgewise word. This country, paradoxically, had transformed him into a professional lecturer, at least in his own scheme of things.

It was becoming impossible for her to get any peace and quiet at this point. Such was the constant, nonstop chatter that she was finding it impossible to hear herself talk even in her own head. It was drowning her out completely. It threatened to obliterate her identity (if that was not explicitly his purpose).

She'd tried to be patient. Oh, heavens!

Actually, he was spoiling the situation for her because he was not aware there was such a thing as a sense of humor in this world, so in the place of being amused by his big-shot speech-making now she was just really provoked now down to her very bones—yes, it was that bad.

"Indisputably, they are the best of chums," he went on hotly. "All the time he is sending for her some fruits to eat. Oranges, pineapples—"

"Pineapples, my big foot! What you talking like a big shot for? I am afraid you will forever remain one worm with the queens and the greens and whatnot that is festering in that head. Well, as long as you do not say I have not warned you about the consequences of this kind of a behavior, as long as you do not come with that, then I am satisfied. That is my only desire, that you cannot recriminate at a later date."

Chapter Eight

For four days they lived on bunny chows from the café on Victoria Street: loaves with their insides scooped out and replaced with a steaming dollop of curry, meat, fat butter beans, and potato coins. What bread remained was wet and crusty. It broke easily in the hand. Ismet went and ordered them in the afternoon and later when he came back they gave it to him in a carton for him to carry home to his wife.

Overall a satisfying repast, washed down with a bottle of Suncrush or a cup of sweet tea. But a man cannot live by bunny chow alone: It was time, to start shooting off roots, to set seeds in the patient earth, time to husband their pool of resources. Had they traveled so far to embrace stagnation? India is a portable country, to some extent, which moves as people do, accommodating itself freely to new environments, but if they started off forsaking her, forgetting her in this and that detail, what would happen at the end of time?

Ismet saw suppers, Sunday dinners, snacks on the weekend-time, curries, *biryanis*, *bhajias*, *pathas*, and *pooris* as the first

essential step, the harbingers, the bringers of a new order among
things and a new set of relations among men.

Philosophically, what was a family if it didn't sit down together to table? Where was community to be found if not in
the breaking of a *nan*, the passing round of a pickle dish?

Anyhow, they couldn't be squandering shilling after merry
shilling at the Gujarati café for bunny chows with pale, white-
speckled butter beans and tea in short cardboard cups. Although
he was not in the least a stingy man, anyone would admit, Ismet
could see each and every precious thumbnail-sized shilling in
his head as if he'd had a photograph taken.

No, a man had to have his tea at home in his armchair while
mopping the brow-sweat inexpensively, a bowl of *chevra* maybe,
now and then a dish of *kheer*, a *phirni*, a *falooda*, a *laddoo*. It
must be possible to invite colleagues home for one teacup chat,
that was a lesson all through history.

Whatever . . . Goodness gracious sake, she was his wife!

Anyway, he had forgiven her already from the bottom of his
heart for her snake-tooth ungenerosity, her cheap-shot outburst
Parthan-style. In a minute's heat they had exchanged unhappy
words.

A silly mistake—bootless abrasion—heedless, needless wit-
lessness!

Henceforth he would be simple and straightforward. That
was what was going to be different from this moment forward.
Cards on the table. A clean break, a clean breast . . .

He waited for a convenient moment, calming himself so that
his heartbeat cooled, then he confronted her.

"It is still our agreement that you will cook for the two of us both. That will be your responsibility in this house. That is what we have agreed, am I correct?"

She didn't seem to hear. Squatting on her knees she was busy with the cupboard Pravina had borrowed for her, taking out the hinge screws with a screwdriver to lay them out neatly on a white oblong cloth so she could oil them, grumbling quietly to herself.

"You made an agreement to cook. Now is this a true fact?"

She looked over her shoulder but didn't get up, "Ismet man, to be honest I thought you would have forgotten about that affair of agreements and contracts. Really, this is not what I expected, how you have gone on and on to remember and remember and to keep on with the remembering like this. I would have hoped by this point you had learned what it is to forget."

"But I put my trust in you. I believed it when you agreed to cook in the future. Admit then. Admit you made this promise, I did not dream it up out of thin air. At least admit, do this one little thing, make me happy," said Ismet, feeling the record must be straight (that was the absolute minimum for preserving his sanity).

"Fine. I admit. You made some threats and the only option for me under those circumstances was to make some silly promises. That is the history of what has taken place in the past. Now you are happy? You want to talk about what is the meaning of the word 'duress'?"

"That is not the point."

She stood up.

"Wait-wait. Hold on a second. Didn't I hear right this minute, 'Admit, admit and we will put this behind us'? I have made certain admissions. Now the time has come to put a stop to what has become a festering sore virtually," she declared.

"Look, Khateja, as a family we cannot be getting by on some bunny chows. That is not a healthy thing, plain and simple."

Immediately Khateja pointed her arms out into the air like a starfish.

As if in a dream she soliloquized, "Funny thing, my own personal eyes cannot see a family. As if it has become invisible or what. Most unusual. Oh no, there is one family that is here?"

Moving very slowly, very warily, she opened up the cupboard and poked about inside to make sure she wasn't missing something. She lifted up each folded-up sari, shook it out, checked suspiciously underneath, and then put them back one by one on the order in which she got them out. Clearly, she was shaken.

More animatedly she took down her yellow rubber raincoat on its hanger, pulled out the pockets, scrutinized the hood, and hung it up again, patting it down on the off chance. But nothing turned up.

She was crouching down to see under the bed when he interrupted her.

"There is no cause to behave in this fashion, Khateja. What a charade! Going on like a what-what madwoman here."

She threw her hands into the air.

Coldly, "Understand this: I will not be called Madwoman. It is not my purpose on this earth to be insulted. Shame! You cannot treat woman like dirt. The sooner you learn that lesson, the sooner there will be peace and happiness in this household. There is no room in this day and age for prejudice!"

Then she pushed him back with her hands straight out of her room and slammed the door fleetly, missing his fingers only because he snatched them out of the way.

All in all, she thought, she'd handled it with a certain savoir faire, a certain strategic brilliance.

In this country she was going to need every single last ounce of experience and intelligence, no doubt.

Lucky she had Ismet to practice on.

Later on, when he went to take a walk outside, her door was still closed. Though he was trying not to listen and get riled up—how she was banging her cupboard doors with extravagant force, opening and loudly closing her window—really it was too much now for his nerves.

Open air, otherwise he would go completely crazy with the opening and the closing and the banging. Also, it was the perfect opportunity to get a fix on the town, Ismet reminded himself, going to borrow an umbrella from Vikram for emergencies.

He wandered over to Queen Street, on the Field Street corner where there were newspaper printing presses, a bottle store with crates of Castle Lager in the window, an off-track tote.

He went into the bottle store and bought a packet of Lucky Strikes, a pink-striped licorice box, a glass bottle of orange crush. Then he stood on the street corner, lit a cigarette, and drank from the bottle, which had the name stamped in white ink around the middle. He examined a newspaper he found lying on the ground, sports events, changes in the government, but his heart wasn't it. Politics, despite its supercharged quality in South Africa, never really intruded on his consciousness, which was otherwise occupied. . . .

Now if Khateja were to spend the coming years sulking away in her room, all black moods and sallies, giving him funny-funny looks while he subsisted in the main on wet breads and fresh fruits—no, he'd not be given the roundabout. Rather give ground, lure back the opposing, spike the froward artillery under armistice—then with quips and laughter in the air redress surrender's stain.

Oh yes, he had taken strides, great strides as knower of the hearts and hounds of women, as gender gamester. Indeed, he was a veritable Assyrian, a flogger of chariots and a wielder of bronze!

Taking a roundabout way home, he picked up a set of yellow stapled pamphlets by Lloyd George that were on sale in the window of Adams Book-Sellers. To give him strength.

"Can I come in? I wanted to have a little talk."

"If it is a matter of life and death."

He opened the door and went in.

"What you want now, to cause some more commotions? Better you go straightaway in that case."

"Look, Khateja, I am sorry. I lost my head and I expressed some feelings and emotions when it was better for me to keep quiet."

"This behavior, really, it is most unacceptable, that is the real issue," explained Khateja, ticking off points on the mental list she'd composed with great care while he'd been away. "In this day and age everyone can expect a little quantity of respect for themselves, that is the meaning of the word 'democratic,' " she declared. "Everyone on the earth can ask for the insults to stop at some point along the road."

"No, it was not a nice thing and I can simply apologize," he repeated, bewildered, despite his mental preparations, by the global-political angle she was putting on things. "Please now, my dear. We cannot be at each other's throats in this fashion."

"I," declared Khateja, kicking the cupboard shut very hard and going over to open the window so she could bang it again, "I am not the one who is fighting and struggling. I am not coming out with the big-shot lectures. I have not made certain accusations as if I am one mad crazy lady, even though that is the word that has been used. Oh no, that is not the case. It is you. Fighting and battling and up to tricks, but my patience is running thin now."

She shut the window definitively and came to the final item on her agenda, "It is not my fault that you are a what-what misogynist and a Hater of Womankind."

"If that is your impression, then it is most unfortunate. I also am a human being, Khateja."

"Hey, I hope you do not think all that is necessary is for Ismet Nassin to wave his magic wand in the air and then what he has done will go away in one puff of smoke. This psychological abuse is responsible for many scars on the inside. There is a process of healing which does not happen in one minute," Khateja pointed out.

"Well, fine, I will not hope for forgiveness right-straight-this-minute. That I will hope for in the future, I will look forward to when it will come. But meanwhile the cooking remains your responsibility, as we agreed."

(About to add, "This thing is on your plate," he thought better of it.)

Well, she thought she'd headed him off at the culinary pass. She'd thought so but clearly this thin madman had taken this cooking thing straight to his thin mad heart, tilted four-square at the gustatory windmill.

Mad Nut!

Berating herself with both hands, "And my belief was you were coming out with a sincere apology. My mistake! With all the I-regret-this-and-that, all what I have seen up to this point is knavery and deception. You are just going to have to learn the hard way that I am an intelligent lady who does not bow down in the front of such wickedness."

"Fine, fine, Khateja. Do not even bother to continue, I am not arguing anymore. I am not quarreling in the least. I am not contradicting so, please, you can stop now, too. Only thing, in this house here you will do the cooking unless you want to be on the ship directly back to India where you will find the arms of this Ahmedu waiting too happily! That is the end of this one story."

Then he turned smartly and left the room and huffed down the stairs and went to complain by Vikram who would be sure to listen, still holding in his right hand the brown paper bag containing the licorice he'd bought specially for her from the bottle store, to try and butter her up.

This was his idea: stand the fractious Khateja before an iron pot and a paraffin stove, have her stirring with spoons one-two hours a day, washing meat, dicing vegetables, slicing up loaves of brown bread on a cutting slab, frying, ladling, marinating—at some point, indubitably, lo! a real traditional Indian-style home-country wife and gentle-fingered lady would emerge from the membranes of dissension, would cast them off, chrysalis-like (or so Ismet imagined). Ushering a new race of beings onto the world-historical stage without first pausing to refit the original mother, truly that would be real madness. Did he not understand full well the significance of nature-nurture?

My grandfather clung to one strand of belief throughout his life. He set great store in cultivation, invention, making, manufacture, in what the Germans called *bildung*. But first the foundations . . .

As for Khateja, it came as a wicked cold-water surprise to be trounced on points. Here he had actually beaten her in a conversation. It was her last line of defense in this world. Next thing (she told herself) she'd wind up lifelong adding a pinch of this and a spoon of that, testing with a finger, down on her two bruised knees scrubbing, chattel-faced, whittled down in the kitchen, rubbing at her red-rimmed eyes at the close of the day only to face the burning connubial bedsheet!

"Is there maybe a special dish you want for the evening time, some craving that is in your heart, my dear?"

"What is this now, Khateja? Day before you were telling me what variety of a monster I must be for requesting a little supper. And now you are actually asking if it is possible to fix a few snacks, is this my correct impression?" he inquired, reminding himself he was not one foolish fellow to be gift-horsed with such ease.

Khateja sat down on the bed next to him and (oh tangled web!) she reached out and tousled her husband's hair with a crooked arm.

"Ismet-Ismet. You have become so fearing and fearful on the inside, so pickled up. Fearing and fearful. It is no good to have paranoias with your own wife. It is not the ideal situation. You must learn to have some trust. . . . Oh, what has happened with the two of us?" she asked, standing up and looking out the window at the setting sun into which the muezzin was crying. "Oh, what has taken place to create such an atmosphere of distrust and a gulf between two people? In fact, what will there be left for us in this world when there is only Hatred between individuals?"

"But this is so true. So true. My only wish has been that you would see this in the same way also."

Oh beauty, oh blessed form, oh Khateja of the dimpled shoulder and the discretionary ankle, sharp-nosed Khat-Khateja, Khateja of the shining eye and the eyebrow elliptical—oh Khateja how would it require more out of you than one single kind-shining word, one gob of affection, before Ismet and his defensiveness, his distrusts and suspicions and hotheaded paranoias—how would it take more than a tender solicitude to overcome his intellect, to subdue and smooth over his twice-bitten empiricism?

Yes, yes, a tousling of the hair, two soft-ruffling palms turned this Ismet into one bowl of *falooda*. One bowl of *falooda*, he offered no resistance. Suspicions passed out from his mailed hands like green butterflies. See, he'd never fallen out of love with Khateja his wife.

Take a clerk of moderation, a reader of Ricardo, an admirer of Malthus, a good and decent chap with a certain amount of resources in the bank—take this fellow and slap him about a bit. Wallop him invisibly upon the head, positively knock the stuffing, hurl him headlong four feet across a railway carriage, exhibit no restraint!

Cast him into a village made wicked by nuptial ambition with a problem five feet two inches in her bare feet. Censure him, this tomfool clerk. Make wild charges. Bring together family in-laws rapacious, uproarious, a father with fanciful high ideas of personal rickshaw and chicken curry, an irresolute mother of no consequence.

Offer money. Send this man and his bride blue-murdered across the breadth of the land, confine them to a carriage and one another's conversation, make some jokes, lead him on, coax him across the Indian Ocean (the Indian Ocean!) and into a position in fruit. Web and spider.

Remember, he was enchanted. Khateja skating across the floor with a brown chamois rag and a bottle of silver polish wrapped in a stairway of fingers, Khateja beating down the door of her cupboard with an impassioned fist, Khateja tapping him insistently in the middle of the forehead early morning—it touched the heart inside him with violence. Oh, he might gain the upper hand briefly, but it meant nothing. He offered her everything, he offered her his heart.

A new race? What better tribute for the most beautiful lady? A journey southbound on the sea face? For love.

A few snacks? To be shared on a plate with Khateja, those self-same snacks that had sprung in the first place from the hand of Khateja.

Leaving the room with his wallet that was lying on top of

the windowsill, she vowed, joyously over her shoulder, "Oh, Ismet, how pleased I am that at last you are thinking straight and correct, you have no idea. No idea. Tomorrow we will eat like kings, my love."

(Though she came in a little later on a second thought: "Is there a chance you will give for me the right amount of money for expenses, eh? You think it will all come out of thin air, Mr. Bombay Education?")

Pravina referred Khateja to "the general store here-here, that is where I am getting most of my groceries, Khateja, for your information. That Charm Soolal owner-manager, you will see for yourself, he is one true Indian gentleman. Do not worry, I will tell him you are going to come one of these days. He will be most delighted to make your acquaintance."

Mr. Charm Soolal, owner, manager, administrative director of Charm's General Store—"the Store of Generals"—was smoking outside on the pavement when she went the following morning first thing, his shirt-sleeves rolled up past the elbow with arm-braces. He was a large man, a beauty spot on his chin, gold fillings in his front teeth, a stiff brown hat with a strip of black ribbon above the brim.

His son, Disraeli, had just swept the pavement in front of the store before going off to school and the six-foot length of tarmac was looking very neat and clean, a definite plus in today's world.

He finished his cigarette as Khateja came up and moved to one side of the doorway, revealing a door with a pane of double glass inset, a frame of chicken wire.

A friendly, chatty man, he held the door open for her, triggering an electrical chime within. "With me, Khateja you will find it is a moderate price." (One time he told his wife, Dorothy, "I am not even interested if there is in existence such a term in the business world as "bargain hunting." I am not even interested, please do not bother to inform me if this is a true fact.") "It is because I am here for my regular customer, you see, so it is only necessary that my profit is small-small. As long as it is steady, then I am happy."

She listened politely, but with only one ear, and went in when he suggested. The shop counter was a glass-fronted desk, the inside shelves crowded with jars of turmeric, *dhunia-jeera*, green chilies, cinnamon sticks, brown-helmeted cardamom pods, pointed red peppers of artificial aspect, purple-edged white boxes of Chinese fruit with their white powdered surfaces (she appreciated them when she could afford to), a large bottle with a pyramid of *bohr* in dark water, red packages that made fizzy juice when mixed with water.

Sitting in open shirt boxes were yards of calico, yellow-rimmed shakers of Keating's Famous Insect Powder, fist-sized bales of Morning Cup Tea—"The Cup That Cheers But Does Not Inebriate"—candles, needles, petrol tins, rubber bottles of calamine lotion.

She piled up four pots, an iron skillet, a big box of chemical matches, a pound of wet red beef wrapped in newspaper, and an ounce of turmeric, cinnamon sticks, black pepper, each tied up in a white paper sleeve. She piled one on top of the next on the desk as she lighted upon them, along with *elachi* and green *dhunia*, which Charm happily folded in a strip of wax paper he tore from a long roll under the till.

As she brought each thing, Charm congratulated her at some length on her precise eye (prizes, appreciation, applause—that was why people bought in his experience).

With a yellow pencil he added up the prices in a ledger book he kept at the back, drawing a line under each item with a wooden ruler he got out from under the counter.

"If you are interested in keeping an account, Khateja, then I will give for you special discount three percent. Cut out of the price. Very special favor," he offered after he totaled up everything finally, and double-checked.

"Ten."

"Ten?" wondered Charm, grieved to his very heart (oh, he knew what the world was, he knew, but still it sometimes came as a shock).

They settled on seven and three-quarters. The extra quarter Khateja insisted on despite Charm's warning of possible bankruptcy: "Seven and one-half percent for Mr. Naidoo, who is the top notch of my clientele, always in here for his toothpaste or the tobacco, or his wife, Pravina, she will come. Extremely sweet lady, that one. But now they will say, 'What is this three-quarter-three-quarter business which we have missed out on all these years? Where is the trust we thought we had, Charm?' My God! Then I will be finished and washed up, and it will be the end of the faith people have put in me, which is even more important than business capital, and it will be the finish and the end of my business!"

They shook hands and packed everything carefully into three brown paper bags, which Charm offered to help carry home if she just gave him one minute to close the store and put up a notice in the window on the off chance. After he'd locked up

Khateja realized she'd forgotten about a chicken.

"I will drop one by chop-chop," Charm promised, "Malvern chicken, very best top-rank Natal chickens, I can guarantee. Yesterday evening only they were cut. What fine birds." He brought his fingers to an appreciative point. "If I wasn't getting for you, I would take one for a pet. Keep company with the childrens and so on. Such lovely fine chickens they are."

They shook hands again outside the door and looked forward to the chicken's delivery. Charm laid down the two bags he was carrying on the mat and disappeared happily down the stairs, patting his hat into place.

Khateja put out her footsoldiers by the sink, inspected them with great satisfaction: pot, ladle, wet meat, spice, a sheaf of paper napkins, a concertina of paper plates.

After putting on Pravina's borrowed apron she chopped the meat into strips in a metal bowl in an inch of water. She steamed the rice until it broke through the white-boiling surface rich and yellow. She fried slices of onion till they were thin and black and aromatic, made a *masala*, tomatoes, *dhunia-jeera*, circles of green chilies. She sliced and diced and chopped and steamed, she sizzled, stewed, simmered, pickled, sampled and spooned. Bubble, bubble . . .

When Ismet got up he was most impressed.

"But it is really not necessary. I had only intended for you to make a mutton curry you know, maybe one-two *rotis*. A few snacks. But as far as I can see this is a feast you are cooking up over here."

She waved a hand impatiently over her shoulder without

turning around. "Shush now please, Ismet. I do not have two brains on me so I can cook and also listen to your chit-chatter same-time," because broth-spoiling was one thing she'd not be a party to.

He went down to have a talk with Vikram and ended up spending the whole morning helping to check the electricity meters in the building. Thinking of a late lunch, he popped upstairs after that, borrowing Vikram's newspaper, which he hardly read anyway, to find she was still busy, brushing him off without a word from her one brain.

On the skillet *rotis*, brown-dotted, flour-smelling, rounds of rinsed wet carrot in a finger bowl, ghee in the copper pot, black buttery slabs melting away over the paraffin. In the yellow rice she stirred peas, blackened onion, *elachi*.

Ismet sat on his bed and tried not to feel hungry and looked out the window. But his stomach growled. It raged and roared, pressed him to shoulder his wife on one side, to devour meat in the red.

"What is that noise in there, man? Hey, it sounds as if it is a rhino-rhinoceros in there."

"I was only coughing, you see," he yelled above the clatter of lids as he closed the door in a hurry. "There is something that has gotten into my throat, that is all."

"Well, it must be a very big something for a throat," she theorized, unveiling a pot in a flourish of steam. "Better be careful you do not choke away in that room as a result of that something that is there, it would not be the first time in the history of the world.

"You cannot choke away, you have a meal to eat," she reminded him.

"Otherwise I am cooking for nothing then," she observed but he kept quiet and lay in bed on his back. He felt like weeping, he was that hungry.

"Hey, this is too much. Check under your bed, please, Ismet. Give a quick look, I am thinking probably two-two snakes are what-whatting under there. Getting up to tricks, that is my guess. Best to be careful in these situations dear," she counseled (not wanting him to get ideas in his head from whatever source).

Emerging from his room, he smiled. "No, no, everything is fine. Actually, it is just the coughing. I think I will just take one short walk down the street. Work up an appetite hopefully."

By the time Ismet got back, after going with Vikram to collect a crate of cheap broomsticks the landlord had ordered so he could sell at a profit to street hawkers, Khateja was busy serving. Already set out were the bowls and enamel blue-edge plates and the one rim-serrated crystal glass Rashida had given. In the glass she'd folded a napkin into a triangle just as she'd seen in a Portuguese restaurant on Mohammed Ali Road in Bombay, with a lace doily underneath.

She was keeping the paper plates for later in the week. Then they'd come in handy. Why must she tie up her hands and her head with the washing when there were more important issues at stake here?

She said, "You, you are just not looking right. Maybe we

must call a doctor? Horrible cough, trembling like two leaves, looking like one glass of the *lassi*. Might be tuberculosis."

He denied it.

"Well then, you are waiting for the bishop to come?"

There was a lamb curry, soft meat awash in peas and potatoes, cinnamon-sticked and sour with green chilies. There were thick buttery *rotis*, hot-smelling and brown-circled, slices of mango pickle, green-skinned and orange inside, smudged with thin yellow oil, heavy yellow rice, wet and steaming with saffron, every grain alight.

On the left was a white bowl brimming with *dahl*, thick with whole eyes of lentil, lemon-topped. To the right loomed a stack of *patha*, with the green and black leaf-sides still visible. To the fore, *kachoomber* listed creamily. Beyond nestled *bhajia*, crisp-fried brown *samoosa*, *falooda*, cold, pink, encrusted with almonds.

And *kheer*, swollen with cream and raisin, *chevra* new with nut, a pot of Ceylon tea made with unseparated milk and seven tablespoons of white sugar, a pile of date-filled biscuits covered in coconut flakes—and, wonder of wonders, miracle of miracles! A large round *laddoo* rising like the sun on its own saucer, orange-proud, rolled about in sweet colored sticks, smooth and close-packed.

Mere words couldn't convey. Leap to his feet and kiss her once-twice on every cheek, that was the only possible way. But clearly she was not accustomed to that kind of an exhibition. It was not only his cold-fish attitudes in front of Rashida. What it would do, it would end up just making her embarrassed. (Ha, sometimes he could read her like a book virtually!)

Maybe he'd undo the bottom two buttons on his shirt just as soon as he was finished.

An odd thing struck him as he picked at a *bhajia*.

"But you haven't eaten, Khateja?"

"Oh me, I am not hungry, you know. Only in the mood for one *roti*."

The following night Ismet was presented with a pot of chicken *biryani*, a saucer of lamb cutlets, a mutton chop, a methi *roti*, *kebaabs* with a lemon slice and a dish of red chutney.

(Only thing, Khateja tossed three bags of dried red chilies in the *biryani*.)

"It is quite spicy tonight, *ne*, Khateja?"

"But that is the way you like it?"

"Yes, yes."

He returned to his plate.

She watched him.

"It is only my duty to feed you, dear. What I mean, with this new job and responsibilities, I am well aware. So please do not make me embarrassed by thanking and showing gratitude like this. In itself this makes me happy. I am not lying, otherwise I would not do it. That is my real reward."

She went over to the window, opened it, and, looking out onto the darkened street, she sang a bittersweet *qawali*.

"Yarrah, this is what-what strong," he noted after a while.

"Ha. Not even a dry chili in there, hardly even one," she estimated from her corner of the table, without looking up from her poached egg.

"Can I have a glass of water if it is possible, please?"

"Here." She handed him the glass she had kept there specially. "But you mustn't go and fill yourself up with water."

Then she went and stood halfway in her door so she could keep tabs and also stand in front of her full-length dressing mirror to brush her hair out properly at long last with the tortoiseshell brush she'd picked up in Bombay for a song virtually.

On Friday morning, on an empty stomach, Ismet took his *namaaz* mat under his arm and set off for the Grey Street mosque. It wasn't far but the streets were busy, men leaning on walls, calling out prices from shop doors, smoking, *paan*-chewing, spitting in the road, since it was two hours out of the day off from work.

He went straight past the jewelry stores with necklaces and Elgin and Madix pocket watches on display in red velvet boxes, the *halaal* butchers selling cold meats and sausages, the Butterworth hotel on whose balcony men were drinking from dark green beer bottles. He was starting to feel perfectly at home. He looked at the blacks in blue overalls, light-bodied men sweating in the heat and moving boxes or grumbling, and he wanted to put his arms around them. There were a few Indian men out on the pavement, shopkeepers and clothing discounters, smoking and talking, laughing.

On the corner of Grey and Bond Streets, by the back of the fish market, he saw a man selling *goolab jamus* on a gray blanket, single or six to a thin tin box that came with. He crossed over in a celebratory mood and bought one and devoured it in three fast bites from between two fingers.

Sugary orange paste ran down his chin. He wiped it off with

a hand that he rubbed against his mat to clean, but only managed to ensure everything was a little bit sticky.

Coming home time he managed to get lost. He went past Campbell's Automotive Works, where men in blue overalls squatted on concrete amid pistons. He paid no heed to the Kubendra Universal Provisions & Refreshments Café with its shelves of brown bread wrapped in paper and the oven with a glass front full of curried chicken pies in foil flowers, hardly having noticed the warehouse on Stamford Road whose large rolling door was up, revealing dusty, white cloth sacks filled with sugar. A backstreet factory-surplus garment vendor accosted him and wouldn't let him go without a ten-minute lecture on bargain-basement pricing. Hurrying away, walking backward from the man who wouldn't stop with the chatting, he barely avoided treading on a nail that someone had left lying there in the street for anyone to impale himself on.

Reaching home after what seemed an eternity, he shouted, "Khateja, my dear! I am absolutely famished."

"Hey, don't yell like this. Everyone will think I am married to Yelling Ismet, Shouting-and-Screaming-and-Going-on-Like-a-Mad-Ismet. In future you must realize that this abuse is unacceptable. It is a simple question of respect. Now just sit and be quiet in your room and the food will be ready in its own time."

He kicked off his shoes and flopped down on the bed and took his bleeding feet in his hands. She came in and wanted to know "what has happened with those foots," so he had to tell her the whole saga, beginning to end, because she insisted.

At the end she chuckled and went back into the kitchen. "It is almost serving you perfectly right for going and filling yourself up with the *goolab jamus* when I am slaving away for your sake only in the kitchen. Yes, yes, those *goolab jamus*," she zeroed in, "that was the root of the problem. But then you mustn't come and take it out on me with the shouting and the demanding. Please, it is too much to take from an emotional level. Well, we will just put it behind us this once. It is time to eat."

She went into the kitchen to fetch the dishes with the distinct impression the outside world was on her side.

The Distinct Impression, it cheered her up immensely.

Thinking about it, she very happily spread out her fine repast while he went to wash his hands in the outside basin: mince *pilaau*, fried *brinjal*, vegetable *samoosas*, *chana puris*, prawn curry, *phirni* in a serving bowl, a whole orange-fangled *jalebi* she'd bought for a penny from Charm Soolal, whose wife, Dorothy, had fried and drained a whole tray the night before.

"Carry on," she muttered impatiently and drew back from the table, seeing two great dice lying in state on purple felt in her mind.

Ismet took in fingers a red-eyed prawn, half a *brinjal*, and a mouthful of *pilaau* and pressed it into his mouth with great enthusiasm and hope.

He screamed, "Aargh! Ahye! Ahye! Ayssh!"

(Six bags red chili powder, twelve grated green chilies, a big glass bottle of black pepper that had a broad maroon label with a pirate ship and skulls on it, for good measure a fifth of a pint of Tabasco sauce in the prawns.)

Khateja shouted back, "Ismet! What is this, what sort of behavior do we have here, I am waiting for a reply! Did I not ask you now this second to stop with the shouting and the yelling like it is some sort of a madness, putting me to shame so I will never be able to show my face in public because of these up- roars? Must be you are blockheaded and wrapped up in perversity, must be, to be all the time ready like this to put shame and embarrassment on one lady! That is the real issue! Total inconsiderateness! Won't listen to what I am saying, won't help with the housework, will not lift one bone to make things easy on my shoulders, oh no! Meantime I am here slaving to make nice-nice for you while you are with the *goolab jamus*, and this is what I can expect in return!"

It seemed to Ismet that his heart had stopped beating. His eyes bulged out like red cherries. The world had come to a standstill. In his slow-motion head he saw framed pictures of himself as a child in Bandra and Breachcandy. Then an immense fire and flame bore down upon his small dry tongue. There was a hammering on his ears.

(But why extend unnecessary sympathy, did not Mark Antony in love, did he not gulp down the stale of horses, did he not drain the gilded puddle at which the creatures sniffed, in the pursuit of love, did he not feast on the bark of the trees for love only?)

Briefly, vaguely, Khateja wondered if she'd done something: Could she be held responsible for irresponsible spicing?

She dismissed the idea. What man had ever been laid down in his grave by a good strong *masala*, she wanted to know. Oh, she doubted there was even one Indian all along through history who had perished from one good hot curry, admit. Show if there was, then she'd believe.

Still (and she must stop it with the chuckle-chuckling,

please) if there was going to be one such victim, then it would be this one *gaderi* in front of her with the fingers right in the nose and the tears falling in the lap.

She'd never have realized at all how the eyeball was such a blood-veined thing, oh no, literally thousands, you could almost count each and every one in this Ismet's eye. Well, it was all part of the process of learning and getting an education, which was lifelong.

Lifelong.

Allowing herself a quick, hot glow of triumph, well deserved, she decided to go visit Pravina, who was making *rotis* for Diwali beforehand.

He groaned.

"No, Khateja," he seemed to be saying but she couldn't be sure and no wonder he was talking funnylike, he was all slumped up in his chair. "Don't leave me . . . water . . . water . . . ple-please."

"Oh all right, so fussy, always wanting something else, always in the mood for something that is not on the table in front of you," she grumbled and got him a glass. Just before she left for Pravina's for a chat, maybe a *goolab jamu* (she had a taste for one now in her brain), she said, very patiently, "Look, Ismet, if you are trying to tell me with all this drama and funny-peculiar play acting that you do not like the way I make my food, then it is just not necessary, you know. You must just come out with what is on your mind straight away. My heart is not made out of stone you should be aware." She sighed. "Sometimes I am really worrying about you, dear."

Chapter Nine

My grandfather, Ismet Nassin, was bred into mildness. Mild were his inclinations, mild was his philosophy, and mild his passions, or so he imagined. Possibly this mildness was to be put down to the operation of the survival instinct. At the Bombay office his boss laid into him with tigery enthusiasm if he made so much as a calculating error after the decimal point, these episodes leaving my grandfather with a case of migraine and a black pessimism about the animal that skulked in the breast of man. His friends joked and jostled him. Even his mother, Rashida, would bicker him down into the bitter earth. And in that fateful village on the very nipple of the world, his inlaws had robbed him blind in under three days.

Seen in this context, the violence and retribution sought by his wife was but the ultimate misfortune in a life in which misfortune was a constant. His nature and his education in the matter of the sentiments coincided in making a virtue from what was necessity. To dwell under heaven is to suffer; he considered this a noble truth. Such is the lot of man.

Not that you needed to keep quiet about it. India is a nation of sufferers, suffering under the seven fates and the glaucomal countenance of destiny: rocked and buffeted, besieged, ensnared, rooked and robbed, cheated—and enchanted. And in equal portions it is a nation of complainers and howlers, moaners, grouchers, and grumblers.

My grandfather explained this philosophy of his to anyone who would take the time to listen: to the landlord, Vikram; to Pravina, his wife; and even to the uncongenial Charm the shopkeeper. There were months in which this was his chief disquisition. When he went into a long explanation of his history of tribulations, his long brown face lit up, numbering the events on his hands, with Yusuf Haveri counting for a finger in his own right, and his wife, Khateja, taking up his whole right hand. Then he would laugh out loud, surprising everyone. What did it matter!

Of course he believed this himself, yet it is just as certain he never behaved according to his own precepts. Ismet was a man of action, a savage, precipitate, suspicious, bullheaded creation. He bought a woman and abandoned his country, he wept and screamed for this woman and watched her with all the fascination of a naturalist. Words and passions and interests and the speed of events prevented him from seeing the truth about himself, as they blind each person about his nature.

In truth, Ismet was more resourceful, cagier, and more cunning than he had any idea and, for that matter, than his wife suspected. But what did it matter what she suspected or believed! They were in dire straits (he reminded himself of it every waking minute of the day). Their marriage had never yet settled at such a pitch of remonstration and diabolism. A complete dead end.

In leaving India he hoped to find romantic solipsism with his wife; he had hoped for the solitude and communion of mind and blood that was impossible at home where, wherever you happened to be, there was sure to be some uncle or a cousin swinging in the next tree. The discrepancy between his hopes and this outcome brought my grandfather close to the blackest despair. All that preserved him was his work, into which he threw as much spiritual energy as it would absorb.

Recently Khateja had been in an exceptionally difficult mood. Part of it, no doubt, was that she had a natural aversion to being indoors this much of the time, a hangover from her days in the village when Khateja, a child of nature, became instantly content dipping her feet into the brown stream, lifting her sari so the water wouldn't reach it, or, with a paper umbrella in one hand to shield her from the temperature, walking into the cultivated hills on an afternoon on which the weather made productive activities impossible.

All of this was the sum of what she had no longer. She had lost it irreparably, this separated creature of the earth. In Durban, South Africa, the stovepipe roof and the plaster walls made her feel like nothing so much as a chicken in a coop. *His* chicken in his coop . . .

Then she went and stood by the door of her husband's room simply in order to wreak terror and devastation:

"Well, I hope you have worked up an appetite," she remarked. "Could I be fixing up a few snacks on your behalf, sweetie?"

Ismet ignored her. If this was what it had come to (indeed, it had come to this!) he would be well advised to keep his cool. He would be as cool as a cucumber. He went on with what he was doing, hunched over on the bed, trimming his nails with a silver cutter, collecting the splinters in the palm of his other hand.

"How about that one nice-nice prawn curry like I made for you that one time? What are your feelings about that, my love?"

At this point his feet tingled from the mental frustration, so Ismet got up and put on his sandals and stepped around his wife—very politely, very exquisitely—on the way downstairs to the landlord Vikram's flat. He left her to close the front door behind him, congratulating himself on his sauntering exit. How her expression was! (She thought she was some sort of vampire now, with her big pointy teeth and upturned collar?)

Ismet found the landlord to be a most sympathetic man. Vikram lived below them in the building with his wife, collecting rents from the tenants and selling broomsticks on consignment to various shops at cutthroat rates as a sideline. He was a large man with slow movements, infinitely genial, infinitely tender, inspiring confidence by the mere fact of his presence. Indeed, he lit up the mood of a room when he appeared and relaxed himself into a chair. They had seen a lot of him already. He had been coming up to their apartment to visit: to fix a plug that was in a state of disrepair, to coax the wires out with a steel comb or to donate a plant or give them a bowl of some frosted dessert on behalf of his wife, Pravina, or just to talk.

Actually, Vikram was lonely himself and felt underappreciated. He was the kind of man who was happy to talk and he would go on speaking even if the person he addressed was busy, appearing from and disappearing into the next room. He talked and looked at the ceiling, looked around, assuming that the other person must be listening although for the good of all he never checked up on this by asking questions or expecting a reply. If he came to a point where the other's response was likely, he paused for a time and if nothing was forthcoming, he continued with his ideas with no apparent loss of cheerfulness. Oh, he had a thousand ideas! In his spare time he was drawing up plans for the Beachfront-Development Brainchild. Yes, Vikram Naidoo, two-bit landlord, had schemes and notions brewing. Schemes and notions and wild ideas!

("Your brain, man," Pravina his wife exclaimed. "The speed with which it manufactures these ideas! The real surprise is it does not overheat and make you sick"—touching the side of his head with a respectful thermometer of a hand—" Must be you are exceptionally gifted and they did not understand one fact at that horrible dump of a school. Must be. Otherwise you would be sitting as a lawyer or one pediatrician at this very moment. This top-floor Khateja is clearly a most intelligent character, I noticed it immediately, and yet your brain is just as good a quality for a brain. This Beachfront-Development Brainchild! After this I am absolutely convinced.")

When Ismet went down to Vikram's flat he discovered that there was a brown cloth bag of lentils standing outside, open at the top like a shirt. Pravina must have left it there to dry. He considered giving it a good kick. Such a kick would relieve the dynamism pent up in his head that would only damage his health in the long run. Two fast-fast kicks. Chop-chop, like lightning. No one would notice a thing and then he would be out of there, much relieved.

But he immediately felt wretched. What kind of a person was he! To take it out on a hapless sack of lentils! He satisfied himself by three sharp knocks on his friend's door, and when Pravina opened up, he went inside to talk to Vikram.

Because there was such a thing as privacy between two people (why must he rattle his friend by making a circus out of his personal difficulties?) and because he was still a confidential man who didn't easily speak about his personal life, my grandfather simply closed the door so Pravina couldn't tune in:

"Vikram, my wife, Khateja, and myself, we have been on each other's head for too long. Cooped up on top of each other's head, it would happen to saints that they must get a little irritable. Must get, that is what it is to be a human being. I was hoping you would come for a walk so it is not necessary for my mind to dwell on this nonstop. In addition, my Vikram, there is some anxiety I have about this job now I have got it," though his declaration of mutual trauma was undercut by the peals of laughter from upstairs, her peals of laughter (what peals? What Peals! Rumbles and Roars!).

Vikram looked at him and spoke with perfect gentleness, "My friend, what is the problem?"

Then of course Ismet's calm evaporated and he broke down and told in hot sobs the story of what his wife had been like, while Pravina circled embarrassed in the living room and put the kettle on for tea (calculating the beverage would be emotionally necessary).

Vikram didn't hesitate when he heard about these dreadful events transpiring upstairs in his building. Despite the nature of the world, he had never been able to harden himself to the suffering of an individual, especially not if this suffering presented itself on his doorstep. And he was fast becoming attached to his upstairs tenant Ismet and his complex and impious spirit, to say nothing of his whiz-bang financial mind.

"Listen, my friend. We will certainly take a little walk together. It will have a restorative effect. Look, I have just contracted for a new broomstick model and I will have the pleasure of demonstrating it for you, for heaven's sake. That way it will be half business and half pleasure, isn't it?"

He stopped only to put on long trousers and a stippled cotton vest, short on the arm. They went and sat in Lockhart Arcade, in the middle of town, where there was a tea room that served chicken drumsticks on paper napkins. People went there late to sit and eat. Vikram got a *lassi* for them to share, appreciatively wiping the frosted top of the glass. He went back and purchased a plate of butter biscuits, which he put down on the table before sitting down himself.

He showed Ismet the broomstick he had brought with him, directing his attention to the salient points: pinewood shaft, a rubber pad for the bristles, the staples and the pins. Vikram had only recently become the regional agent for these broomsticks, which were produced in Cairo. It was the ideal product, essential to everyone: black, brown, white, purple, you name it. He would sell them by mail to the Indians who owned stores in the black areas, small-time on Grey Street and Commercial Road, in bulk delivery to the white shops on Smith and

West Streets. He would make sure everyone had one. He was going to clean up!

The landlord stopped himself and folded his hands.

"One-two pounds on the retail side, Ismet, that to me is of no importance. This broomstick is of real quality, man! Top notch! I have been struggling and striving to get this one point across into the heads of our Durban Indians and, believe me, it has been a terribly frustrating process. To imagine that poor, soft-hearted Gandhi has to see us in this condition, it breaks my heart. If I told you, still you wouldn't believe the climate in this town. The backbiting and the jealousy, they are phenomenal. We are living in the Dark Ages, my friend."

By now Vikram was both exhausted and exhilarated. They sat there in silence for a while and he fidgeted with his fingers, one of which bore a green cut-glass stone that he put on whenever he went out socially, to mark the occasion.

How he could trust this Ismet to interpret his thoughts correctly, he marveled to himself, perhaps without much justification. How telepathically Ismet understood! He leaned back in his chair and went on, putting his arms over the side,

"This is a new world for Indians, Ismet. We cannot imagine the opportunities. The next generation will be all professionals and whatnot. Doctors and solicitors! This country is literally made out of gold and diamonds. Tell me if it is a law of the universe that the Indians should not cash in also? My friend, is that a logical fact? You must decide. If we stick together as Indians, then the sky is the limit. That is the only proviso. We must be together as Indians. The blacks and whites do not have the time of day for us. Soon you will come to understand this."

Now, in a happier time, my grandfather would have instantly refuted these words. What India did this Vikram imagine was there? Throwing around this talk was irresponsible. The only India he had seen was a million squabbling fiefdoms and hostile tribes quarreling over the land. Where were these "united as one man" Indians going to come from?

Moreover, Ismet never exactly planned on leaving India forever and all eternity. He still thought of himself and his wife as tourists on an extended pilgrimage. Oh, it was a miracle that you could live here as you would in India, but that didn't mean you should rock the boat. In this country they had nothing in common with the blacks and the English. They should keep to themselves, pacifically, and then they would return home (such was my grandfather's line of argument in his private moments).

But he was too tired and troubled to want to break his friend's heart on top of all his other adventures that day, so instead of raising these issues he changed the subject.

"Vikram, you want to hear about the greatest businessmen of India?"

"Most definitely!"

Vikram was actually worn out from all this talking that he had undertaken simply to cheer his friend up and hold his mind in a state of listening and suspension, free of misery. He was more than happy to sit and listen now.

Ismet told him about the Gujarati merchants, brown-headed, pea-eyed men with whom even the British were impressed, despite all their economic sciences.

The Gujarati men were traveling salesmen who arrived at the door of their house Bombay-side shining from ear to ear with quips and flattery for the lady of the house. Oh, they produced wallets of testimonials and printed guarantees, urging Rashida to buy this and take that and help herself to a little of those. How well Ismet remembered them! They reappeared in his brain to dispense their paper-wrapped confections and biscuit tins filled with needles and thimbles and cotton on cardboard fingers, free of charge as a gesture of goodwill. They had taught my grandfather the essential lesson, that goodwill is everything in the business of business. They sang wedding songs, played tops with the boys in the yard, folded sheets of paper into roses and ships.

As a matter of fact (he explained to Vikram) one of these merchants had played a most important role in his childhood, performing virtually as his substitute father, one Mehmoud Ghani from Surashtra who had befriended his mother, Rashida, over a number of years.

Taking him into his lap when Ismet was just a boy, Ghani made an observation that was indelibly printed on Ismet's brain: "Man has a very short memory and he tends to conveniently forget, Ismet, my son. Conveniently Man tends to forget. That is in our nature. Yet for this very reason I must take an interest in you who is virtually my Own Son growing up in front of my eyes. Owing to that is the backbone on which the business environment operates. Human Connections between people. Now that is the beauty of this one profession, my child," and then Mehmoud presented him with a castanet tastefully glued where it had been broken one time at the top, which Rashida kept to this day in a drawer draped with and protected by a polyester handkerchief.

Later on (he explained to Vikram) Ismet wrote letters to Ghani when he felt he needed advice. The Gujarati had retired to Varanasi on a commercial private pension: holed up with tuberculosis, bringing up blood in a silk handkerchief, wasting naked on the sheets in the afternoon, rinsing with mint. On the recommendation of a local sage he took only sugar water, a plate of prandial nuts, and apricot preserve by the spoonful. Actually he was bored to the point of total distraction not being able to sell a red cent to anyone, and he was thrilled to receive these respectful inquiries. He sat on his balcony at a wicker table and formulated responses, dispensing business advice and practical thoughts. On the opposite side of the street was a tea seller who brought him milk-tea at a moment's notice. For inspiration he read Tagore in Urdu. He wrote everything down in pencil on lined paper which was ultimately handed to Jorthi by the vegetarian restaurant around the corner, Jorthi who—for two *rupees* and English lessons—typed with one hand between rolling out *parathas* on a chopping board. From there they were forwarded to the Bombay office, where they were devoured with great interest by everyone Ismet read them aloud to. They were treasures of business wisdom and wiliness.

My grandfather laughed to remember all of this, not out of a sense of irony but from the pleasure that recollection affords. And his past was slowly but surely being reduced to a collection of such stories and maxims, as the flood of new experiences and new struggles entered into his brain. To come fully into its own, the present necessarily expands at the cost of the past, no?

"In India they have ten thousand years' comprehension of

how to sell in business," Ismet concluded. "We must learn from
their example, my friend Vikram. That is our one greatest asset
as Indians."

Vikram was hypnotized. For his own reasons he was particularly susceptible to this talk of Indians. He was something of
a lighthearted nationalist. He sat there paddling his hands on
the tabletop, lost for words. Then he said, "My friend, one thing
you must promise me?"

"Anything, Vikram."

"You must come and work with me. Help me with these
broomsticks. Together, with your brainpower and the contracts
and orders I have collected already, we will put one broomstick
in every house in this country. No jokes!"

He looked at Ismet anxiously. Misinterpreting his expression,
he went on, "No, take the time to think it over, Ismet. You
must have an opportunity to reflect, I can understand. But what
we will do! In the daytime still you can go and work at that
Campbell's office but afterwards you will come and we will be
together in business. We will make a fortune and become millionaires."

My grandfather took the landlord's hands in his own.

"What you worried about, Vikram? Of course we will be
together and united in business. We will be millionaires, man!"

Once they came to this understanding they started working
the very next day. Ismet made his way down to the basement
when he got off work, the basement where Vikram was sure to
be busy, crowded with filing cabinets and a short writing table,
a few chairs, boxes everywhere, everywhere brooms. There was
an enormous amount of labor involved, work that Pravina

couldn't be relied upon to perform since she wasn't expert with figures and practical items.

Their shipments came into Durban at a warehouse on Aliwal Street, next to the beachfront among the cheap seaside hotels and Portuguese bars where people stayed on permanently. Unable to get a truck, they had to pick the goods up by bus, the two of them carting plywood boxes on board while the driver grumbled and spoke in a foreign language and the passengers fiddled in their seats suspiciously.

Once they got everything home and arranged in the basement, all of it had to be catalogued. Ismet took care of this, entering numbers in a double-entry accountant's book with a red leather spine that he found on a sale on Grey Street somewhere and that impressed Vikram by its authoritative character. They unpacked the cartons and checked each and every broom because sometimes they were defective, the bristles virtually falling out in the palm of your hand, and they had to be returned to the manufacturer by express post with an angry note.

When this was accomplished, the most important part remained: to sell them off at a reasonable rate of profit and in quantities that might assure both of them a decent income. Vikram had a few contacts, but up to now it had been a sideline for him and the money was peanuts. It was transparently obvious that they had to expand.

"We must practice selling them," Ismet announced once he familiarized himself with the details of the operation. "We must practice down to the last word. Before we can just go out there into the world we must arrive at a scientific technique, otherwise we are simply wasting our precious time."

Vikram observed that his friend was transformed. Ismet was by nature a thin, pale, lean man and the result of a physique like this was that his inner conditions expressed themselves fully in his appearance. When he was dejected there was nothing more indubitable, and touching, as his hangdog expressions. On the other hand when he was puffed up with optimism, as he was now, Ismet had the spirited look of a greyhound, alert and whiskery and ready to pounce. It was such a show that Vikram was almost ashamed to contradict him.

"What are you talking about, Ismet? What is this scientific technique?"

Ismet looked disappointed. He got up and stood next to Vikram and punched him lightly on the shoulder.

"What did I tell you about Mehmoud Ghani, man! This is the work of a lifetime. We must know how to sell this so everyone will feel the need for their personal broomstick, not to have to borrow from the neighbors or whatever. This is what we must teach them. It is a work of education and experiments. Everyone must chip in to help. We must sell to Pravina, to Khateja, to Dorothy. Then we will know what is successful and what is not, to reach someone's heart. That is the only way, Vikram."

"Hey, you are getting into hot water," countered Vikram, who had no clue what his partner was proposing but disliked high-flung conceptions as a matter of principle. It was Ismet's mastery of imaginative details, not his abstractions, that appealed to the landlord.

"Nonsense. You will see. This experience will prove most valuable."

As it turned out, there was some truth to both sides of this dispute. Vikram might flatly refuse to participate in these practice runs, but Ismet was determined to press ahead. The following morning he popped into Charm's shop after spending the whole night reflecting on it while Khateja slept as soundly as an ox in the next room.

Charm was labeling bottles of milk with red stickers and mumbled something as he went on, not looking up. Ismet said, "Just one moment," went into the back of the shop, and from a shelf in the darkest depths he helped himself to a packet of knitting needles tied up with a loop of string, in order to praise them to high heaven to the shopkeeper's face. He went up to the counter exhilarated, clutching the needles in one hand.

This was his thinking: He would sing their advantages because the ultimate miracle in this world would be to be able to sell Charm something that belonged to him in the first place.

But Charm made no bones about not appreciating his merchandise-stock-capital being manhandled. In a very nasty tone the shopkeeper inquired whether he Personally would want for Khateja to arrive back with knitting needles which had Everyone's Fingerprints On due to such Enthusiasm from any chap in the future who was making a performance for the public benefit?

Ismet, shame-faced, bought two packets, "for domestic purposes, Khateja asked last night, you understand, Charm." Laughing it off, he explained that Charm had misunderstood his joke.

Inwardly he cursed the provincialism of these folks and

vowed never to return to the premises, not—at the absolute minimum—for a fortnight, to give the *baniya* an opportunity to regret his vicious onslaught.

"That is the difference between us and this fellow Charm, who is the typical provincial shopkeeper," he explained to Vikram. "We have the modern outlook and he is stuck in the mud. He is out of another era, from the Dark Unremembered Ages, as you so brilliantly pointed out. Well, it will be a hard lesson when he discovers that we have sold more broomsticks than have previously been sold in the course of human history."

(Oh, Vikram worried about these abstractions, he feared them, but how could he tell his partner?)

When Vikram and Ismet ran into Charm at the backgammon club on Somerset Road, the first Thursday in August, Ismet remembered the insult all too well. How this Charm festered on him!

To punish the man for his bloody-minded peasant stubbornness, he raised the issue of "customer relations" out of the blue, flooring the table, which was more accustomed to chitchat about prices. Ismet explained how crucial it was to develop a rapport, and so on. Otherwise you were just ruining your life and your prospects in the business world. What a pleasure it was to hear the shopkeeper confessing his total ignorance of the idea and needing to attend as he personally briefed them on the going trend, which he picked up on by reading American commercial journals! (My grandfather increasingly became a self-educational reader, laying his hands on almost anything that promised to aid his commercial enterprises.)

That encounter with Charm pleased Ismet. It put the day in a different light. He went home and smiled to himself for an hour with a vegetable *pakora*. Chuckled and Grinned. Ah, the little things that made existence delightful . . .

My grandfather's campaign continued in parallel with the nitty-gritty work of loading and unloading brooms and taking boxes to shops that had committed themselves to buying. At Christmastime—visiting at the house of Pravina and Vikram's auntie in Isipingo because Pravina's nephew, Prakash, was getting engaged—Ismet's eye lighted on a silver sweetmeat dish on the sideboard.

Like a flash out of a gun, Ismet seized the thing and chit-chatted with the hapless Prakash for a quarter of an hour about Quality, polishing it up with Prakash's handkerchief, taking it into the light to twinkle and wink, handing it to the bridegroom with a flourish for his renewed appreciation.

"If you didn't have one already, Prakash, you would have to go and buy one this very night. That is how magnificent it is. Truly magnificent. What, you should have two in the bank, you will never regret it. Take my word for it."

That was the Last Straw for Khateja (although she couldn't come and give him Two Kicks on the Backside due to how the room was staring in shock).

On the way home it was obvious from everyone's expression that they were furious. Even Vikram wouldn't catch Ismet's eye on the bus and spent twenty minutes tying his shoelaces and fixing his cuff links. Without saying a word Pravina thrust upon him an egg sandwich from the foil block she unwrapped. Next to her, Khateja steamed up the seat and tossed balls of foils down the aisle into a string bag of potatoes that belonged to the driver, who didn't catch on since he had to watch the road.

So Ismet bided his time till they were at home, in private. (Tactical thinking, it was a prerequisite for the game of life, he reflected. The chance desire occurred to him to strangle Yusuf Haveri until his eyes bulged out like marbles and his feet kicked useless in the wind.)

Khateja was beaming a red glance at her reflection in the outside window.

Totally outraged: She was playing with her ears, it was a clear indication.

"It is my work, my dear Khateja. Vikram and myself are committed to this business and we have decided together that this is essential to our success. Preparing in this way is all part of the discipline. Learning to sell the least item to the most unsympathetic person, it is a question of survival. I must keep up even if it will cause some embarrassments along the road. Believe me, there is no alternative. We must all learn to make sacrifices."

Khateja brightened up at the mention of "sacrifices," except that for her, the word conjured the idea of a chopping block and a great stone-headed axe, which she'd know exactly what to do with if they came her way.

No, she hadn't listened to a word. She'd been waiting for a lecture opportunity, which was precisely what he was afraid of—that was the obvious deduction from how she held her exasperated hands up high.

"Now it has become impossible to take you with us anywhere. Quite impossible. Out of the question, my Ismet. We want to include and to keep you by us, that is who we are. In this country we understand you are alone and lonely and we want to include you into our group, believe me we want to, and then out of nowhere you must go and do a thing like this. Really," she decided, "in this life there is no end to pain."

Feeling how Pravina was precious, twenty-four carat in fact, and that she must be totally put off by this crazy-in-the-head oddball—what was his case?!—in the company of a dish and two ferocious white stars in his eyes, she wondered, why was she to be mortified and put to shame. She wanted to know, What is this Impulse rooted deep inside that you must cause Embarrassments to those to whom you are close?

Khateja repeated herself, tapping her feet against the edge of the table and moving the vase so he couldn't escape into a corner.

Then he closed his eyes and kept quiet while the smell of fuel oil spilled on the road and hot rubber and brown chickens close in the slatted pine box behind the tea room came in through the windows. And that made her really cross.

This might all seem a little random, a little peculiar, but when the truth came out it was clear that Ismet had some idea of what he'd been on about, strange as it might seem. A large part of their business involved him and Vikram going to talk to shopkeepers in a personal way, people they decided might be vulnerable to ordering fifty or a hundred brooms from them. The two of them would walk around with their prospective client, gossiping, smoking cigarettes in the back of the shop, laughing. Then they would ask him to sign up and promise him infinite sales. These broomsticks would make a fortune for all concerned.

Now, my grandfather had suffered throughout his life from verbal brickbats and so on. Despite his relatively superior intelligence, the chatty, vituperative race amongst whom he lived ran circles around him in personal life. It was only now that he had schooled himself deliberately, that he had looked back on his past experience and come to certain conclusions about its nature, that he could reveal himself as a man with a certain charm all of his own, a nervy and feverish kind of personableness. After a while Vikram would just keep quiet and let his partner talk for the both of them, resigning himself to the post of a large man who brought confidence by his mere presence. Ismet was more than happy to show off his newfound prowess, taking the shopkeeper virtually in his arms. Having his heart's courses blocked up at home meant that the language of love naturally infused his bargaining manner.

"You should see," he explained, "how my wife reacted when I brought one of these broomsticks home for her sake. One look and coo-cooing like One Dove, What! One Dove! Then it is Honey-this and Honey-that. Then it is a totally different situation. All because of this broomstick we have here. Now that is the beauty of it, my friend. She has become an Affectionate Thing with Stars in her Eyes. Stars Virtually!"

The other man took the broomstick and examined it.

"No, it will really come in handy, my friend. Vikram, you will give us two on account, isn't it? You must come in for tea, man, you and this witty customer over here."

Or Ismet would say, "This broomstick has kept my Khateja

looking like one youthful-youthful twig, that is the opinion of everyone by the house. No, have a look for yourself. It will keep these women in their original condition, you understand. They don't have to bend over and creep over the floor. You and your customers will have the same identical experience, I can promise it!"

"Stars Virtually!" exclaimed Vikram out of pure excitement.

"Well, are you going to play and wave your broomstick in the air only? Or you want to sell us one-two? This unnecessary delay is Nonsense-Business," they told him, tapping their feet and scratching their arms.

Vikram's personal back wasn't up to traveling, so while he took a bucket filled with brooms and sold them in the park next to the City Hall of a Sunday afternoon, Ismet went out of town to sell large orders to the storekeepers and owners of department stores who couldn't be expected to travel all the way to Durban. He took fruit from the company offices, available at almost no charge to employees, and gave it out to people whom he thought might be persuaded to purchase from them. And he was only too happy to have the chance to leave the city for a while.

He traveled via delivery van down the coast to a general dealer in Ifafa beach; Umkomaas; the open-air market in Port Shepstone; Ilovo, where there were wild banana trees and egg-shell bridges on the rivers. They went north to Tinley Manor, the Tongaat steam mills, Adams Mission, Camperdown, Nagle Dam, the Umvoti mouth stitched by mudflats, sugar plantations, great empty land filled with flame lily and African violet.

In town on his day off from the office, Ismet was to be found on Bond Street sharing a tube of mint humbugs with school-children, one hand in his pocket on the corner of Aliwal and Pine, smoking Bangalore Ganesh *bedies* under the water gutter, handing around a sampler of guavas to shopkeepers in Salisbury Arcade, a carton of strawberries at the Baker's Biscuit factory-shop off the Old Main Road. Then he would produce his broomsticks and wheedle a good price out of them. Accountancy was all well and good, paying off the rent and the necessaries, but entrepreneurialism corresponded to the infinity of his desires.

To celebrate their partnership Vikram held a dinner party, paid for out of part of the proceeds. He invited Charm of course, doctors, lawyers, a man he knew who worked in a bank, a wheeler-dealer and a fiscal shark, and all their wives who were seated at the other end of the table between Khateja and Pravina, who served as the bookends.

They were laughing, talking. Ismet was telling them about Mehmoud Ghani. Khateja turned to Pravina and said, quite loudly, "Of all the husbands who are in existence in the world, it is my belief that this particular individual is the very worst of all the husbands." Ismet expressed his appreciation of Vikram, "who has been the one who introduced me to the business arena." Khateja said, "Capitalist Exploitation, Pravina, Capitalist Exploitation, that is the real enemy in this country."

Of course he heard it. But Ismet, despite his slow self-education, was ultimately powerless. Before Khateja's grandeur he would be helpless for many years to come. The chamomile breasts with their miniature saucers of mud that he glimpsed through the hallway bathroom door shining with water—to him they were avocados, smooth and swollen and scaffolded in white petals. Her trunk to him was as an hourglass mango, her head willy-nilly a peach, her dreaming toes apricots bunched up and bigger in the middle, lined up alongside one another like piano keys when she rose barefoot in her shift.

Chapter Ten

When Khateja, irritated to her very teeth by her husband's big-shotting around the place—only because why? because he was selling a few grapefruits and broomsticks here and there cheaply on account—when she, arms akimbo, wasn't expressing her total and utter contempt for fruit-trafficking knaves—when he wasn't making up stories about her cooking, or threatening to send her on the next ship back to face the music—when Pravina wasn't accompanying her in the kitchen with a box of peppermint crisps in their silver wrappers, a bottle of mango pickles, a few slices of white bread—when Vikram hadn't invited Ismet down to sit out on the patio by his flat for a Suncrush, a *lassi*, and a cigarette . . . then, by and large, things were quiet during this period of their coexistence.

Ismet lay on his bed reading the newspapers, checking through the accounts from the previous day to catch any mistakes, eating fruits with a cheese knife or a bunny chow on a paper plate, legs crossed, rising now and then to smoke cigarettes on the balcony, to watch the evening delivery vans, the water floats bearing rows of glass bottles in red open-face crates.

Now and then he would pick up his cherished novel, *Don Quix-ote*, and read through one or another episode to regenerate his moral strength.

Later on he stayed downstairs in Vikram's basement office until late for peace and quiet, particularly when Khateja got into one of her feverish summer fits that reduced her to near-catatonia, ice presses, a jar of pickled figs, a tablespoon of honey in black tea, soliloquies in her room with the door ajar.

When her head was really troubling she simply stayed in bed for days on end, shedding red tears, speaking to Pravina while submerged beneath the sheets, as if via a periscope, emerging with boiled face and fingers with pink panels, breathing steam, her body trembling like a berry, to lay her head weakly on the breast of Pravina, which was as cool as a hedge of cucumber and as steady as the Rock of Gibraltar.

Recovery from these migraines was slow. There were white marks in her vision. She was nauseated, subsisting on water and jam and eggs. She went about in a slip. She completely var-nished the room furniture that she'd bought secondhand from Charm Soolal's cousin, pouring ointment from a silver-necked bottle into an open cloth. She boiled herself soft eggs and ate them with salt and pepper. She muttered out loud to herself sometimes when the flat got too quiet for her in the daytime and Pravina was busy working with the children.

At night mosquitoes thronged about her bed, ran her through with metal snout and forked foot, padded about her on springy legs, hiked hairily across her chest. Wolflike. If she woke up in the middle of the night they glared at her with red eyes; they would not be moved.

For a while she became convinced that the mosquitoes were farming her.

Brandishing the stigmata, she complained to Pravina, "I am their personal vegetable dish."

"What burns me up inside?" she hinted.

"The loss of blood?" Pravina ventured, "the itching, *ne*, it must be the itching?"

"This man! Happy like one *gaderi* in the morning with his big smile. One day I will just go and strangle him with my own two hands, killing him dead in his chair with his head in the porridge."

Pravina was suddenly frightened.

"The day is coming."

Pravina was puzzled. Sometimes she felt she couldn't keep up with her neighbor's mind. It moved too quickly, too treacherously for her own (oh, she knew it) slower block of a head.

"It is as obvious as this nose." Khateja tapped Pravina's nose with a finger. "He instructs them. 'There is a feast of snacks there, in the shape of my wife.' One of these days I will catch him, then . . . Mr. King of the Fruits!"

"What he will be up to next, that is the real cause of my anxiety," Khateja explained further, aware that she was outdoing herself in her paranoia.

Anyhow, she was exaggerating, relieving frustration, Pravina knew, with "I will kill him dead in his porridge." It was merely a question of blowing off steam.

She, Pravina, was there after Ismet's first episode, when Khateja had wiped her teary face and had spoken in a low voice of how she had triggered the whole affair by her teasing.

She, Pravina, had listened as Khateja wept onto the shoulder of Dorothy in the next room and remembered in a broken voice the afternoons he'd come home with special fruits to please her.

She, Pravina, was conscious of how Khateja had written a letter to the London doctors for further information on her husband's condition. So please do not come to talk to her of the heartlessness of Khateja.

As a matter of fact, her friend Khateja was discovering as slowly as one discovers anything important that it is impossible to live without tending to the demands and ambitions of the heart. Of course she would never have put it in these terms and there was even a certain horror-chill she felt when she realized the reality of her emotions.

Khateja was accustomed to pure emotional astringency, because no one had ever called upon her feelings. If these novel sentiments weren't so overwhelming at moments—her heart was breaking inside of her—she would have been able to ridicule herself back into her former state and confine her heart to its formerly thin condition. But here she found herself thinking fond thoughts concerning her father, Yusuf, who had at least entertained her with the misery and poverty of his spirit, about her mother and the rapacious uncles and her mentally addled brother, Ahmed, and even, now and again in a flood of charity, about her one-time fiancé Ahmedudu. She tried to dismiss these thoughts, but it was a losing battle. What else did she have to occupy her?

If things got really slow, she composed letters in her head, keeping every punctuation mark in the right place, checking and rechecking the grammar of sentences as she paced through the flat. She hoped that by writing these letters her judgment and bitter memories would be restored to her. She recited them out aloud to herself in the kitchen, watching herself in the window, her heart rising in jubilation. This went on for some months until she frightened herself into believing she was on the brink of losing her mind, and cut back her output. By then she could hear each and every word played back in her brain as if it were a note played exactly upon a piano.

To Rashida Nassin,

Perhaps it would be of some interest to you how your son's head is festering with fruit. Festering, I have consulted my dictionary. My belief is that he has forgotten behind his brain in your house. If you could please locate and forward to this address, it would certainly be the most wonderful development. Only thing, please exercise a considerable amount of care if you do put the brain in the mail. Apparently these items are quite sensitive and damage may be done very easily.

To Yusuf Haveri, erstwhile husband of the unhappy Shireen, possibly the father of Khateja Haveri, though this is by no means an established fact since there is a chance there was dilly-dallying and fooling around,

I can only hope this will come to you. Your daughter, Khateja, who I know personally to be a highly intelligent Indian lady, is starving to death in the south of this world. That is the place to which she was dragged by a misguided lunatic who has already been put into the pot by the cannibal tribe. What you have done to her is a betrayal of everything that the word "family responsibilities" means. And to think how she always had a smile and one joke for you around the clock. She possessed many wonderful qualities in addition to this, not least that she had the biggest heart out of individuals in this world. In conclusion, a daughter like Khateja is a great gift and not a piece of tissue paper to be thrown away. This misogyny, it is not a laughing matter. It is my hope you have gambled up the 200 rupees and in the future you will not even once ever again lay eyes on one more additional chicken,

> From a Friend and a Well-Wisher
> who has Observed and Seen a Few Facts
> Because her Eyes have remained Wide Open.

To Shireen Haveri, faithless mother without a heart,

How is it you have been able to get even one minute of sleep?

> From a Daughter who has Known what it is To Die a
> Thousand Deaths.

To Ahmedu Akhbar,
Choke Die Choke worm bastard choke choke Die!

No one had to tell Khateja that writing these letters was immoral, even if they were only composed in the sphere of the imagination. She knew perfectly well how wicked they were, and how coarse in their intent. She wasn't so locked up within her own concerns not to recognize that in her hatred and bitter spite—which paradoxically went hand in hand with her new spirit of mercy and remembrance—she was reverting to a phase of her childhood. These epistles were but the symptom of her decline, locked, as she was, in these three rooms.

Oh, she would never inform him of the fact but the truth was that firing back at her husband constantly did neither of them much good. She had lost the pleasure of it, whatever small pleasure she had once derived from it. She didn't know what she thought!

At times she believed that this exile from India, which had been so cruelly and crudely forced upon her at pains of marriage to an idiot, this exile had sapped her strength and left her defenseless. Who is not a creature of the local environment? In the village, even in Bombay, Khateja was a creature perfectly adapted to the culture and the tempo and the justifications of the land, its vicious assaults and feverish provocations. That she was a master of, as was only natural. Perhaps it was just as natural that here, in this South Africa, she was condemned to be a fish out of water her whole life: a misfit, a social joke.

Her state drove her to take up reading again. Books had always been a comfort to her, historically speaking. From perusing them she had learned half the lessons of life, and without them there wasn't a snowball's chance that she would live to attain the other half. Indeed, when you took into account her circumstances and rural education, she had been reading from a remarkably early age.

Even as a young girl of twelve, tugging at his *dhoti*, she had said to Yusuf, her father, "*Daddyji*, Uncle Shikant from the shop here, he has said he will teach for me the way to read, the basics and the essential facts, if that is all right. Only little money you will give for him each week if it is possible, *Dad-dyji?*"

Yusuf glowered, "Sorry this is not possible. That Shikant, he is a bloody Hindu!"

She climbed into his lap and put her hands on his cheeks.

"In that case, what about Uncle Rabbindi Singh here by the station? He is an educated man and he has made an offer to assist. You may not have been aware that he has been a teacher in the schools until quite recently?"

"He is a bloody Sikh!"

She got up and went over to Shireen (her own mother!) and clasped both her hands in her own.

"Ma?"

"Hey, listen to your father now, Khateja, that way you may actually learn some things about the facts of the situation," Shireen insisted, drawing her hands away. "Only do not come out with these plots and plans on a second occasion, you hear. We are not millionaires for your information, that you can gallivant like this and spend money up as if it is water. Another thing, these people are not your uncles—the sooner you understand this, the better."

In the final end, tears in each eye, she had gone off to see her grandfather Mahmoud, who was always sending her to the store to buy *bedies* in brown packages and giving also one-two *annas* so she could buy for herself in addition a packet of jujubes, hopefully a butterscotch roll.

With him she begged and pleaded and wheedled a contribution, and then she sold her brother Ahmed's train set on the q.t. to the next-town *maulvi*. All together, it worked out to be enough for beginning lessons with Shikant, a middle-aged man with copper eyeglasses, philosophically inclined, devoted to the study and exposition of the Mahabharata, who as a young man had done studies in Madras with an English tutor.

Afterward, to keep up by herself, she bought two pamphlets of grammatical and vocabulary exercises, a handbook of stylistic pointers, a fist-sized, secondhand cloth dictionary and a looseleaf notebook, a pen, a rubber balloon of ink, navy-colored. In the afternoons she studied secretly by the ticket booth after she'd finished beating the clothes by the river and fetching water.

Give him this, when Yusuf found out from Shikant later on that year, he was magnanimous in defeat.

Everyone who visited he told, "This Khateja, she is definitely the one with her father's brains. Her father's brains. I have realized only recently that she is the one. Read and all, I may not have mentioned. As a matter of fact this Madras Shikant was so impressed he taught to her everything which he knows, and for free! Now how many Indians? It is a true pleasure to converse with a girl who is so sharp like this, like one razor blade, you know, those were his exact words. Yes, yes, she is not like this boy Ahmed for whom we had hopes initially. Such a scatterbrain he has turned out to be"—glaring at his son in the corner who was still in disgrace after eight months—"losing the toys and whatever we bought for him to stimulate his mind. While his sister is out getting an education, that is the real irony. Expensive things he must just throw away as if they are made to go down the drain, really it has hurt me right here in my one heart. Well, at least we have one bright spark, at least there is that consolation," and he'd take her on his lap and pinch her cheeks for the general benefit and then send her to get raspberry jam biscuits, one packet.

"She is my chicken over here," he'd say.

"Definitely, she is my chicken."

In fact, the only thing that rankled her about her father at this stage—putting to one side the whole business of threats and coercion that had soured their relationship at the finishing end—what rankled was the way he'd swooped down a year later on her one treasure, the folded copy of *Moby-Dick*, concealed behind the dressing cabinet, which she had bought from the store with the funds derived from Ahmed's train set.

How she doted on that book, rubbed out the pencil lines on every page, brushed every last page clean—and because why? Because, lying in a square of sunlight by the river with the Haveri cow and goat, or sitting quiet-quiet (not a squeak!) by the stationmaster in the morning with her father still asleep and her mother, Shireen, gone to soap her hair under the tap so she had the opportunity to read, then she was in ecstasy virtually.

And how Yusuf Haveri had seized her book, worth a couple *anna*, how the bloody man (his face lit up in every quarter) had taken away her book by main force and sold it back to the storeowner for half-price return, saying, "Take this and give one chicken drumstick, my friend, maybe a *samoosa* also, *ne*?"

Sold, fallen under hammer, bartered away for a miserable

chicken drumstick and, yes, a *samoosa*! A batter-fried drumstick, granted, a good thick *samoosa* fattened with good mince
and good pea and good carrot, oh, a veritable prince of a *samoosa*, a Hamlet gone among *samoosas*, that much could be
said without fear of controversy, but a *samoosa* nonetheless.

At the time, needless to say, this rash piratic action of Yusuf
Haveri caused a certain amount of strained relations between
father and daughter. For weeks they fought like cats and dogs,
recruiting the entire family onto one side or the other and
creating havoc in the village.

Yes, it was an extraordinary saga (she explained to Pravina).
She thought of it as the day before virtually, now that she
thought of it at all. How the words brought everything back!

Khateja had been in the process of recounting her entire
life to Pravina. Someone should know it from start to finish,
that would be her only monument in this world, and who
better than her downstairs friend? Being isolated in this new
country made Khateja, understandably, feel that memories
and a culture couldn't be left to themselves; instead, each person had the responsibility of being a practitioner. And where
better to start than oneself? Accordingly, Khateja went to the
downstairs flat every afternoon and continued from where she
had left off the day before, regaling and exalting Pravina, like
a minor-key Scheherazade.

She told Pravina, "All along throughout my life, I have
been concerned with my own education. One way. It was my
responsibility to save up a few-few *paisas* here and there and
do some jobs even as one small-small child so I was able to
afford reading lessons, I may not have mentioned before?"

"Your hard work and determination, hey, it is an inspiration for Indian females in this country!" exclaimed Pravina.

Hadn't she always respected Top-Floor Khateja, who made intelligent comments that she, Pravina, would never have come out with (not one time in a million years!)?

That evening Pravina said, "Vikram dear, you think it is possible for me to go with top-floor Khateja to the cultural evenings at the British council? She has said she will get an invitation for me. Hopefully I will learn and it will pay back in rewards since this is a modern age in which knowledge and education plays a big part?"

"Pravina, man! What you want to go running to listen to these pinky-pinky English chaps for? But they have absolutely nothing to do with us as Indians, man. No, no, there are better things you must do in this house. You do not have enough instant agitations to keep your hands away from the idle mischief and the time frittering?"

Vikram (a good-natured man who wore silver rings on his fingers and silver fillings in his mouth) spoke sternly because he worried about top-floor Khateja's influence.

Initially it was a Cultural Evening one time off. And the next thing it was petitions and placards. It was a slippery slope from the very outset. At the end of the day, where would his Pravina be? Better to clutch the bird before, *ne*?

In Victoria Arcade, at the center of the commercial district reserved for people of Indian descent, Manilal's Used Books and Spice Emporium sold used books, religious materials, primers for a shilling, lightbulbs, pots of white glue. There, standing next to a copy of *Moby-Dick* that she latched onto for sentimental reasons, Khateja found a copy of Samuel Richardson's *Clarissa*. When she pulled out *Moby-Dick*, it came out as well, so she took it on the off chance, as well as a bound copy of Mary Wollstonecraft's letters. Manilal himself with a *cheroot*, standing at the till in his pale blue safari suit, made a few remarks when he saw the novel that Khateja had chosen.

"Hey, the lady in that book there, that Clarissa, she really gave them hells! Hells! I have not read myself but that is the impression I was given by my cousin-sister, Babs auntie. But she enjoyed that like nobody's business. Many interesting facts," he recommended, nodding and smiling and clearing a space on the counter with his free hand.

"As for that Moby-Moby what-what, there I cannot help you. Up to this point I have not heard anything but if there are any reports I will be in touch," Manilal conceded, putting her receipt in the bag with the books.

He gave her both books together at one-third discount and sent his regards to Ismet.

She sat cross-legged on her bed, sari hitched up over her knees, bundling her hair back when she turned the page, a glass of water by her so she could drink without stopping to go all the way to the sink, even sipping with her eyes glued.

Eventually she went and sat down on Pravina's patio. She closed the sliding door to fend off her friend's nettlesome children, dragged out Ismet's soft-topped ironing board, put it in a patch of sunlight and bathed her feet in comfort, a pencil tucked behind one ear the way the municipal workers kept their lunchtime cigarette.

Always it happened to her after an hour though. Her bee-bonneting fingernails strayed into her mouth, her feet itched in her shoes. It was a problem with her concentration possibly. Her brother, Ahmed, had suffered from a much worse version of the identical phenomenon. In fact, she'd picked it up in herself but didn't want to make an issue out of it, even as a small child. (The sad truth was that she was getting to the age when it was not feasible to correct such difficulties.)

She stood Ismet's ironing board back against the wall so he wouldn't know she'd taken it (a little thing, but this world was won by attention to detail, at least that had been her own father's experience and she had no reason to doubt the validity). She went and interrupted Pravina, who was busy with a *sorgee* for the children, cracking eggs wholesale on the side of a metal bowl.

"Carry on, I will just talk into your ear," she told her friend, though she was well aware Pravina couldn't do two things same-time.

Pravina: Listen and make *sorgee* simultaneously, it was completely out of the question! Did she, Pravina, have two brains to be working with? No such thing unfortunately, so Pravina turned over her full attention. She put her whisk symbolically on a saucer and closed the tap.

While Pravina put the stove on low, Khateja, her hands moving quickly, explained how Clarissa's sensitive heart had been exploited by land-grubber brothers and bloodsucking leechlike suitors.

"After, then they came with their stories. When she was already dead and gone and passed away."

She put the book down on the clean part of the table.

Because she was a soft-hearted lady, Pravina burst out, "Oh ho! When Clarissa is dead and passed away, the time has passed for apologies!"

"But also there is the question of moral victories," Khateja put in calmly.

Pravina was a simple woman and drew simple lessons from literature, but you had to think about it more carefully, Khateja reflected, before you made these sorts of outbursts. Invariably the meaning of a book wasn't lying naked out there on the surface, like a surprised sunbather.

(The week before, bumping into Gandhi on Aliwal Street, had she not insisted to come and chat with him in the carpet shop where he was going for a visit, telling him very sadly, "Intelligent conversation, my Gandhi, that is what I really miss. Our Durban Indians are too busy with business-business-business. Everything today is just business?")

"Moral victories, moral victories," Pravina mulled, and broke into a smile that made light. "There I cannot help you, dear."

Although she wanted to agree, "There, my Pravina, you have taken the words right out of my mouth, it is most extraordinary," Khateja reminded herself, as she was going over to have a word with Vikram, that "forebearance was the better part," for the nth time.

She was going to explain this to someone if it killed her. She couldn't say why exactly this idea had made such an impression on her, but she admitted that there were obviously parallels with her own life. If no one understood the simple fact that you could lose utterly and entirely on the material, practical plane and yet triumph at the same time in the moral and spiritual sphere, why then she was wasting her time. The world would never appreciate her philosophy! (Although Gandhi's face had certainly lit up.)

Vikram was busy cleaning up the basement. He had laid out his box of electric lightbulbs and his spirit-level on the ground and was making the new shipment of broomsticks neat and tidy.

Finally they had arrived from Lourenço Marques the week before, after months of negotiations over price by means of expensive telegrams. Then, when he and Ismet and Charm checked, four were defective. The bristles were falling out practically in the palm of his hand as he watched in dismay, his heart in his mouth, on the verge of sobbing. They had to be sent back parcel post for replacement.

Nevertheless, despite his business concerns, he heard out top-floor Khateja, nodded and smiled to encourage her through her story and sat on the stairs thinking after she finished, the sleeves of his blue shirt rolled up to the elbow.

"Well and good, that she achieved one moral victory. But it is not enough to end there, that is my feeling. I am only one simple man, my Khateja, not to appreciate these moral victories."

Vikram laid out his palms in the air like a deck of cards.

"Ah, my Khateja!" he sighed, "what a simple-simple man I am."

Chapter Eleven

nderneath the multisplendored trappings of costume and language, if human nature remains constant, it would be impossible to tell because the circumstances of life are all too capricious and ever-shifting. History is not a thought experiment, nor a cosmic laboratory—resembling instead, in its infinite specificities and particularities, a large handful of spaghetti. Since the most constitutional republics convulse from time to time and since even kings and courts prove to be addle-headed and contingent, then how much more inconstant is the immigrant's lot! How could such lowly persons expect stability, fixed moorings, and unchangeable institutions, especially from their mercurial companions?

Oh, it might seem as if Ismet and Khateja had reached their penultimate destination in the three small rooms at the top of the stairs in Vikram's building. It seemed predestined that they should always be mindlessly at each other's throats, duplicitous and wordy and red-throated in battle. Having founded a life composed of two solitudes, they wrestled against one another in a self-contained bubble, sealed off from their neighbors, from India, and from historical time. Yet only the wealthy and very powerful (finally, only the immortal, really) get immunity from contingency.

Around these star-spangled anti-lovers, South Africa started to burn, a slow ignition that would continue for the remainder of the twentieth century. There were political disturbances against the segregationist government—boycotts, petitions, demonstrations, and brutal policing—although Nelson Mandela had yet to try on a pair of boxing gloves.

In Natal province, around Durban, the African National Congress distributed leaflets and dispatched an emissary from Johannesburg to speak at the city hall and in the Anglican churches that would have him. There were furious editorials in the English-run newspapers fulminating against foreign rabble-rousers and homegrown bolsheviks, immigrant Jews and foreign-educated Indians. The provincial council made armed preparations. There was a demonstration on West Street calling for political equality, led by churchmen and broken up by cavalry. An Indian-owned grocery burned down in one of the townships. It was agreed that the end of days had come.

Charm applied to the authorities for a gun permit, believing that he could hold off the blacks at the doorway of the General Store. Vikram wrote a letter to the editors of the Natal *Mercury* on the subject of the Asian question and repatriation, and he dispatched a copy to Gandhi. He asked Ismet to check the spelling, hoping that his friend could be persuaded to add his name at the bottom, but my grandfather refused since he couldn't say what it would lead to, also because he couldn't make head or tail of what point the landlord wanted to make. Since no amount of education could straighten out a dispute between two loving human beings, what chance did the landlord have to unravel the cussed destinies of twenty million? Political fiddle-fiddling, intellectual log-rolling and stone-casting, according to Ismet, merely further blackened the pot and the kettle.

"I will say this, Vikram," Ismet told him. "You are playing with dynamite here, and one day in the near future it will explode in your hands and then where will we be? Tell me that!"

Now Vikram knew he couldn't match this level of eloquence, so he made no response; he contented himself with fuming to Pravina about "this shortsightedness in the hearts of Indians who will only have themselves to blame if the road to freedom in this country is built over their heads, I can tell you," something he had heard discussed in church two Sundays before.

Despite Khateja's addiction to the newspaper, and to any reading material in fact, she always had too visceral a grasp on humanity to comprehend politics. What was in front of one's eyes and stepping on one's toes and sticking its fingers in one's nose, was real injustice, *ne*? The turbulent situation in Durban mostly affected her by ruining her free-ranging dispensation. She deeply relied on freedom of movement—a motorized expression of her capacious inner liberty.

In her childhood village Khateja took herself to the stream, up into the red hills, to recover her serenity when it was seriously threatened by other people's machinations. In Durban now she had eventually begun to adapt herself: She bought a toffee apple from the vendor on the beachfront; she went into the hotels and got kicked out of the back entrance because she had not read the warning signs about which races could be ad-

mitted; she spent an afternoon in the Oriental Imperial Carpet
Finery Display Exhibition Emporium investigating the patterns
and visiting the workshop; she arrived at Manilal's and searched
for a used book, turning everything upside down before she was
satisfied and agreed to leave before Manilal's headache got
hopelessly aggravated and put him straight under a tombstone.

The bleak political atmosphere that curtailed Khateja's ex-
cursions also subverted her delicate mental equilibrium, which
relied on continuous socializing. Indeed, Khateja was a kind of
perpetual immigrant. Her restlessness with each individual person meant that she needed access to a new supply of human
experiences. She could hardly talk to her own husband, could
she? His head was propped up to the brim with broomsticks x
and broomsticks y, and fifteen wise sayings on business prospects and business proficiency. Oh, he was a limited creature
with a limited fund of notions and propositions, and even if he
hadn't been, it took two minutes for their conversation to de-
generate into a dispute of some sort. To be honest, that level of
endless disputation only made her wretched. (Later on Khateja
became altogether allergic to argumentative speech making.)

Then there was Pravina in her life: Pravina who was so ob-
tuse, so shallow in the matter of an imagination and fine dis-
criminations, that, more often than not, talking to her was a
trial of one's patience. Sheer torment drove Khateja to itch and
fumble and curse Pravina to her back.

Despite her aversion to unfiltered sentimentality, of course,
Khateja, like any human being, sympathized with her sympa-
thizers. The pack of them, including Pravina, Charm, his wife
Dorothy, and Vikram, outdid any previous form of consolation.

What had India given except for a pair of curtains snagged from Yusuf's nonexistent window? But immigrants, notoriously, lean heavily on one another, such are the mental vicissitudes of a traveling life, a tendency redoubled by South Africa's colonial peculiarities. During the state of emergency in particular, Khateja confronted the under-sufficiency of consolation in her existence. Alarmed, she listened to the rumors and whispered stories that passed for a political consciousness at the time.

From Charm Soolal (whom she was definitely getting to be sweet on, somehow), Khateja heard about incidents of cannibalism. Seeing the impact of his predictions on his audience of one, the shopkeeper even exaggerated his creepy possibilities. (Oh, how Charm dished it out!) If the Europeans didn't send them all back to India on the next vessel—as the parliament threatening to do—the blacks were bound to revert to their customary version of hospitality. So ran Charm's line of argument.

Her husband did his best to reason with Khateja:

"You are completely mistaken, my dear. Their complaints are directed against the government in its madness. What do we have to fear? Vikram will tell you, only ask him. Please do not worry your one brain into total oblivion."

He stepped back and looked at her and, upon his countenance, a smile shook itself together. Ismet's newfound confidence, derived from his success at peddling a large consignment of broomsticks, revived that mood of expansiveness that he had occasionally suffered from in India.

He put his arms on Khateja's shoulders, lightly holding her at a distance.

"Whatever is the case, they are not about to take a helping of Khateja. You are virtually one skinny-skinny bone. First they'll have Charm up there on the spit, roasting, and we will have time to escape. Your great acquaintance Charm will suffice for the hungriest Zulu. It stands to reason."

"Ah, now you are the comedian in this family. On top of it all, now you are a political pundit on the side, what a revelation. Well, go and entertain your Vikrams and whatnots with your little stories! Please do not think you are going to make a fool out of your wife, who knows every truly wicked morsel of your organism!"

Some notes on the balance of power. In this time of troubles (as opposed to all the other times of trouble that together constituted his brief existence), my grandfather derived considerable security from his two jobs. Unlike Khateja, he got to know the local inhabitants beyond their small apartment building doing Campbell's accountancy. And he and Vikram were making money hand over fist in their afterhours broomstick enterprise. My grandfather, as everyone was starting to be aware now, was a world-historical salesman.

Success meant little to Ismet, however, if it wasn't immediately leavened with filial gratitude. So once a month he sent Rashida a small bank draft. At the very minimum this newfound opulence allowed them to be more closely in communication. Rashida installed a coffee table that Solly Ghani, son of the famous Mehmoud, organized for her at cost plus ten percent. It was handy whenever she wished to compose a letter to her son in pure comfort, reclining in a chair next to the table and

soaking her old feet in a basin of water salted with half a tablespoon of mentholated Vicks ointment.

Oddly enough, in these letters, which Ismet read aloud, close
to weeping, Rashida referred affectionately to "my daughter Khateja." Rashida was one of those people who suffer through each
day with incredible acuteness and yet remember the circumstances of the past in an optimistic fashion, more and more
happily as the temporal distance increases. History was all in
the past, no?

This tender mode of address left Khateja at a loss, feeling
almost flattered for a moment until she suppressed the thought.
She recalled Rashida's stunts and the box of delicacies reserved
for herself and Ismet which Rashida slept on top of in her Bombay bedroom, supposedly to prevent Khateja getting at them.

Then, as was proper, Khateja took it out on her husband:

"I have discovered who really occupies your heart's center
stage: your conniving mother. How you speak about her, as if
she is a goddess from the stars. You idolize her, Ismet. I look in
your eyes and must I tell you what I see there? Rashida!"

In this case Khateja wasn't entirely deluded. Ismet had constant thought and constant dreams on the topic of his mother.
The only way of quelling them was to send her gifts, which he
did almost every month along with money, sealing something
up in a pinewood crate and hauling it off to the post office with
Vikram's assistance. For her fiftieth birthday he ordered a picnic
hamper for her through the pages of the *Illustrated London News*
(Dorothy's brainstroke). Rashida stretched out the sardines for
a fortnight, having them with plates of cream crackers and water
biscuits. Included was a bottle of white table wine in a cone of

silvered paper that she passed off on the next-door neighbors, a Hindu family who didn't object to a drop of alcohol.

He sent her a portrait of them by Crown Photographic Studios. (Khateja insisted he pay her at an hourly rate for her voluntary participation and actually tacked on a surcharge when she was forced to smile.) He got several Parker pen-and-pencil sets from a broomstick importer, printed with the man's commercial details, and mailed one to his mother, and others to Tejpal Reddy, Solly Ghani, Yusuf, his father in-law. Also a down quilt for his mother's four-poster marital suite, a silk dressing gown in which the old woman lounged about, an egg timer.

Rashida was quite delighted by all the attention. She took her pen-and-pencil set to the bank, opened it out on the counter to reveal the red-felt surfaces inside the case. She blessed the name of her son every time she tied a bow knot in the belt of her dressing gown. She fantasized about Khateja's head while cracking open a hard-boiled egg on the souvenir coaster from the Tower of London.

But Rashida Nassin was not averse to India's contradictory and melodramatic style of manners: that is, combining doses of ferocity and unsquanderable love in one unseparable bundle. So one morning a neatly constructed package arrived with purple stamps and Khateja Haveri's name on it. When it was cut open with scissors, the cardboard panels opened out like a flower to reveal a lamp bandaged in tissue paper and tied up with a purple ribbon knotted into two bows at the top, a modest thing with a tin base and an enamelized receptacle for oil.

Khateja (generally bewildered by the significance of symbolism but tolerant of its role in the psychological makeup of others) saw instantly that it was an exact cousin of the lamp whose destruction had, in her contemporary opinion, sent her across the ocean initially. At first she didn't know what her feelings were. For a minute she started crying. Then she dried her eyes.

It was at times like these that Khateja most needed a sympathetic ear, and who better was there than Charm Soolal, the shopkeeper from over the road? She went to see him. He had been a comfort to her at every new and dire turn she experienced crashing down on her ears in South Africa. Charm, a self-conscious ladies' man, was good with her and good to her. In a nonsexual way they cultivated a soft spot for one another, miraculously.

For example when Ismet had brought that silly gramophone secondhand from Grey Street and put it on his windowsill and played his one Vivaldi record (that came with as a bonus) one whole Sunday at an extremely high volume so her teeth were shaking in her mouth—then how he was beaming with one big smile after his work promotions, talking like a big shot about community responsibilities.

During that particular episode, because she was on the verge of tears, breathing hot breaths, Charm took her hands and told her, "I am well aware of how you must feel since I also have suffered. I am selling only half the fruits from before. That is across the board, mangoes, watermelons, what-what all sales cut in two halves! Ismet is only with the big shots and the companies who can swallow up a little bloke like Charm in two-twos. So do not worry you are alone, Khateja. Take, take a few peaches, go on, I will give them for you free at no charge," he insisted and walked her home around the corner.

He could come with her and even take longer walks in the afternoon because his oldest boy, Disraeli Soolal, had grown up old enough to be trusted with the counter. Already Disraeli could add and subtract and all, ever since his eleventh birthday.

("Also he will multiply," Charm said with a grin. "Also he will multiply from time to time.")

Yes, Disraeli was a boy of great promise, that much was evident to anyone who walked in the store and conversed with him, detected his neatly parted hair and his unscuffed school shoes with the metal tags in their laces. Charm (a believer in the power of names) saw him as an engine mechanic with a technical diploma, an industrial foreman, what maybe a doctor! A lawyer! An independent businessman!

"My Disraeli," he'd mumble, tousling the boy's hair. "In the future to come maybe it will be Disraeli the prime minister of Africa and then you will come to collect your father from the shop in your big-big limousine-automobile!"

Indeed, in later life Disraeli rose to the dizzying height of vice-chairman in the government-instituted Indian Council, and he drove in a red tax-free Daimler Benz with a one-digit license plate until a young Marxist named Kubendra Govender—going under the nom de guerre Leon Troshottam—stuck a Soviet hand grenade in the swinging garden chair on the vice-chairman's patio.

But the ill-starred idealist slipped while tying a piece of string on the grenade pin and erased only himself and an inexpensive outdoor tea chest. Savvy to the political tide, Disraeli nonetheless resigned his post and returned to his chain of bottle stores and *halaal* butcher shops.

Meanwhile the vice-chairman-to-be administered the internal affairs of Charm's General Store (hadn't it always been "the Store of Generals"?), taking inventories on Saturday morning, heaving around bags of nuts after school, pouring out washing powder by the cup into brown paper wallets while his father sat cross-legged on the mat in front, smoked, greeted passersby, dipped a modest finger into advertising. (Following Ismet's exploits, it had become clear to Charm that the modern age demanded an investment in the advertising side of business.)

Good customer relations, word of mouth, small profit margins weren't good enough for today's young people, oh no. They wanted something more, a bit on the side, love with their *achaar*, beauty from their *bharfee*, glamour right along with their one *goolab jamu*.

Oh ho! Man's appetite was increasing (Charm could see that), growing prodigiously, the world was crying out for more, more this and more that, and if the owner-manager of a general store wasn't to respond to this new climate, then who would? There was the tough question shirked by proponents of mildness and meekness like Gandhi. Who would sink, that was the real issue—and who would swim?

So there was now the Charm General Store's Lottery of Millions. The prize? Ah, genius, true-true genius and Indian forethought had stroked Charm's forehead with its blessed claw: a full lifetime's supply of *paan*, as many chewy green triangles of bitter leaf as one person could stomach, day in, day out, freely available in quarter-pound stacks wrapped in rubber bands and newspaper from the counter of Charm's General Store, corner of Queen and Victoria Streets.

Just fill out an entry form obtained from a cyclostyled stack
behind the counter: one per person (no children, sorry), name,
age, address, hobbies, and particulars.

Only thing . . . the prize was for personal consumption only,
not for relatives, neighbors, husbands, cousin-sisters, and aunties
for their teatime snacks also. Since there was such a thing as
limited resources in this universe.

A new winner would be drawn every single year on New
Year's Eve, a brand-new lucky recipient of endless quantities of
paan—though this would in no way affect the rights of previous
winners, which were 100 percent guaranteed.

Now the thing was this, as Charm saw it: true, the giveaway
offer smacked of a heat-touched head, what unusual extravagance, what whirlwind generosity to virtually give away the
store!

But then, this was Charm's point: how much *paan* could a
claw-footed, shrunken old woman munch and splutter her way
through? Truthfully not much, even when inspired by greed and
infinite abundance. It wasn't as if much valuable leaf was in
danger, oh no . . .

. . . Because of course he had no intention of letting, say, a
portly thirty-five-year-old *paan* addict get his green fingers into
his, Charm's, daily *paan* supply purchased from Victoria Street
market in precious bales. Certainly not (and support the swain
in comfort and luxuries for a further thirty-five years at painful
expense, hard-earned cash automatically out of the window, it
was out of the question!). He was a decent man, a good, upstanding, canny-fingered Indian businessman—but no fool!

No fool was going to go around calling him fool and spendthrift. That wasn't about to happen, reason being he quickly tore up the entry forms of anyone under sixty-seven years of age, and threw them away in a special bin in his house—and still had a sizable number of forms to choose from on New Year's Eve (because why must he take all the fun out of it for himself, when there was a better way?).

The first time, the previous year, he had been stupendously fortunate. Yes, the bitch-goddess had descended for him. He had put on a firework show with the help of the boys from Disraeli's school, three tax-deductible trays of ready-made sweetmeats, a spittoon contest, *kulfi* in shallow tins, and a whole crowd of *paan* addicts with their red-stained gums and orange teeth and fingers (including those unsuspecting callow youngsters who were, unluckily for themselves, below sixty-seven years of age).

With a rented bullhorn and notecards that he drew up with help from Dorothy and Disraeli, Charm made a short speech and then he paused for a moment above the bucket, around whose rim ran a string of colored Christmas lights, scratched his chin while the excitement mounted, especially among the younger generation, and then drew out a stapled form from near the top and read out the name.

A Mrs. Ronnie Haripersad, tottering bravely on her eighty-four-year-old feet, came up proudly in the clapping and the singing to collect her specially printed certificate, embossed with "Official Winner, 1st Prize 1st Time, The Charm General Store's Lottery of Millions, Held on this day of New Year's Eve in the City of Durban, Natal Province."

Mrs. Haripersad turned out to be just visiting the country

(which caused a certain amount of disappointment, since it was felt a local champion was preferable in the best-case scenario). She had come away from her home city of Calcutta to spend six months with her sixty-one-year-old daughter, Kubeshni (disqualified).

The victor beamed in front of the crowd and said out her name and address in Hindi through the bullhorn before sitting down, drained from the excitement. Afterward she went with her daughter and asked Charm if it would be possible, seeing as she herself was in the country for so little time, if her daughter, Kubeshni, who had also entered, could receive the first prize in her stead?

"Sorry, Mrs. Haripersad," he said firmly. "Rules are rules, you understand. Otherwise, if we can all decide what is personally best for each one of us without obeying the rules, what will happen a few steps down the road? It will be anarchy and chaos, I am telling you. But"—he smiled and congratulated her again for a moment while Dorothy took photographs—"if you want *paan* when you are in India, now and again when you have the taste, then all you must do is to drop me one line. On a postcard or whatever, I am not a fussy chap. It will be straight with you, virtually same day, that is my promise."

Mrs. Haripersad's heart packed in on the return voyage. She expired with her disappointed eyes wide open, still chewing. The certificate in her hand luggage that testified to her lifelong entitlement was discarded without a second thought by her whippersnapper daughters in Calcutta, who had taken up smoking instead as part of a modernizing trend.

All in all, Charm reckoned he'd spent one pound, maybe

one pound two shillings, on the lottery and accumulated thirty, forty times that much at in extra profits, at least.

Energized by the success of the first competition, he was preparing for the now annual Lottery of Millions, new and improved, and hoping to entice Gandhi into delivering the keynote address. This year he calculated on giving a goat as a second-place consolation, a small whole live bleating goat. His brother, Rajendra, had given the goat to him for his birthday. So far it had done nothing except eat good hay, grass, expensive sugar cubes. And Charm wasn't up to cutting it himself, being a fastidious man.

When Khateja arrived he was working on a pasteboard: The Lottery of Millions, Great Prizes & Opportunity of a Lifetime, Enter Today Only at the Charm General Store.

This was painted black in fancy block letters on a background of neat green and yellow squares, which Disraeli had finished off that morning, getting up extra early on his personal initiative. Charm was planning to chain it by the *madressa* in Lockhart Arcade, since his sister kept the books for the school and could also keep a watch on his board. That way it would be seen by the Friday mosque-goers, the wealthy ladies who went to the jewelery stores, the cost-price cloth merchants who bought wholesale from the Prince Edward Street warehouse.

His shirt was off and yet such was the heat that he was sweating, whistling happily as he dabbed deftly here and there. There was paint running down the pavement and into the gutter by the fire hydrant.

Quite a sign (Charm congratulated himself). With luck it would double or even triple the previous year's takings, which were extra sweet because he didn't declare them for tax purposes. (That was the advantage of cash sales in South Africa, where no one paid taxes if at all possible.)

People would stroll by, take a look around, pop into the General Store, and leave with their entry form and a bunch of bananas to go a liter-bottle of orange drink, a big packet of multicolored gumdrops for the children.

But here was Khateja who just wanted to talk. Since he was busy, she would just come by later on. But he said, "Sit, sit, what problem for me to have a chat with our Khateja," and rubbed the paint off his hands on the newspaper underneath and pulled his shirt back on, buttoned it up expertly without looking, stood his board in the sunlight to dry.

Wanting to talk, wanting to have a little talk, it was the curse and the cross and the characteristic bondage of Indians in business, Charm reflected in a moment of irritation. He suppressed it immediately in favor of his cherished commercial suavity. He put his arms on Khateja's shoulders.

"One cup sherbet?"

"This morning I had a cup with Pravina Naidoo."

She pulled her sari up her legs and sat in the shade under the awning, her arms around her knees. How could she explain her feelings about Rashida to this rock of the ages? Charm was famous in her mind for standing up for family togetherness as the most important value in life. She feared he would write her off as an emotional cripple. In an odd way, Khateja's heart was closer to exploding now than ever before—why she didn't know and preferred not to inquire.

Instead, she talked to Charm about the book she was read-

ing, how Clarissa stood up for her own rights even when it
meant she must go against everyone, including her elders who
bundled her into a trunk. At the end of the day, in her considered opinion, that was the meaning of the "true heroism." Ah,
the sweet delectable joys of rehearsing a familiar theme!

"My Khateja, why you letting yourself get so worked up over
one story for, eh?" Charm wanted to know, talking over his
shoulder as he examined the surface of the sign board.

Sensing that she was embarking on a profound measure of
self-exposure, Khateja went on to explain the narrative's significance in her own existence, time and again. Up to this moment
she had never thought of herself as an autobiographer, because
her life didn't lend itself to analysis so much as the defiance of
repellent injustice. Now Khateja found herself rather enjoying
the process for its own sake, talking about the village and Ismet
and Rashida and the lamp almost as if she had a book of photographs in front of her.

Charm sat down next to her in the sun and listened intently,
a discipline he practiced while keeping a part of one ear open
for prospective customers. He took his hat in his hand and studied the brown ribbon on the brim, reflecting intently.

So much he never knew about his friend top-floor Khateja,
so little he understood! Now the picture was becoming clearer
and the pieces fell into place. Up to now he thought of her as
a private person, consumed with her husband and the problems
bottled up under one domestic roof. Up to today she never
volunteered information about her past history, her parents and
her Indian past and the scandalous manner in which she had
been sold as a bag of chattels with a pretty face on it to this

rapacious, boggle-eyed, entrained husband for thirty Judas pieces. Most extraordinary! Occasionally he coughed or made some innocuous comment or an expression of commiseration, but for the most part he was silent until Khateja finished with her catalogue of horrors: the peach pips of shame, the banged-up lamp, and the diatribes and suspicious minds of Bandra on Bombay's oceanfront.

He exclaimed, "What a golden opportunity!"

"Excuse me. What?"

"Yes, my Khateja. This is a golden opportunity in a million. In one moment you can renew your love for Ismet."

He spoke with a smile for, beneath the vulturish financial exterior, Charm was truly a sentimental man, believing in ultimate reconciliations and the power of the iron bond of family to restore itself to a proper level. (In fact, Charm's capitalistic prejudices also, just as much as Vikram's genial socialism, grew out of the conviction that the universe could be happily organized.)

Although Khateja went around cursing her friend the shopkeeper for a blockhead and a "Gujarati typical moron" for some time until she cooled off, his words had the effect of disposing her to avoid more quarreling with Ismet—not because of the content of Charm's advice but because, like human beings generally, Khateja followed her instinct to avoid simultaneous conflicts in multiple theaters. Reasonably speaking, it was necessary to struggle with every person at some point but suicidal to fight everybody at the same moment; otherwise who would guard your back?

◆   ◆   ◆

One-legged Sonny Govender, their old friend, invited them to his daughter Sharmila's fifth birthday party. Sharmila's mother taught history and maths in a Bombay girls' school and had sent her child to spend a few months with her father while she went for a typing course. Sharmila came on the coal-burning steamer operated by the British-India Steam Navigation Company, traveling with an auntie who was herself off to get married to a practicing pharmacist in Johannesburg who'd corresponded with her family through the *Times*.

Sonny was thrilled by his Sharmila. He held her up in his two strong arms for a photograph to be taken. He passed her around for inspection. She'd been bought a special dress with a big pink bow and mother-of-pearl buttons, as well as shiny black patent-leather shoes, size three, that were open at the top and had a metal strap and buckle so they were easy for her tactless five-year-old fingers to open and close.

"In the future shoelaces will be a thing of the past, that is what they are saying on the street," the proud father explained to Khateja. "These shoes Sharmila has on." He put one arm around her and leaned down and picked up one slender, glowing foot and displayed it sitting in the middle of his palm like a butterfly. "You can see. That is what we will all be wearing shortly. Already it is the fashion in America."

"Hey, man. There is always a new thing on this planet," observed Dorothy, arriving from the other side of the room, Disraeli in tow (wearing flannels, a schoolboy tie, and a white cotton shirt with a button-down collar).

My grandfather found himself alone in a corner of the reception area, a common occurrence for him at social gatherings when no one decided to pick on him and make him the center of everyone's attention forcibly. Not that the sweet man minded. He never failed to come out of it with something valuable, some observation on the nature of humanity in groups and so on that would be useful in business, although he invariably forgot these bitter conclusions later on. In a philosophical mood, Ismet got to thinking about the succession of generations on this earth, the old succoring while being devoured by the young, like a stork cheerfully feeding its hatchlings on servings of its own blood. Appalled by this image, Ismet spent the remainder of the evening thinking about his wife and her quirks, his wife who so fascinated him at the intellectual level. A lock he couldn't pick, as yet.

Chapter Twelve

Although, "We must not be the ones to take sides with Ismet or Khateja," Pravina had insisted. "If they want to come to sit with us to have a few snacks, then it is important that they must come together as one couple, Vikram. Otherwise it is just a recipe for disaster, I am telling you," it was enough to see how his friend could not share in his own ground-floor felicity to make the landlord unhappy.

Wanting to help, with an arm slung around Ismet's back had Vikram not suggested in confidence, "I am always bringing my Pravina one chocolate from the shop when there is the opportunity. It is only a little thing, but she appreciates it, Ismet. Especially when I can afford one top-quality chocolate, then her whole face will light up with excitement, I have experienced it. One top-quality chocolate, for her it makes all the difference"?

So Ismet pilfered twenty-four feathery peaches, wrapped them up individually in tissue paper, arranged them carefully on a white cardboard tray, and left them strategically on the middle shelf of the kitchen cupboard, next to her packet of chocolate digestives and her bottles of marmalade jam and homemade chutney. Without a note or anything.

A score of strawberries, pink and pitted, large as thumbs, their green stems and sharp leaves spread out like paper napkins. A dozen perfect pears with fair green swan's necks and beauteously curved and dimpled bottoms. Five plums, cold-frozen. A threesome of aristocratic avocados, silver lines radiating across their white faces. Two golden bananas with their yellow toes curled up, stocking peels, with warm meat and straight black striations. One perfect *papino*.

Flirty Helen, was she wooed by such a repast?

Patiently scheming, innocent-faced, Ismet left hatboxes on his set of drawers, where her curious eyes could not but catch sight of them, sliced up peaches in tea saucers to keep by the sink, took a dishcloth and concealed a plate of skinny litchis in the middle of the table, where she would have to move them to enjoy her midmorning poached egg since the saltshaker was under the cloth, the edge of the pewter base showing (she would know where to check).

"Look, Khateja, my wife."

He picked out the best plate, the one with Arabic letters printed in green ink around the brim that had been Shireen Haveri's favorite. On the raised outer edge ran a fine silver line that he used to line up the guavas he'd brought. Then he opened the curtains so there was a good light. He stood back and admired the presentation gift box that was his particular stroke of genius in this case.

"I have brought something really special to delight you."

Then she screamed from behind the closed door where she'd been saving up her breath, "Is the world burning down that I must break up my legs? My only hope is that you have not gone

and brought your fruits again, since it is my belief I have developed a big allergy. There are allergies in my family. It is a
private matter, that is why I have not previously mentioned it."

He brought bananas with him. She peeked through her key-
hole first, watched him lounging about with his hands in his
pockets, perfectly offhand.

Theatrically: "My only hope is you have not brought bananas
again."

When guavas were his gift, "For your information, Pravina
has told me how her cousin-sister Sattia has contracted a serious
illness after one guava recently. Deadly in fact. One guava and
it could be *charlo*, Khateja!"

So then the plate would stand unattended on the table, covered over with a cloth across which insects pricked their way.
Ismet sat in his room in a blue sulk. Pravina came with her
carrom board and the two women would go laughing to play
with Ruwayda from next door. Then (what profit in despair?)
he would steal back into the kitchen, pick up an exquisite *gren-
adilla*, buff it against his shirt, and, saying, "If you sure you do
not want this" to no one in particular, take a bite.

On one occasion she explained to him that he must stop wasting
good money arriving with these wasted oranges.

She said, "Wasted oranges, that is what they are," and looked
disappointed that he would indulge in luxury.

"Wasted oranges . . . Since when must you waste food in this
fashion?" she wanted to know.

She told him, "It has always been one of your virtues that
you are one thrifty-thrifty character. One thrifty-thrifty char-

acter. Your mother, too, don't think I didn't notice. Now you must spoil this also?" and opened the door-chain so he could come in from the outside hall and put his box in the kitchen.

The book she was reading lay open on the table. He pushed it aside, found himself a saucer and a butter knife. He sliced up an orange and put a little bit of salt on it.

Still concentrating on his orange he said, "You think I do not know the meaning of the word big 'allergy'? I will not be troubling up my wife with oranges. There is such a thing as respect for women. For your information, I have brought this one box oranges so that it is possible I can have a few snacks."

"You never know when you might want one snack," he added, sucking out the juice from his slice.

"Hey, do not carry on like this, Ismet man, it is very out of character," Khateja chided, helping herself to an orange. "With the shouting and the screaming, your heart, one of these days it will stop and I will have to take you and bury you away and the polices will have some questions to ask."

"Please, Khateja, help yourself to an orange. I do not want to intrude. As long as you are aware that you are welcome."

She put down her orange and leaned back and tapped him on the chin one-two-times.

"This is a sweet fellow! Oh yes, I am a very fortunate lady to have one funny-funny husband who makes me laugh and smile nonstop and on top he brings oranges for me. Ah, a humorous husband, it is no joke. Only thing?"

"What?"

"Please do not spill juice all over, the whole morning I have been scrubbing and cleaning and at this point I am utterly exhausted. Just be a little careful, that is all I am asking. Only don't be waving that orange around like it is a tennis ball."

"Hey! I just do not like it full-stop."

Bit by bit Pravina was getting accustomed to her friend and her quicksilver disposition, her soliloquies, dolorous moods, the off-the-cuff quips. Still, she needed to concentrate to keep up.

Khateja had been standing by her while she washed clothes in the tin bath on the patio with a beater, a bucket of warm water, a box of pale blue soap flakes. Why this out of the blue?

"It is a feeling in my bones. It is difficult to express," admitted Khateja. "Perhaps it is me who is what-what paranoid."— ("If you are what-what paranoid, if that is really the situation," Pravina declared valiantly, "then I have not seen one indication. I have not seen that indication, so do not worry, my Khateja. We will cross that bridge later on down the road.")—"I am convinced he is up to tricks."

"Up to tricks?" asked Pravina.

"Oh ho! It is the cross on my head that I must watch and scrutinize constantly. Otherwise he will start with the funny business. There is a very sinister side to him that has come out, I am telling you. You must thank your lucky stars that you do not have to worry about Vikram. Go home and thank your lucky stars, Pravina."

(That fellow Vikram, he was as open as two windows, Khateja reflected, a sharp green flower in her heart. She experienced a sudden, deep relish for domestic bliss, almost like a strong craving. The world didn't have enough sugar, indisputably.)

Pravina was most flattered by Khateja's remark. She blushed and coughed.

She return-complimented, "But it is a totally different case to Ismet who is one of our great smooth talkers."

"I am surprised you would come out with this Pravina, out of everyone. It is as a result of that Bombay accent he has picked up. Ah, our Indians! It is a pity there is this kind of prejudice in the world today."

Pravina apologized. She knew that voicing her high opinion of her friend's husband in front of her was a recipe for danger. On the other hand, she had noticed recently that running the old charmer down didn't seem to do much for top-floor Khateja's spirit. Oh, she baited and complained about Ismet, but it didn't provide her the pleasure it had in the past, when it had once been an instant restorative.

"I did not want to say, my dear, but I have had a similar experience."

"What experience are you talking about, Pravina?"

"Vikram! Vikram, you wouldn't believe! He gives for me one top-quality chocolate, then after that his face will light up and I must listen there while he comes with stories about his ancestors who are lying dead in the grave and all. Dead in the grave, my dear! In exchange for one skinny-skinny chocolate in rice-paper wrapping, it is getting a little excessive at this stage, my Khateja."

Khateja called from her room where she had a full view of Ismet reflected in the window above the sink:

"What you poking up with your fruit for?"

"If you want one banana, then all you must do is to ask. Then I will give you one-two bananas. I will provide several bananas if that is your wish. I will go out in the street and buy for you a banana tree, no problem," Ismet vowed. "Ask and you will get. Only, why is it necessary to shout in my ear?"

She waltzed into the room panther-footed, her hair hanging down gloriously over her shoulders.

"Hmph," she sniffed, half-asleep with black half-moons under her eyes, "sneaking in with your bananas all secretly and quietly. Hushed up, you know."

"I didn't want to wake you up, that is a crime?" he countered.

She flipped through the bananas.

"Well and good, well and good but the lesson you must learn is to draw a line. I have brought these bananas away from work specially with you in mind. So please let us have an end to these suspicious stories. I am taken aback by the degree of suspicion this episode has revealed."

At his anniversary party downstairs Vikram proudly showed off his stainless-steel wedding ring, which he'd snagged for cost plus ten from the Jaffrey family, and then, struck by the difference in their situations, he took his friend into a corner and told him, "You know Ismet, Pravina and myself, we are talking almost the whole time. More and more I am convinced that that is the real secret. As long as there is a dialogue, as long as one party can listen to the other party, then there is communication. Then mutual understanding is a possible option. I am the first to admit that maybe we are not an intelligent couple. Maybe we do not have philosophies but our hearts are open with each other, that is the essential fact. It does not matter what is the issue, Pravina will come and sit by me and explain what is her perspective. She will say what is on her mind and then"—he spread his symmetrical hands with their proud happy bands in front of Ismet—"I will say what is on my mind. It is that simple."

Ismet thanked him (actually he muttered "One Top-Quality Chocolate" under his breath, actually, but Vikram didn't catch) and wandered off to stand by Dorothy and Ruwayda by the salad bowl.

Later that evening, after the in-laws and brothers and snotty children with their india-rubber cricket ball and red spinning top and the wallet of marbles had left so it was now safe to walk on the carpet again, Charm and Vikram and Ismet went to the Red Hill Billiards Club, where Charm was a member, and played one set before they got into an argument with two London-trained lawyers about socialism and the inherent temperament of the street Indian. A more just system of organization, according to the Londoners, would bring out the finest, cultivable elements of human nature.

Clearly impassioned after listening to the debate for five minutes, Ismet rocketed to his feet, his voice half breaking. He asked the barristers, "How we all going to agree what is right for the world in one country when it is not even possible between one man and one woman? How will we say this is the correct procedure and no, this is not correct, and this is where the money must go into this man's pocket? Eh? How is this possible, please tell me right now! Tell, I will be only too pleased to hear," before Charm and Vikram made him sit and calmed him down and Charm went off and got him one nice whiskey with a slice of lemon in a shot glass that had a coat of arms printed in white ink on the bottom, because clearly he needed it.

Ismet was sitting one evening on the balcony with his worm-wood rocking chair that he'd brought out from his room. By his feet a half-empty glass of *lassi* purchased at the store.

Charm, flush with surplus investment capital from the lottery, had imported a *lassi*-making machine from overseas, and was proudly charging a shilling a cup. Out it poured from a nozzle, white and foamy and tasting of soap. Only thing, it was convenient.

Honey-spirited from her badminton victory in the competition organized on the rooftop by the building's women, Khateja swept in after leaving Pravina (who'd retired after the first game of the round-robin due to a back condition) at home with her feet in a bucket of ice, propped up in her living-room chair with two goosefeather pillows and a cold cloth for her head. She lit instantly on the bunch of seedless green grapes spotlighted on a platter on the sideboard. The riots had been smoldering down, the weather was delightful, and Khateja felt exorbitantly well.

"Really, it is most delightful that you have come home with these grapes at this moment. I am just in the mood for one-two grapes," the victor said, picking the seeds out of her teeth and spitting them in her hand, when Ismet came in from the balcony.

"Now I can see why you are doing so well on the business side. Must be it is a question of timing. Now I understand."

"You don't mind I am eating up your grapes like this?" she
inquired with great charm.

"Go straight ahead."

"Why you don't have a grape, eh? Don't be shy now, please."
He declined with his head buried in the newspaper.

"If you don't pipe up now I will finish them all and then
there will be no point in regrets," she warned, rewinding the
morning's glorious moments.

He threatened to explode.

When she was finished Khateja left the empty white plate
and the saucer by the sink. The lamps in the flats opposite were
visible as dishes of light, yellow-brown cones on the brown brick
walls. Below (she could detect them individually!) the mosquitoes gathered in their vast black armies, furry, crook-legged and
red-eyed. Razor-toothed. She closed the window and drew the
curtains.

"Ismet man?

"Ismet? What you are saying to me with this whole performance?"

"Me? The point behind this? That is not how I operate. At
this stage of the game," he objected, and went on, "Metaphor,
metaphor. My dear, it is not my cup of tea."

Like the universe itself, everything seemed to be in flux with
the two of them. When they got into a blazing row about
money. "At least when I am at my work there is the respect I
have earned, and people do not always believe I am on the sly,
busy with the plots and the plans. At least in the business world
there is a certain amount of respect!"—("Hush, Ismet, next

minute the neighbors will be in here also for some conversations," she suggested.)—"I do not care if these neighbors are breaking the door down. It does not make a difference to me since apparently I am committing crimes in this house no matter what! Now you have eaten up all my grapes. Next thing you will probably kill me flat!"

Feeling quite shocked, Khateja went downstairs and collected Pravina to go visit Dorothy, who had just delivered her baby in R. K. Khan hospital. She reassured herself of the baselessness of his charges. It was a question of paranoia here.

It was after Charm and Dorothy celebrated the first birthday of their daughter, Lady Mountbatten Soolal, that, following the third afternoon of shopping for the baby, Khateja came home in a new beige cashmere jersey she planned to wear with trousers.

"What an apple you are. You are an apple of the apples. For myself I can say honestly that I have never seen such an apple with my own two eyes. A crisp new thing. And you are not one skinny-skinny apple that I must come with one microscope and one magnifying glass."

If she hadn't seen this spectacle herself—her husband kneeling on the bathroom mat, declaiming to his apple-topped palm—then she would have been sure he was dilly-dallying with another woman on the side.

She must keep on her toes, *ne?* (Although that also, all it was leading to was an early grave. An early grave.)

He looked up, blushed, and closed his guilty fingers around the apple, cobra-like!

He tapped the apple onto a saucer and got up and stretched.

"I was not, ur . . . aware you had arrived, you see."

He smiled secretively between two discreet cheeks.

Khateja answered him in great serenity. (Heavens, self-control was needed for a minimum of one person in this asylum!)

"It is part of my work, you understand."

Very subdued, she agreed.

"Do not humor me, my dear wife."

"Well, I was only taking an interest," she pointed out defiantly.

"If this is true, then I am only too happy to show you. If you are interested?"

She informed him that she would be most delighted. He insisted she make herself comfortable.

He held his arm out and opened his fist to reveal the green shining apple with its gray squares, flourished it beneath her nose, spread his end-gaming, apple-topped palm level with her chin.

He sliced off the top of the apple with a cheese knife, exposing the white.

"Take a look inside, my Khateja. Put one finger there. Take one little nibble. How soft, *ne*? How sweet, this is the sweetest and softest apple. The sweetest and the softest. On top"—he clicked his fingers under her chin, a smile in both eyes—"since it is chock-full of vitamins and minerals, it will take years off. You will feel like one new lady," and he handed it over to her, still in its skin.

◆　◆　◆

The following morning the city smelled like a butcher's shop—
meaty somehow with the confection of human needs and desires and unquenchable appetites. Steamed bark on the bottle
palms along the beachfront, holiday makers with underarm tow-
els and shallow, round ice-cream tins in their hands, old white
women from the old-age homes behind Addington hospital on
the promenade sporting liver spots on their arms and cockle-
shell clips in their hair, sardine vendors crouching by half-wet
cardboard boxes, girls in cotton dresses holding toffee apples.
Steam in the gray-block tenement buildings with ventilation
slats and washing hung out on the cracked balcony walls.

She woke up and went to open the window. She saw that
she'd fallen for the man with the apples between his knuckles
and the silver lines in his hair. She'd gone and fallen for him,
after all this time.

Beginning at what stage?

When he'd appeared in the window of a certain train, his
fez set at a rakish angle, when he'd bobbed up and disappeared
with a violent motion? When he'd trailed her home and forced
his unblushing way into her hut, embarrassing himself by pushing so hard on the door it was broken until Yusuf unscrewed it
from the hinges and put it straight again? How he escorted her
around the *nizam*'s castle, reading the information on the bat-
tlement aloud in a strong voice because he thought she could
not comprehend? When he calmly filled a bucket outside and
poured it over his incandescent jacket and the pair of Rashida's
carpet slippers she'd torched with a paraffin-burning lamp? So
recently he'd kept her up half the night—yes, half the night—
with his half-delirious talk to the extent he'd woken Vikram in

his dressing gown and borrowed two watermelons from their

pantry for illustrations?

There were the evenings she'd waited, bored stiff, just to tease him about the bottle-green corduroy trousers that Vikram gave him after some admiring comments, the way he'd sit on his balcony chair and toss plucked, rinsed strawberries into his mouth like a trained beachfront seal. . . . She wanted to feed him things.

She went walking. A spring day (the season for love). Poking up through the concrete paving were the heads of daffodils and dandelions. They had gray feathers on them and made her sneeze. The tap on the opposite pavement which the *halaal* butcher used to wash his meat, was leaking into a red puddle.

She ignored the shop selling shoes on imitation mahogany stands covered in purple felt, the hardware dealer who had put a crate of lightbulbs out on the street in front of his shop, each bulb in its own square package. Instead she bought a tin of shortbread and three sugared Boudoir biscuits in white paper sachets from the general dealer. She stood outside in the alley feeding them to the goat tethered there to a roll of chicken wire.

"Ahye," Charm groaned when he came out to smoke his pipe. "Those are costly biscuits to be feeding that old goat. Costly biscuits. Imported from Scotland. Now how is a goat to know all this?"

"Charm, do me one favor? Stop with the spoil-sporting. There are other things in life. I am perfectly happy here in this alley wasting up my tin of shortbread. Truly, I have become quite fond of this goat in a short period of time."

"Now, Khateja. What is the need to poke fun?" Charm asked, aggrieved, "Nonstop?"

She reassured him.

The goat sprang onto its hind legs and snatched a whole biscuit from her hand. She shook another one into her palm but held it higher up, protectively.

Charm was still doubtful.

"If you are liking this goat so much," he said, helpfully, "maybe I could fix a price, ay? Never know when a goat will come in handy. Superb curries you know, with the *brinjals* and the *mudumbes*, ah yes. Dorothy has made a great curry from a goat one time. Quite spectacular. But second thought, I cannot sell away this goat since I have already advertised it as the second giveaway prize in my lottery. It is a pity but those are the facts of the situation."

"That is fine. I would not think of taking away this goat and cutting it for a curry. It is much too friendly, really. Almost intelligent, I swear, just see in those eyes and then say for me I am wrong, go ahead."

Charm looked at the goat.

The goat stared steadfastly back at Charm, forgetting for one moment Khateja's ready biscuit trove.

Charm stared at the goat.

The goat stared at Charm.

"Ahye, what an ugly goat this is, too ugly," exclaimed Charm.

Oh ho! What an ugly, ugly man this is being. Oh, what an ugliness is this! thought the goat. Above all he is rude and ill-mannered. Those eyes, all swelled up and red, wouldn't be taking a sugar from this one, oh no.

With great dignity it turned away from Charm and looked up at my humanitarian grandmother.

"Charm! What is the point to these insults, eh? Running it down to its face for what?"

"It is not as if it can hear," Charm pointed out, weakly.

"Ha!" said Khateja. "You would be surprised."

That evening Ismet pushed open the green door at the top of the stairs with his raincoat in his arms and a punnet of strawberries in a brown paper shopping bag.

"My dear? Great stuff. Great stuff. If you would please step in here for a minute."

And then?

Yes . . . and then a finger was raised and what a finger it was and how far it was raised! What a rolling about there was, what a lifting of legs, a tumult of thighs, a nesting of navels, a knitting of knees! Slabs of iced feet, bright-blazing ears with the thrice-nibbled inch, the leaning on elbows when he went to fetch the strawberries, the subsequent spreading of sphincters, the beating of breast, a burning in the chest. . . .

He fell back against the headboard, felled like a great rooting tree.

He grasped at his heart.

Khateja's face appeared over him like a kind balloon.

Then, a slow fluting, a gentle needling, a silence, a pause, a junction, a sliding in and a sliding out, a tunneling, a burrowing, a shunting and a shuffling, a downing, a muffling and diving.

But why mince words, why foot with the pussy, why struggle to keep under wraps what is private between two people. Aren't I the proof, me the egged gamete (at two removes), me the irrefutable, unmistakable evidence and ramification?

Yes, there's no getting round it.

My grandparents made love.

And not once either.

Several times in fact.

Over some days.

NORTH

Chapter Thirteen

I n his marriage's many heavenly months, my grandfather, as an upstanding entrepreneur and a modestly accomplished backgammon player, discovered that his boisterous apprenticeship with Khateja had befallen another person, a different Ismet Nassin. Time sapped those incidents of their brain-shaking intensity. Scrutinizing his wife when she was sleeping next to him, Ismet couldn't conceive how this same creature once tied a goat to the frame of this very bed with a frayed piece of string and two safety pins while he stood protesting—and complained to the animal about his conduct the evening long. The remarks and the comments, the hints and quips, words that came bearing daggers, iron-smiling! Oh, not that he resented the wasted socks it got its beak into, the breath of the goat on his neck as he lay beneath it, or the stench, or the superfluous exhortations: "If you move this goat that is my one true friend, then I will accompany it. So much I promise you. We shall venture out together, the two of us. For the sake of proper companionship, I have brought this animal into the house."

Now practical issues occupied his thoughts instead, enough

to forestall his unproductively dwelling on the past. Vikram, his business partner, needed to be restrained. In Vikram's unspoken competition with Charm Soolal, the landlord's ambitions had broken all reasonable limits: He wanted to borrow working capital and build new buildings right, left, and center. Plotting a Beachfront Marine Water Development, he could only be stopped by the combined resistance of Ismet, Khateja, and Pravina. ("A Big Splash!" Vikram kept repeating, as if that settled anything.)

In his heart of hearts, Ismet had never envied the arena of great men and grand ideas, apart from moments of passing delirium. Tutored upon Rashida's brown-teated breast, Ismet was a temperamentally domestic man. The private life was the true glory: His lovely wife floating across the earth with her coconut cheeks, her fancies of gold and silver, glorious, gimleted Khateja! Wisecracking, rambunctious, mouth-like-a-bright-green-chili, rolling-boulder-past-moss Khateja whose feet impeached the pillars of the universe itself and put all things into question . . .

My grandparents, by all accounts, flowered into a rather conventional couple, burying their youthful emotional radicalism under ordinary thoughts and ordinary words. This gentling desire to refrain from absolutism—from skating right over the edge when riled up and sticking the dagger as deep as it could go into the other person's gullet or belly—meant that, to their surprise, they were capable of kindness despite the temptation to malice and puncturing that is present in every marriage. A comedy necessarily ends with the renunication of arguments— even with the disavowal of one's conversational powers. The rest is silence, no? Accordingly, my grandfather, decidedly easy-

going with Vikram, tolerant toward Charm and his mad, vituperative wife Dorothy, preferred to speak after taking time to
ponder internally. He put his hand in his hair, he looked away
into the middle distance, he tapped his other hand against the
tabletop reflectively. And only then would he say something.

The communist party began to organize in Durban and dispatched its Indian cadre, Yusuf Dadoo, to visit with my grandfather. Yusuf was then a minor functionary in the party (later
buried in Highgate Cemetery in London in the lot on the right-
hand side of Karl Marx, a lot that Joe Slovo won in a poker
game in 1957 in the Soviet Embassy in Budapest). Yusuf was a
charming man, elegant and philosophical, and made friends
with Khateja. He came to see them on a second occasion accompanied by Mr. Slovo and by the nephew-by-marriage of Mohandas Gandhi, a big buttery man with a poxy complexion who
had gone into the insurance world but had never relinquished
his relative's ideals that indeed continued to burn in his breast,
affording him no rest.

Vikram and Charm, wearing tennis uniforms and holding
rackets, heard through the grapevine about the communists being there and arrived to invite all of them to a festive dinner,
but they were forestalled by the nephew, who kept them busy
with stories about his uncle and his exploits against the British.
Meanwhile, Khateja invited Yusuf Dadoo into the kitchen and
quizzed him about the place of women in society and the role
of British culture while Joe Slovo explained to my grandfather
the mechanics of historical development and the iron laws that
determined a man's possibilities. He was also a pleasant man for
all his ideas and notions; in fact, the communists were generally

likable individuals, and Ismet gave him a donation on behalf of the business, hoping that it would pay off if they ever did come to power and wanted to nationalize every Joe and his uncle.

However, he refused to sign their petition. Communist universalism, for one thing, didn't recognize the distinctions between peoples, which couldn't be practical in his understanding of the universe.

"Our Indian businessman, of which Ismet is a classic example!" Yusuf fumed to Joe outside. "They must come round to recognize which side their bread is buttered on, before it is too late and the tide has swept them away."

Because they were enlightened men, both because of doctrine and from their inner convictions, they considered asking Khateja to attend the weekly meetings they held in a room of the Anglican church in Asherville. On the face of it she would be an ideal recruit, she could be a showhorse, but Yusuf dismissed the speculation on the grounds that his ears were still ringing.

"Realistically, Joe," he insisted, "we are only asking for trouble to come down on our heads if we have Comrade Khateja around. We are asking for trouble!"

Later on, the Durban City Council, acting on recent legislation enacted in Parliament, appropriated my grandparents' new house on Wills Road because it was scheduled to become part of a white neighborhood, handing to Khateja Nassin a titleholder's check in the amount of seventy-five pounds, which my grandmother promptly donated to the Communist Party in what was, for her, a unique gesture of political protest. It was never invoiced. It was in fact cashed two weeks later by a senior party member who needed spending money for a trip to Johannesburg to meet a committee of gold miners with the most progressive notions—and also to spend a few days with his mistress, a flirtatious red-haired little thing who had visited Lithuania and shaken the hand of Beria, the chief of the secret police.

Having lost most of their wealth as a result of the government confiscation, my grandparents eventually moved into a small house in a segregated suburb on the hills about ten miles outside Durban, next to the reservoir. In the next decade Vikram, out-leveraging himself in an import-export deal, would go bust and open up a Chinese restaurant. Ahmedu emigrated to Australia. Charm made a good deal of money from a chain of discount liquor stores, and invested much of it into educating Disraeli at a British boarding school. The government outlawed the Communist Party, sending Joe Slovo and Yusuf Dadoo into exile in London. Mehmoud Ghani's son, Solly, opened a hardware business and was busy printing up his father's aphorisms in salable pamphlets as a profitable sideline. Jayraj and Tejpal founded a luxury cruise travel liner that went between Cape Town and Ahmadabad.

There were fewer letters back and forth to Bombay and Rashida—imagination, which is capable of joining together countries ten thousand miles apart, must be admitted to be a mercurial power. Like any deracinating system of forces and energies, the imagination sponsors moral and filial disorderedness. My grandparents got mentally denationalized, so to speak. If something's been muscled out of the future, it's only a matter of time before it loses its grip on the past, no?

Little in the way of material possessions had survived their years in South Africa. The silk goods, those that accompanied them on that long ago ship sealed in a green tin trunk, were getting to be worn and thin, water-marked, so that Khateja could hardly put on an old sari to wear inside the house or spread her familiar tablecloth in their lounge without her heart breaking. The tea chest popped its copper bindings. The curtain from her father's house had long since been taken out of the window and folded away in a cupboard, a poor slip of a thing. My grandfather's cobbled shoes, the toes of which were kept in by a narrow band of tin, were cracked and hobbled by years of use. He put them away in a drawer, inserting a sheet of blotting paper into each shoe to secure them from the humidity. One day Khateja took them out to inspect them and to her horror they literally fell apart in her hands, unfurling their old brown leather petals.

After having racked up so much motion, my grandparents seem to have surrendered any further ambitions in that direction. In fact, my grandmother still lives in this house, but Pravina has moved in for the sake of true companionship. Outwardly Khateja is a religious old woman, filled with Muslim pessimism and crotchetiness as far as the modern world is concerned, silent except when she complains about Pravina. To tell the truth, they complain about each other, twit one another where possible, and pass in the corridor like ships.

I half suspect that it's a kind of performance that my grandmother adopts an old woman's habits. Khateja wears a penitential white scarf around her head and loose quilted clothes on her body, takes *paan* and snuff, counts through her prayer beads. Affecting a lofty and philosophical tone when she remembers, my grandmother resorts to an irritable demeanor most of the time—which I guess is the elderly antidote to pervasive bodily pain and to their inescapable jealousy of the young. But the mask that's worn into my grandmother's face has a symbolic function: by rendering her more or less anonymous, more or less interchangeable, it indicates that her story is no longer really her own. It belongs to our common history.

I should admit that my grandmother, now thoroughly nononsense, displays minimal sympathy for my style of interrogation and my curiosity. Why do I expect anything?

"Your grandfather was a good man," she tells me. "He had a good heart."

"Which doesn't mean anything to me."

"Why are you so insistent? Previously you didn't want to know anything."

"So I've changed my mind."

"You rascal! Don't cheek me," she threatens.

The temperature between us rises quickly, unusual for grandmother and grandchild. In our mutual dealings, I am just as much to blame as she is. It does suggest that, not far beneath the crust, Khateja's quicksilver nature is still boiling away. Because I believe that time never really passes for human beings: Each moment is self-contained, like a walnut in its shell—and enduring to infinity.

"I want to know about my grandfather. I want to know how you came to this country. It isn't a crime, ma. Please see that. This knowledge belongs to me. I need to find my bearings."

"But you are asking the impossible, my dear. There is always a limit to understanding, which you must come to accept. In the end how much can you know about human trivialities? And it is not as if I have been keeping secrets from you. You humiliate me by reminding me what condition my memory has deteriorated to. Well, you must fill in the blanks for yourself now." She examined my reaction to this. In frustration she called into the other room, "Pravina, my persistent grandchild has certain inquiries. You may be able to provide the required information."

"Look, don't trouble Pravina."

"What trouble! Tomorrow she will have no recollection of what transpires today."

"I give up."

"Well then, my dear, it seems we have reached an impasse. Tell me what occupies you overseas. Your father offers only the sketchiest information. I am firmly convinced that he keeps secrets away from me. The important thing is, have you found a suitable girl?"

It isn't that Khateja is not fond of me, of course she is, but it's in her removed style, as if proximity to the next world substitutes for intimacy with this one. I can recognize such a state intellectually, like looking at my grandmother through a telescope.

A word or two about eloquence. I believe it is reasonable, in light of my heritage, that I am extremely suspicious of people who are quick with words. In general, I would say that I am skeptical about the powers of talk, at least the positive powers. If I have an ideal to substitute for the dead hand of language, it's nothing fancy. I would wish to be released, to wind up the ball of string and follow it out of the labyrinth. For centuries the Nassins have suffered from a tyranny of voices. Even now— in the confines of my head—they assail and torment and discourse on every topic conceivable. Khateja, a master of words, understands their treacherous character for this reason. Words— flighty, insubstantial creatures—are liable to veer from the true state of reality in unexpected directions, like a cloud of swallows breaking across a hillside.

But I do not want to leave the impression of final reconciliations. Dear reader, I have been withholding information for dramatic purposes. I have concealed the one fact that is primary about the afterlife of my grandparents' marriage, the evidence that convinces me of the fatality of fate.

The truth is that my grandfather Ismet Nassin married again. Yes, he found himself a new wife, Yasmin, a second wife—for nothing that stirs the soul is eternal. Charm lent him the money for a proper wedding, and the black-edged invitations to the ceremonies of Yasmin Jaffrey, of Jaffrey's Emporium of Jewels, Gentleman's Watches & Precious Stones, and Ismet Nassin, formerly a resident of Bombay, were sent out during a summer of big rains in the valley of a thousand hills, a wildcat strike in the textile factories put down by the Natal Carboniers, a flash flood, a daytime moon.

On the day before the *nika'a* there were people at the new house, lounging about in the pine sofa-chairs, handing around cigarettes, drinking imitation orange juice, taking down telephone numbers. It was an afternoon of white light spreading among the bottle palms and the great black firs on the Berea.

There was a telegram from Bombay:

Many congratulations on this auspicious occasion. Hope
business is good. We hope to make the journey soon. Many
here have fond memories of our friend who is apparently an
important man overseas. Rashida is always giving us the news
snippets.

Your Friends for a Lifetime and Beyond,
Jayraj & Tejpal Reddy

Charm Soolal in copper-rimmed dark green sunglasses, and
his boy, Disraeli (so grown up, wearing a bow tie and all!),
appeared to shake hands, distribute business cards, offer congratulations.

"What an inspiration Disraeli has found in you Ismet."

"It is true, you have made the greatest of impressions, sir,
the greatest—" Disraeli started before Charm cut him off with
a glare. Then he continued, "You are a genius, he has informed
me of it, a model for Indians who are working in the retail
industry!"

Overcome by emotion, Charm insisted on renaming his
Lottery of the Three Thousand Millions on the spot, to be
known from this moment forward as the Ismet Nassin Lottery
of the Three Thousand Millions. At Ismet's suggestion, Charm
settled for Yasmin-and-Khateja's Own Sweepstake-Lottery of
the Three Thousand Millions and went among the throng
shaking hands and spreading the news.

Charm had been stocking some London-published political
pamphlets of interest to Indians, and, thinking Ismet would

appreciate them, he brought Mr. Gandhi's well-known *Conditions of the British Indian* and *My Soul's Agony.*

Vikram embraced my grandfather and wept on his shoulder. He shook from emotion. He would not move until eventually he retired to a corner of the house, crying.

Later, "Vikram still has not arrived at an understanding of the development of manners in this day and age," Ismet complained to Yasmin. "Am I," he inquired, "am I a rattle that I must be shook and shaken up? It is time to put a stop to it, I must make Vikram understand."

On the day of the wedding my grandmother was in top-top form, roaring around in her motorcar, gray serge cap pulled low on her brow, Pravina in pink shoes in the passenger seat, handbag clutched to her lap. She spilt sweet yellow rice over Yasmin during the lunch. She left the *nika'a* early with what seemed to be tuberculosis. In the evening she ploughed down a folding wooden table and ran over Ismet's right foot with a soft white tire, narrowly missing burying him deep within the earth with the big rubber bumper on the front of the Ford. Khateja was in a grand, rip-roaring mood, loosing herself from the blackest pessimism, outstaring the universe and prepared to stand gladly against the polygamous fates. A manifestation of sublime powers, she was far beyond moral criticism.

And Yasmin was beyond even Khateja's reproach. "Poor Khateja," she told her mother while dusting rice off her sari after lunch, "all elbows she is today. All elbows, I am really feeling for her. Probably she is the most nervous one out of all of us."

After the *nika'a,* as she sat next to Ismet and greeting everyone with a smile and a kiss and a thank you, she leaned over to the groom, "That was quite a nasty cough Khateja had. When there is the chance we must find out if she is okay, maybe she must see a doctor. We can't only be thinking about ourselves all the time, you know."

Then, with Ismet lying on the ground in his double-breasted suit tugging at his shoe, groaning loudly, Yasmin rushed over to Khateja, pulled up the Dodge's hand brake, and enfolded her in the solicitous yellow cloud of her sari, "Dearest dear, I have been worrying about you the whole day and I was correct. Your arms must be shaking for you to have run off the driveway like this. You have not suffered any injuries, that is the important thing. But sit, we will have tea now."

Yasmin, my grandfather's second wife, was famed for her beauty and equable character. Khateja (in the late afternoon before the whole drama of the car crash) was moved to whistle. Then she turned to Ismet, who was standing with Vikram and Charm Soolal and Roderick Campbell, and said, "Under this camouflage it would be possible for a man to marry a buffalo! How could he know? Afterward he would come to the realization that he is married to the buffalo. Up to then that fact has been totally invisible. What a dreadful shock to discover that he is in the bed with the naked buffalo ultimately!"

"Ha! Ha!" Ismet laughed nervously, turning to his friends with outstretched arms. "That is Khateja's sense of humor for you. That is Khateja for you, and her sense of humor. It is half her charm for me."

He felt magnanimous. Ayesha Jaffrey, his new mother-in-law, in a rare exhibition of sympathy, had massaged his affronted foot with skin cream and bath oils. The classical dancers and the *qawali* band with their red silk *kurtas* and sitaars had been a great hit.

"Having them perform for us," he announced, "it is the little I can contribute to keep our Indian culture alive for all of us. Our Indian culture, that is what really counts at the end of the day. Remember that it is only the beginning at this point. We all of us have a responsibility. So please do not offer me congratulations, that I am not concerned with. Go out and do what is possible with your own creativity and imagination."

The architect Enver Hassan, tactful as ever, had been vanquished by the groom twice in a row at the draughts board. Roderick Campbell winked in admiration at the bride and brought them a stainless-steel bowl as a wedding gift. The throbbing purple bruise on my grandfather's foot was throbbing a little less. He pinched Yasmin's cheeks effusively and insisted on feeding her sweetmeats morsel by morsel.

Khateja leaned over to Pravina and whispered audibly enough for Ayesha and Yacoob Vowda to hear, "At least, since a woman is really the product of what she eats, one day we can be making, oh, an excellent curry with this Yasmin." She fed herself a handful of *chevra* and smacked her lips. "Yes, what an excellent curry she would be making, tender you know. Exceptionally tender. Even Ismet would be enjoying it and asking for a second helping, until he came to the reali-

I was thinking about my grandfather riding atop his train while
going downtown in a taxi, to see a movie. Strange coincidence,
the driver was a Sikh, a young man with a scraggly beard,
jowls, and a clean white turban. He had a thin, square head,
wide-set eyes, long legs in nylon trousers, a piece of black
elastic wound tightly around his ponytail.

"You from India?" he asked, peering into his mirror and
swerving around a corner.

The flannel dice hanging from the mirror bobbed up and
down. The rain slid down the windshield. Outside everything
had turned dark and and indistinct.

"Well, sort of."

Thinking better of it, I said, "Not really."

"Weren't born there, eh?"

"No."

"Father?"

"No. My grandfather was though. Ismet Nassin," I offered.

"Which part?"

"I think the bit on the top, you know. On the one side."

The flannel dice hit the driver smack in the middle of the
forehead. He flicked it aside.

"Gujarat? Maharashtra? Punjab?"—the last hopefully.

"It might have been Kashmir?"

"Kashmir, eh?"

He looked back at me suspiciously.

The car squealed and shot past a Toyota in the same lane, missing it by a fraction. It hooted but our driver didn't seem to notice. He turned back to the road.

"Well," I prompted, "where are you from?"

"India, yes."

He didn't seem as communicative. Was he sulking? Had I said something against some custom?

"Where in India?"

"Delhi."

He shook his head from side to side.

"And how long have you been in this country?"

"Seven years now almost." He sighed. "I came after the riots. After Mrs. Gandhi. Nineteen eighty-five."

"And you like America?" I asked hopefully.

"No, not really. Too dangerous. Expensive. And the blacks, *ne*? Hey! They're too cheeky with us. Robbed my uncle Tej two years ago. Right in broad daylight."

"Oh."

"Yes. Right in broad daylight, just like that. Stuck a gun in his neck. And him being a small man." He smacked his horn for emphasis and frowned at the BMW next to us. "Problem with his heart. And they with a gun. Could have killed him out."

"No?"

"Yes. Yes, could have killed him. Snuffed him out. Later on it turned out the gun was plastic. Water pistol, left it lying in the back seat. But Tej couldn't be working for a week. Nerves shot, you understand. Just sat there in front of the T.V. and watched *Dynasty* and called for his wife to fry *samoosas*.

'*Samoosas,*' he would say, and she must make them in the frying pan. Straight away she must put them on. A whole week, every two hours. Must have eaten hundred plates, two hundred plates, who knows? Never expected such things in America. Still won't pick up blacks. Can't be too safe."

"That's true," I said.

"And seeing as it was because Tej's brother Logan was killed that we came here."

"Killed?"

"Oh yes. Killed by the Hindus. In the riots. Couldn't even see his body for a week. And then, the polices call us and are asking us to identify him. And Tej and me and his mother go in and then when they pull the sheet up from over him he doesn't have a nose. He does not even have his nose. It is gone, just like that. No trace. Disappeared. Whoosh! We ask the polices, 'Where is his nose? Where is Logan's nose?' Then they say 'Can't help you, sorry.' "

"That's really terrible."

"Tej has nightmares about it still. He calls me, bang in the middle of night, sweating, says he can't sleep thinking of his poor brother Logan wandering around after death without his nose on, humiliated right in front of his grandfather and his dead father. 'Did we grow you up,' they are asking, 'not to take care of yourself? What pride is it you can carry on to lose your nose like this? How is it you can do such a thing to us? What are we to tell everyone here, our own fathers and grandfathers? Luckily we are already dead or this thing would have killed us, man!' I can't sleep worrying about it, Tej tells me. Poor Logan, he says."

"I'm so sorry."

"Hey, don't be worrying about it. Me, I don't believe in these things personally. Superstitions. Superstitions. I was a Communist in Delhi." He paused, edging the cab between a bus and a police car. "And even if Logan was there in that situation, I'm sure his family wouldn't be scolding him all the time. They would get finished with it. In the end they must get used to it. Must become accustomed, that is what it is to be a human being. They would be able to forgive and forget. Forgive and forget. Still, it's a terrible thing. Makes you think what people can do to each other."

He spun the wheel smartly to the right and drew up sharply by the curb. White electronic letters circulated around the Newsweek board. They showed in the glass fronts of the opposite buildings.

A red jeep zoomed past, cutting through the traffic. Its tape player was very loud. From it came the strains of a rap song calling for an end to policemen, FBI agents, the president, Koreans, white people, social workers and, generally, suckers.

The movie had already started by the time we'd bought tickets, so we had to sidle through the aisle and along the rows of seats to find a place. I edged past a veiled woman who glared at me and wouldn't stand up. She pretended not to see me and sulked into her hands so I tripped past her as carefully as I could and stepped on the foot of the boy sitting next to her.

"Ahye!" he shrieked.

"Yarrah," she scolded me in a light-syllabled Pakistani accent, "watch where you are going! That is my boy you are tramping all over with your feet. That is my own personal son over here you have attacked with your feet!"

I apologized (anyway she'd left her little monster luxuriating in the undergrowth with his feet stretched out like badminton paddles, so actually it was her fault as a matter of fact) but she turned to her son, ruffled his hair, and pointedly ignored me.

"These people today," she told him, "in this country tramping around on everyone. They are just not aware whether they are coming or whether actually they are going."

Eventually I found a less perilous seat. The movie was about an itinerant family of Indians. They start off in Uganda, outside Kampala, peddling tobacco and whiskey and toilet paper. There is grass everywhere; the sky is high and clear; there is even the odd giraffe and elephant. People are happy.

Then, in 1972, Idi Amin, struggling with the thought, comes to a conclusion. He furrows his brow and announces, "Africa is for the Africans. That means," and he pauses for a second, scans the paper in front of him, and continues, "that means that Asians have no place here. They should go somewhere else."

So they do. They go.

Oh, first they protest, "But this is our home. We've lived here all our lives, our fathers and mothers lived here. Aren't we Ugandans? Don't we belong here? Isn't this our property?" But no one's listening.

They decamp to Mississippi, a languid, watery, prefabricated state, where the dams are cut out of rock and river delta and the policemen have large, pink faces like balloons and where the soil is fertile, the fields ripe to their tops with corn and wheat and beetroot.

They buy a motel, white the walls, pummel the sheets clean with bits of red soap. Like Robinson Crusoe (the original, archetypal migrant!) they set about scraping their world together again, in the same shape in which they've always known it. Indian spices can be found in the neighboring town. Clothes—those shiny expensive Indians saris and scarves, shiny pink and green and purple, threaded through with silver and gold line—are available via catalogue, mailed direct from India or New York City, Queens. Incense sticks are manufactured virtually next door in Alabama, cheap. With prayer medallions from Hong Kong, carpets from Kashmir, records and videocassettes from Bombay arriving in plain white cardboard boxes like shirts, what else might one's heart desire?

Business is good, the blacks and whites keep their distance, there are hopeful signals in Kampala: Stammering Amin is history; property could be restored. Letters are exchanged with the Ugandan authorities. Things are looking up in the 1990s.

But who can really tell? The future is uncertain for the strongest. How much more for the beetle-browed migrant! It turns out the heart has desires that can't be satisfied by post. The daughter meets a young black shampooer of carpets, by accident.

By accident: A momentary distraction while driving and wham! she smashes into the fender of his van, crammed full with detergents and electric shampooers and polishers. He draws up the hand brake very carefully, checks himself in the rearview mirror, gets out, comes over, and smiles brilliantly in her window.

Nothing left to tell: They fall in love, elope. Her family is outraged. On the other hand, his folks are extremely tolerant. They have a barbecue under the sky that is higher and more clear than anywhere. But after a time (because there's no such thing as a smooth-running course, not in this world) the recession puts a choker on his business. Over his pleas for a little more time to reckon properly his blue file brimming with receipts and bills, the bank forecloses and he loses the property.

Her father flies to Uganda and finds in the twenty years of absence it has put on a face he cannot recognize. The grass has grown up through everything. Meantime, the lovers dance together in a field to the music in their heads and pack their things into the shampooing van and head for California, which is at an infinite distance.

Afterward it had stopped raining. The thickets of buildings looked freshly scrubbed. Under a restaurant umbrella outside there was a couple sharing a plate of oysters.

The oddest thing: Standing there outside the theater, underneath the awning, on the pavement in Times Square, an eternity after Ismet Nassin saw the most beautiful woman in the world, wondering if Uncle Tej had called up our driver sweating about his noseless brother Logan, amid the Hispanic dope dealers and the Jewish daughters and the Irish cops and the Puerto Rican teenagers and the Korean grocers and the Pakistani mothers and the limousine-ferried real-estate magnates and the black rap addicts and the sweatered and suede-jacketed students—standing there, for an instant, I imagined I was at home.